A Sporting Chance

Roland was furious. That slut Maggie had turned him down the previous evening so she could hang out with the team. His team. She and Troy were far too interested in each other for his liking. They'd probably been screwing all night. And now his star player's performance was suffering. She was nothing but trouble: using him to get free tickets, manipulating people and interfering with players' training. She would have to go. 'You'll rue the day you turned me down, you little whore,' he muttered to himself.

By the same author:

FORBIDDEN FRUIT

TAKING LIBERTIES

A Sporting Chance

SUSIE RAYMOND

Black Lace novels contain sexual fantasies.
In real life, make sure you practise safe sex.

First published in 2000 by
Black Lace
Thames Wharf Studios,
Rainville Road, London W6 9HA

Typeset by SetSystems Ltd, Saffron Walden, Essex
Printed and bound by Mackays of Chatham PLC

ISBN 0 352 33501 7

All characters in this publication are fictitious and any resemblance to real persons, living or dead, is purely coincidental.

Chapter One

While Maggie was waiting for her friend to return she glanced around at the posters on the walls. One in particular caught her attention:

THE BRISTOL HUMMINGBIRDS
V THE FAIRWOOD TROJANS
6 MARCH FACE-OFF: 7.30 P.M.

She moved over to examine the poster more closely. It was going to be a crucial match. If the Trojans could just beat the 'Birds, they would be in with a real chance of going through to the finals. What she wouldn't give to see the game live! She glanced at the squad photograph and ran her eyes hungrily over Troy, the tall, dark-skinned ice-hockey player of her special fantasies.

It was a great picture of him: his raw sexuality was practically oozing out of the poster at her. She pictured him skimming effortlessly across the rink with the perspiration beading on his forehead and running down his chest. The image was so vivid that she could almost smell the masculine odour of his body radiating towards her. Ebony and ivory. Fire and ice. What a combination.

Involuntarily, Maggie rested her hand lightly on the poster with her fingers covering his hard, lean stomach. She was surprised and slightly shocked at the strength of her yearning to caress all that hot flesh and feel it pressed up against her.

'Maggie? What are you staring at?' The voice came from behind and made her jump. She removed her hand guiltily from the poster and spun round. Her friend was just coming out of the ladies room. 'Come on. If we don't get a move on we'll miss the start of the film.'

Thirty-two-year-old Janet Nichols tossed her head so that her shoulder-length blonde hair fanned out attractively around her pretty, heart-shaped face. She hurried across the cinema foyer to where Maggie was standing and peered curiously over her friend's shoulder.

'Oh. It's the Trojans. I might have guessed. Don't you get enough of them at work every day?' Jan rolled her eyes expressively and licked her lips. 'Will you just look at the size of Pele's shoulders!' She pointed to a blond-haired, blue-eyed giant with biceps like watermelons. 'Can't you just imagine that giving you a good-morning hug?'

Maggie couldn't help smiling. She and Jan had been friends ever since Jan had helped her to find her flat on behalf of the estate agents where she worked. When Maggie had started working as a receptionist at the Fairwood ice rink, the two of them had also become avid fans of the local ice-hockey heroes, the Trojans. Arguing over the players was a favourite pastime.

'I still prefer Troy,' Maggie maintained loyally, as she thoughtfully traced his outline with her fingertip. She wondered if she would ever get the chance to really know him.

Jan laughed. 'I bet they're the only reason you stay on at the ice rink,' she accused her friend. 'The pay's lousy and the hours suck, so it has to be them.' She squinted at the photo again and then removed her glasses to give them a quick wipe with her sleeve. 'Unless it's because of Justin? As a close friend of the management, I suppose you'll automatically get a ticket to the game?' she teased.

'I doubt it. A home game is one thing, but this match is down in Bristol.' Maggie hoped that Jan wasn't about to start trying to make something of her on–off relationship with the ice rink manager, Justin Edwards – again. It wasn't a subject she enjoyed discussing.

She thought about her friend's comment and wondered if she was right. She did enjoy working for Justin most of the time, and she liked the idea of being near the Trojans even if she never saw much of them. The truth was, it didn't really matter to Maggie where she worked. A job was just a job to her, a way to pay the bills. She certainly wasn't as career-minded as Jan. In fact, she couldn't understand why her friend put so much effort into her work or why she was so ambitious to get on; perhaps even open an estate agents of her own one day. Maybe, if Maggie had done better at school and gone on to college – like her friend – but she had been too impatient. At the time, a steady wage had seemed much more attractive than another three years of study. With plenty of work available, qualifications had seemed superfluous.

Jan was still staring intently at the poster. 'Well, I confess that I wouldn't mind going, but I can't see Marcus being very enthusiastic. You know what he thinks of my interest in the Trojans.'

'Didn't you say that Marcus was going to be away next weekend anyway?' Maggie reminded her. Jan's current live-in lover was in computer sales and often travelled away on business. At least, so he said. Privately, Maggie had her doubts. Jan could be a bit domineering at times and she suspected that sometimes Marcus just needed a break.

Jan nodded. 'You aren't actually thinking of buying tickets are you? Won't they all be sold out by now?'

Maggie shook her head. 'I don't know.' She ran her eyes over the Trojans again. 'I don't think I can afford it anyway. I'm flat broke at the moment. Besides, we'd have to stay the night somewhere, unless you fancy driving back after the match.' She shrugged. 'I guess we'll just have to make do with watching it on your TV.' Maggie couldn't afford satellite or cable. She glanced at her watch. 'Come on. The film's about to start.'

The following morning Sara Williams arrived at the ice rink to start her next shift in the café and stopped by the front desk to examine the large poster. The rink was justifiably proud of their home team's success and never missed an opportunity to promote the star attraction. She was still staring when Claire, who worked part-time as a cleaner, also arrived. Claire stopped and peered over Sara's shoulder.

'I wish I could go and watch,' she commented somewhat wistfully. 'It should be one hell of a game.' Sara turned and smiled at Claire's long, honey-blonde hair and lithe dancer's figure. Even though she was a good ten years younger than Sara or Maggie, the three of them were firm friends and united in their support of the local team. Mind you, it had to be said that they had never had the chance to be quite as supportive as they would have liked! In fact, since the Trojans usually trained early in the morning, before most of the staff arrived, or late at night, after everyone had left, they didn't even get much opportunity to see them other than at a game.

'It's bound to be live on Sky,' she consoled the younger woman.

Claire snorted rudely. 'It's not the same.' She stared intently at the poster and then heaved a theatrical sigh. 'I'd do anything for an evening out with any one of them,' she continued dramatically. 'Especially Pary. He could do whatever he wanted with me.'

Sara's grin broadened. Knowing Claire, she would

probably die of fright if any of the Trojans so much as looked at her. She was terribly shy with the opposite sex. Perhaps it was because she was so young? Sara examined the photo again and began to wonder just what it would be like to actually meet her heroes in the flesh. Every one of them had a body to die for. If their stamina under the sheets was anything like their stamina on the ice . . . Her cheeks began to glow. Truth to tell, Claire probably wasn't the only one who would turn into a quivering wreck in their presence!

She focused her gaze on her personal favourite. As part of their image they all had silly Trojan-sounding names. The one who was known as Ean, short for Aeneas, sort of reminded her of Mark, an old boyfriend. They shared the same dark-brown hair and almost black eyes. Mark's body had never been quite that perfect, of course.

Claire glanced round at the clock and sighed even more dramatically. 'Shit. I'll have to go and get started or Justin will flay me alive. He hates it if the locker rooms aren't swept out before the public arrives.'

Sara smiled indulgently after her friend's retreating figure before returning her gaze to the poster. What would Mark be like now, she wondered.

'It should be a terrific match.' A man's voice just behind her took Sara by surprise. She turned round quickly.

Justin Edwards, the rink manager, was immaculately dressed, as always, in a dark suit and crisp white shirt. His longish blond hair was tied back in a ponytail and his pale-blue eyes seemed to sparkle with mischief as he casually appraised her trim figure.

'Are you going?' he questioned, with a nod at the poster.

Sara flushed under his gaze and unconsciously fingered her short silvery-blonde hair. She knew Justin's reputation only too well. She was flattered by his interest but didn't take it all that seriously. Everyone knew about him and Maggie, although that didn't stop his eyes from roaming when given half a chance. Or his hands.

She shook her head. 'I try to get to all the home matches,' she explained softly, 'but, I haven't got the time or the money to go to the away fixtures.' Sara backed away and walked off quickly. The early morning staff would be in for their breakfast soon and she was already running late. Besides, being Saturday, the rink would be packed with kids later, all starving and with money to burn. As usual, she and her fellow workers would be flat-out serving burgers, fries and hotdogs. Sara took her responsibilities very seriously. She might be only an agency canteen assistant, but that didn't mean she could afford to be slipshod.

Maggie finished her own shift on the reception desk just after midday. It had been a particularly hectic morning and she was feeling exhausted. Shortly after they had opened, a little girl had fallen on the ice and sprained her ankle. It hadn't been a particularly serious injury, but it was rink policy to play it safe, so the child had had to be taken to the local A&E for an X-ray. The girl had been terrified so, when her parents could not be contacted, Maggie had volunteered to go with her and see her safely home afterwards. Although he was irritated by the inconvenience, Justin had been forced to see the sense of this.

Once she had got over her shock, the child had proved to be an endearing little thing, shyly admitting her secret ambitions to be a professional skater. ''Cos, it's only a dream. I'll never be half good enough.'

'Nonsense,' Maggie told her. 'If that's what you really want then you can do it.'

'Do you really think so?' asked the child and her tear-stained eyes had shone with excitement.

'Of course,' Maggie insisted. When she had been about the same age, she had dreamed of becoming a doctor, but everyone had laughed at her. Perhaps, if someone had encouraged her and given her confidence in herself . . . 'You can do anything you put your mind to,' she declared firmly. 'And don't ever let anyone tell you differently.'

By the time Maggie had returned from A&E, her shift was almost over and it was hardly worthwhile relieving her replacement. After picking up her coat from the staff room, she walked back through to the main entrance and gave the Trojans' photo another long, lingering look. If only. As she was turning to leave, Justin came through the door from the rink. His eyes brightened when he spotted her.

'Maggie. I was hoping to catch you before you left. Is the kid OK?'

Maggie nodded. 'Fine. Just a simple sprain. I drove her home and made sure everything was OK with her mum.'

'Good. Thanks. Look, I'm finishing here early tonight. Do you fancy a meal at the Cellar?' The Cellar was the restaurant-cum-nightclub attached to the flashiest hotel in Fairwood. It was so popular that it was almost impossible to get in without a reservation – unless, of course, you had influence.

'We could go back to my place afterwards,' he added meaningfully.

Maggie hesitated. She just couldn't make her mind up about Justin. He was great fun to be with and he could be so sweet and attentive, when it suited him. He could also be totally faithless and unreliable. Their last row had been about him standing her up, supposedly for a business client.

It wasn't that Maggie minded him dating around. She wasn't looking for a permanent relationship with him or anyone else. It was just the way he went about it. In her books, there was nothing more insulting than being stood up; it was as if she were nothing more than some kind of reserve option.

'Oh, I don't know, Justin. The Cellar can be so loud and crowded. I'm not sure I'm in the mood.' Besides, she had already half-promised Sara that she would go with her to an exhibition of local artists' work at the town hall. Sara was a bit of an amateur artist herself and was always talking one or the other of them into visiting galleries or attending evening classes. Unfortunately, she was the only one of the four with any real talent. Maggie's recent attempts at pottery had left a lot to be desired. She had managed to get more clay in her hair than on the pottery wheel.

Maggie stared back up at the Trojans' poster. She wouldn't say no to a night at the Cellar with one of them – or going back to one of their places afterwards! She felt a rush of warmth to her loins. An evening with Justin certainly held more potential than traipsing round the town hall. Jan had agreed to go with them anyway, so she wouldn't really be letting Sara down.

Justin moved up closer behind her. 'I don't understand why you women spend all your time drooling over those boneheads,' he commented dryly. 'Don't be fooled by all the padding. They haven't got anything I haven't got.'

Maggie grinned.

'I suppose you've already bought your ticket?' Justin continued.

Maggie shook her head. 'I'm broke,' she explained ruefully. 'It must be something to do with the terrible wages you pay me.'

Justin's face took on a crafty look. 'If you really want to go, I might be able to rustle you up a couple of tickets.' He put his hands on her shoulders. 'If you play your cards right.'

Maggie stared at him in surprise. Was he offering to get her some tickets if she went out with him tonight? How could she possibly refuse an offer like that? Besides, after her thoughts about the Trojans, she was more than ready for whatever else Justin had in mind back at his flat.

'I can't afford a hotel, either,' she explained cautiously.

Justin's hands slipped down her body and cupped her breasts. 'I think I could sort that too, if you want,' he whispered, as he started to kiss her neck before moving up to nibble her earlobe. His fingers began to tease her already enlarged nipples through her bra. Maggie shivered with pleasure, but said nothing.

Justin snorted contemptuously at her silence. He pushed her body round and pulled her hard against him. 'Well? Do you want to go or not?' he demanded.

Maggie wasn't entirely sure if his question referred to going out with him or going to see the Trojans. Or, were they one and the same? 'Are you saying that if I want some tickets, all I have to do is go to dinner with you?' she challenged him.

Justin nodded. 'And then back to my flat.' He ran his hands down her back and squeezed her buttocks possessively. 'And stay the night,' he added softly.

Maggie hesitated. He was always asking her to stay the night with him. So far, she had always resisted.

'We could discuss it better in my office,' he suggested as his left hand slid down inside the waistband of her skirt. Maggie gritted her teeth as she felt his fingers gliding over the thin material of her panties. He pulled her even harder against him so that his erection was pressed urgently into her flat stomach. She felt her own breathing quicken in response.

'Let me get this straight. If I let you have your wicked way with me, you'll get me the tickets and fix me up with some accommodation?' she teased him. Maggie's blouse was completely untucked now and she could feel his hand creeping back up her body, his fingers drawing intricate and tantalising patterns on her sensitive skin. She melted against him and savoured the little tremors of passion already rushing through her. She felt his other hand leave her buttocks and begin a slow and exciting journey around her hip towards her already damp and swollen sex. She shuddered with delight.

'If you come to my office with me, we can talk about dinner and about you spending the night with me at my flat. Then, we'll see.' Justin pulled his hands free of her clothing, twisted her round and started to guide her towards the door to the manager's office on the far side of the corridor. Without removing his hands from her waist, he kicked the door open with one foot and steered her inside. He let her go while he pushed the door closed behind them and Maggie heard the gentle click of the lock.

'I'll need two tickets,' she pushed him. 'One for me and one for my friend, Jan.'

'I'm sure that could be arranged –' Justin grabbed her from behind and pushed his hand back inside her waistband '– if you please me.' His other hand glided down her leg and his fingers started to gather up the hem of her skirt. Maggie glanced across the room and saw herself clearly reflected in the glass front of a trophy cabinet. She thrilled at the sight of his hand revealing first her stocking top and then the lace of her panties. She trembled as his fingers slowly disappeared inside them, and her breathing again quickened as he began to caress her neatly-trimmed mound.

'Twice,' he added hungrily.

'Oh please Mr Edwards, sir, do I have to?' Maggie put on her innocent-virgin act. She enjoyed playing roles and Justin was always quick to catch on to her games and play his own part superbly. It was one of the things she most liked about him.

'Yes, my girl. You do. If you want those tickets, you will have to do whatever I tell you.' His finger pushed down between her sex lips and unerringly sought out her hardened bud. The palm of his hand began to squeeze her mound rhythmically. 'Everything I tell you to,' he added softly.

Maggie took a deep breath. 'What do I have to do?' she whispered, hoping that he would be explicit. It always drove her wild when a man told her exactly what he was going to do to her.

'First, I'm going to finger you until your juices run down your legs, then you're going to strip naked for me.' His finger started to probe deeper into her and Maggie could feel his pelvis thrusting into her buttocks. She shivered again and closed her eyes.

'You are going to pose for me in every position I can think of, so I get to see you in all your naked glory.' She could hear his breathing getting heavier as his own imagination ran away with him. His hands squeezed her even harder and another tremor of longing shot through her.

'Then, you'll have to touch yourself while I watch you.' He tweaked one of her nipples painfully. 'I might even have to spank you for being such a naughty girl.' He pinched her nipple again and grinned as she cried out. 'Or, maybe I'll hand you around to all my friends? Better still, maybe I'll invite them all to come round and watch you play with yourself? After you've stripped off for them, maybe I'll hire a girl so that the two of you can entertain us?' He was really getting into his fantasy now. Maggie felt herself becoming ever wetter.

'How would you like to sit on their laps and rub yourself on their hard pricks until they lose it inside their pants? Oh yes, you'd enjoy that, wouldn't you?' he emphasised the question by squeezing her mound even harder with the palm of his hand.

Maggie pretended he was talking about the Trojans. 'Yes,' she gasped, helplessly. 'Yes, I'll do whatever you want.'

'Perhaps I'll sell your body to them. Then you'd have to do whatever they wanted, wouldn't you?' His breathing was almost as ragged as her own now, and his cock was as rigid as an iron bar against her buttocks.

'First, you're going to kneel in front of me, with your knees apart, and unzip me,' he continued hoarsely as he gave her mound another hard squeeze. 'You're going to drop my trousers and pants and take hold of my cock.' He emphasised each word carefully. 'You're going to take me in your mouth and suck me dry.'

Maggie half-opened her eyes and again looked at the reflection in the glass. 'No. Please sir, don't make me suck your cock,' she pleaded softly.

'Worse than that, Maggie. You are going to put your hand between your legs and finger yourself. Right in front of me so that I can watch you.' He pushed his finger deeper into her. 'I don't want any faking, Maggie. I want to see you climax.'

His voice was becoming more and more strained as his arousal deepened. Maggie felt him tug her panties down to her knees and pull her skirt up. As he guided her back against him, she discovered that he had also unzipped himself. She couldn't contain the soft moan as she felt his burning cock nestling between the cheeks of her buttocks. What if somebody came looking for him? Well, it was a bit late to worry about it now; she doubted if she could stop him even if she wanted to.

'Oh yes,' she whispered, as he began moving up and down against her. She tightened her muscles around his hardness and stared at the reflection as he tugged her skirt even higher, exposing her mound. She glanced up and saw him watching her watching them both. His face was flushed with excitement and the memory of his words made her clit tingle even more urgently.

Justin pushed her forward and thrust harder against her. 'When I'm finished with you, I'm going to pass you around to all my friends,' he breathed softly. 'Women as well as men. You'll have to please them all.'

'Oh please, no,' she whispered. 'Not women, too.'

Maggie felt his movements grow more urgent at the sound of her pleading, and her own breath caught in her throat. 'I'll do anything you want if you just promise not to give me to your female friends,' she begged.

'You're already doing what I want,' he whispered. 'Maybe I'll make a video of you screwing my friends. Would you like that? A film of you going down on another woman?'

'No. Yes.' Maggie felt faint as she gave in to the images he was conjuring up in her mind. She imagined a room full of men and woman all running their hands over her naked body at the same time, while Justin watched and wanked himself. Her legs trembled and she felt another trickle of lubrication run down her thighs.

'You'll let me watch you licking another woman. Yes?'

'Yes.' She would too. She knew she would. What she really wanted was to be made to do it, so that she had no choice. It was one of her darkest fantasies to be virtually raped by a whole group of men and women.

Justin groaned helplessly as the first burst of his climax splattered across her lower back. Maggie felt him spurt again then again, directing his flow over her buttocks and thighs. She could hear his laboured breathing and see the wild look in his eyes as she stared round at him. She pushed her mound hard on to his hand and let her own pleasure engulf her.

Spent, Justin pulled her limp body up and pushed her over the chair. She felt his hands smearing his spunk all over her buttocks and thighs. She lifted her skirt higher to make it easier for him.

'It is supposed to be good for the skin, isn't it?' He smiled cheekily at her as he stood up and began to tug his clothes back on.

Maggie started to get up. 'I think I need a shower.'

'I'll see you tonight then. About eight o'clock?' Justin started towards the door, then stopped and turned his head to whisper in her ear. 'You can keep yourself hot and juicy for me,' he commanded softly, 'but you're not to climax until I say you can.'

Later, as she brushed her short brown hair and pondered over what to wear, Maggie contemplated how much she had enjoyed earning her tickets. The whole concept of virtually selling herself like that thrilled her. Maybe she could acquire a couple more tickets this evening. She knew that Claire and Sara would both love to go to the match too.

Maggie threw the dress she was holding to one side and picked up another one. It was short and tight fitting with a slit up one side and a low V-neck. The soft, silvery-grey material matched her eyes perfectly and gave her skin a warm, healthy glow. She remembered how Justin's eyes had bulged the last time that she had worn it.

Maggie slipped the dress over her head and pushed her feet into matching silver sandals. As she gave her face a final quick scrutiny in the mirror, the doorbell buzzed. One thing you could say for Justin: he was always punctual. Unless, of course, he failed to show at all. Remembering his unforgivable sin of standing her up, Maggie resolved to give him a hard time that evening. Given the way she was feeling, she decided, that shouldn't be too difficult. Smirking to herself, she picked up her jacket and bag and hurried to the front door.

'Ready?' Justin eyed her up and down and whistled softly. 'Very nice.'

Maggie smiled and gave him a swift kiss on the cheek. She caught a whiff of his expensive aftershave. 'You don't look so bad yourself,' she told him generously. It was true. Justin might not be a Trojan but his body was in pretty good shape and his silk shirt and well-tailored trousers fitted him like a second skin.

She savoured her memories of what he had done and said to her in the office and wondered what he had in store for her later. Would he dare keep any of his threats? If so, would she go through with it? She'd never been with another woman before. Well, not properly, only the sort of adolescent playing around most young girls experimented with at some stage. Still, she knew that a lot of men fantasised about it. Now that she thought about it, it was perfect for her. She'd always been a natural tease and, although men thought they controlled her, it was usually they who ended up desperate and panting for it by the time she was done. This, of course, was just the way she wanted it.

'Is that all I get?' he complained. 'A peck on the cheek?' Justin put his arms around her and pulled her closer to him. He put his lips against hers and forced them apart with his tongue.

Maggie snuggled tightly against him, savouring the moment. She put her hands behind his head and ran her fingers along his ponytail. She loved long hair on men. It was so sensual. Her pelvis was hard against his groin and she could feel the outline of his cock through the tight material of his trousers. She closed her eyes and conjured up an image of the dark Trojan who was never far from her mind. She hadn't forgotten Jan's words and the thought of pushing herself against Troy's huge prick caused a sudden rush of moisture between her thighs.

With a soft moan, Maggie plunged her tongue deep inside Justin's mouth. She wriggled her hips, pushing herself eagerly against him. Justin's body stiffened slightly and she felt his penis twitch against her as he started to respond. His hand slipped down to the small of her back, pulling her body even harder on to him and she felt her breasts flattening against his broad chest. She marvelled at the sheer strength of his arms.

'You're a bit overdressed for what I've got in mind,' he told her, as he pulled his lips from hers and started to nuzzle her neck in a way that was guaranteed to drive her insane. Her legs started to tremble and a flame of lust ignited like a pilot light in the pit of her stomach. She could see the longing in his eyes and hear his breath rasping as he struggled to keep himself under control.

'Take your knickers off,' he ordered her, as he released her body and stepped back to watch.

Maggie put a look of fear and disdain on her face. Slowly, as if reluctant to comply, she pulled her hem up to her waist and spun round on her heels. She leant forward and slipped her fingers through the elastic. Gradually, she slid her panties down over the bulge of her buttocks, taking care to ensure that the hem of her skirt remained well up out of the way. She straightened slowly, sliding her fingers round over her hips and on round towards her mound as she turned back towards him.

Justin was watching her avidly, his face frozen and his eyes unblinking. As she grasped the elastic at the front and began to roll the material down over her crotch, she heard his urgent sigh.

'Now your bra,' he demanded hoarsely.

Maggie stepped out of her panties and tugged the shoulders of her dress down. As she undid her bra, her breasts dropped free and Justin bent his head forward and nipped her right nipple with his front teeth. Immediately, she felt both nipples harden. Maggie had big nipples and she knew from experience that they would not go down again for ages now. What's more, Justin knew it too.

Grinning, Justin nibbled her other nipple and then pulled her tight against him again and started squeezing her buttocks. She could feel his cock straining against his clothing. If she didn't stop him soon, it would be too late. Teasingly, she pushed him away. She didn't want things to go too far, just yet. She wanted to tease him until he was horny and desperate. They had the whole evening in front of them. She certainly didn't want him sated so soon.

'Come on,' she whispered. 'I'm starving. I haven't eaten anything since breakfast.' Her voice sounded shaky, even to her own ears. She realised that she was more turned on than she had been for a long time. She loved this game, loved it when a man lusted after her like this. She watched his face as he tried to cover his disappointment. His breathing was fast and erratic and she examined the longing in his eyes anxiously, wondering if she had already gone too far. She heard him swallow as he regained his self-control.

'OK then. Let's get going before you get me too excited.' Justin tugged at the crotch of his trousers to loosen them and Maggie felt another erotic thrill at the thought of what was causing his discomfort.

Outside, Justin helped her into the passenger seat of his almost-new MGF, and Maggie savoured the way his eyes darted up her skirt as she swung her legs in, and sank back on the soft leather.

For once, he drove slowly, only lifting his hand from her thigh to change gear. Maggie could see that his trousers were still too tight across the groin area: a situation she did her best to encourage by placing her hand in his lap and gently tracing the outline of his zip with one fingertip. By the time they reached the club, they were both flushed and breathless and she could feel her heart thumping erratically in her chest.

Justin parked the car in one of the very few remaining slots and moved slowly round to open her door. Maggie noticed that he was having trouble walking and that he had to stop to adjust his trousers again. This vivid reminder of his physical arousal made her squeeze her own thighs together tightly. She took her time climbing out, deliberately smoothing her skirt over her thighs to remind him that she wasn't wearing any underclothes.

As they headed for the door, Maggie could see Justin glancing repeatedly at her still-swollen nipples poking proudly through the thin material of her dress. She shivered with a mixture of excitement and cold as the raw February wind cut through her clothing and chilled the dampness between her legs.

As they passed a convenient clump of spindly bushes, he grabbed her arm and tugged her into the scant seclusion provided. His tongue found her mouth again and his hands were soon all over her naked thighs and buttocks. She could sense an unaccustomed intensity to his caresses that made her weak with longing as she eagerly curled her tongue around his. It was only when she heard the sound of his zip opening that she found enough will-power to push him away.

'Behave yourself,' she whispered shakily, as much to herself as to him.

When they pushed through the Cellar door the heat hit them like a wall. As they stumbled down the narrow stairwell, blinking in the subdued lighting, Justin gripped her tightly round the waist with his fingertips teasing one of her nipples. Maggie clamped her thighs together, as tightly as she could, and hoped no one would look up her skirt as they descended the stairs.

Although it was still quite early, they soon discovered that the popular club was already packed and humming. Justin forced a path through the swaying bodies on the dance floor as he led her over to the tiny 'reserved' table in the far corner. A perspiring waiter appeared almost immediately, and he and Justin exchanged a few friendly words before Justin ordered two glasses of white wine.

Maggie was acutely aware of the way the waiter was staring at her, almost as if he could see her nakedness under her dress. She wondered if Justin had said anything about her to him. They obviously knew each other. The neckline of her dress was low enough to give him a good view and she made a conscious effort to stop herself from crossing her arms to cover up. He must have been able to see her nipples. She examined his crotch surreptitiously, wondering how he would react if she let her hem slip up any higher over her naked thighs.

As the waiter left, Justin sat back and opened the menu.

'What do you fancy to eat?' he asked. 'Maggie? Wake up!'

'What?' The sound of her name pulled her back from her fantasies. 'Sorry. I was miles away. What did you say?'

'Food. You said you were starving. What do you want to eat?'

Maggie realised that the waiter had already returned with their wine and was hovering over them expectantly, his eyes everywhere. Her stomach was doing little flips as the after-effects of her arousal still coursed through her veins. 'Eh, um.' She glanced down at the menu and remembered the blue-black sheen of Troy's skin. 'Stuffed aubergine with cheese sauce.'

Justin raised one eyebrow, then looked up at the waiter. 'And I'll have a steak and salad. Rare, with lots of mushrooms.'

While they waited for the food, they sipped their wine and chatted about work. Justin, who was a dynamic and ambitious manager, had recently introduced a new quality management programme at the rink. He was anxious to discuss ways in which he could encourage the casual staff to get more actively involved.

Maggie tried to show some enthusiasm, but her heart was not really in it. Although she could appreciate what he was trying to achieve, it was harder to imagine how casual part-timers like herself and Claire could be motivated to give the same dedication to their work as Justin did to his. Jan would appreciate his point of view, but then Jan was as ambitious, maybe more so, as Justin was.

Besides, Justin wasn't exactly making it easy for her to concentrate. Her mind was far too engrossed in the feel of his hand – which had somehow contrived to find its way on to her thigh under the table – to worry about anything else. She marvelled at the casual way in which he managed to carry out a perfectly normal conversation while his fingers crept relentlessly up her leg. By the time the food arrived, she found that she was no longer hungry – at least, not for food. She pushed her fork around her plate, absent-mindedly tracing suggestive patterns in the thick white sauce. The purple-black skin of the aubergine seemed to taunt her.

'I didn't think that was really your sort of thing,' Justin said and nodded towards her plate. 'Do you want to try something else?'

'No. This is fine, honestly. I guess I'm just not as hungry as I thought.' She gave up on the meal and pushed the plate away from her.

Justin finished polishing off his steak and took a swig of wine. He stood up. 'Well then, since you won't want a sweet, how about a dance?'

'Why not?' Maggie greeted the idea enthusiastically. She was still feeling keyed-up and restless. Dancing would be a great way to burn off some of her excess energy. She stood up slowly, carefully rearranging her dress, and took his outstretched hand.

The dance floor was now so crowded that it was virtually impossible to do anything more than stand in one spot and sway in time to the music. Justin pulled her against him and slipped his hands down on to her buttocks. Maggie sensed that he was keen to recreate the thrill of their earlier embrace. That was just fine with her.

She hugged him tight, her own passion quickly mounting at the feel of his cock pressed into her stomach. Her head was reeling with the effects of the wine, the heavy atmosphere and the unsettling images in her mind. She was practically willing him to lift her hem and expose her nakedness to everyone. Excitedly, she thrust her crotch harder against his, grinding her hips against him in an effort to provoke him still further. She felt an uncharacteristic urge to behave both impulsively and dangerously.

Before she could stop herself, Maggie slipped her hands between their bodies and took hold of the catch at the waistband of his trousers. She eased it open and started to slide the zip down.

Justin tensed and pulled her tighter against himself, trying to trap her hand. 'What are you doing?' he whispered anxiously.

'I'm sorry? Is something wrong?' she questioned innocently as she finished undoing the zip and pushed her fingers inside the opening. 'Don't stop dancing.'

'Jesus, Maggie!' Justin jumped violently as her hand slipped down the top of his pants and closed around his expanding penis. He lost his balance and they stumbled against the couple next to them. 'Sorry,' he muttered awkwardly, as he pulled her even closer against him. His hands slipped around her hips to try to hide what she was doing. He was holding her so tightly that her fingers could barely move.

Maggie drew her stomach in and pulled back slightly to create some space in which to work, then slid her fingers gradually down his burning shaft. Justin immediately pushed hard, trying to pin her hand, and Maggie's whole body began to tingle with the erotic stimulation of what she was doing to him. He had a problem. He couldn't back away from her or he would expose himself to everyone. She pushed his pants down and tucked them under his balls so that his cock was even more exposed.

'Stop struggling or everyone will see,' she threatened softly, as she gave his genitals a warning squeeze. Justin gasped and relaxed his body slightly. Maggie smiled and wrapped her fingers round his cock again. Despite his shock, Justin was still swelling rapidly beneath her fingers and she could feel his body trembling as she tightened her grip and began to pump him slowly.

'Shit. Don't. Oh God, woman! What are you trying to do to me?' His voice was no more than a feeble squeak. He tried to pull her even closer against him and she felt his hands tightening on her buttocks. She shivered again and began to pump him harder. His cock twitched in her fingers and she felt the first drops of moisture dribbling from the tip.

A surge of lust shot through her, so powerful that she almost fell over. Her breasts began to tingle and her own lubrication was making a rapidly expanding damp patch between her legs. His cock jerked again and she heard him draw a sharp breath.

'Why don't we go back and sit down?' he hissed through clenched teeth as he tried to guide her back towards their table. Maggie shook her head.

'Not yet,' she told him softly. 'I'm just getting into the rhythm.' She increased her movement still further, so that she was pumping him rapidly. She heard him gasp again as he tried to jerk his hips back from her.

'For God's sake,' he pleaded, 'I won't be able to hold it if you keep doing that.'

'Try,' she breathed, kneading him mercilessly with her fingertips and marvelling at the way he seemed to be still growing. 'You're always preaching about self-discipline. Practise what you preach.'

Perversely, her words seemed to steady him a bit. He took another deep breath and pushed his tongue into her ear. Maggie whimpered and almost lost her balance again as a cold shiver ran down the back of her legs. Justin started to pull the front of her dress up and Maggie stumbled against him.

'What's the matter?' he whispered as he steadied her swaying body with his strong arms. 'Where's that self-control you were talking about?' He nibbled her earlobe and squeezed her tightly.

Maggie realised that Justin was fighting back. He put his hand on the small of her back and pulled her tight. His other hand moved on to her breast and she felt his fingertips caressing her exposed nipple. She was squeezed so tightly against him that, as she moved her fingers up and down his cock, she was rubbing herself as well. The pang of desire in the pit of her stomach was so strong, so intense, that it was making her head spin. She couldn't remember ever feeling quite so desperate. It was all she could do to stop herself ripping his clothes off him in front of everyone. Her fingers clasped his cock so hard that he grunted in pain.

'Christ. Be careful what you're doing,' he gasped as he jerked his hips back. 'What's got into you tonight?' He moved his hand so that it was resting on her bare thigh, then slipped it up under the back of her skirt so that his fingers were lightly brushing the curve of her left buttock. Maggie felt the hem of her dress lifting.

What indeed, Maggie asked herself as she thrust her breasts urgently on to his chest. Her nipples were now so hard that they were almost painful. She thought about her nakedness under her dress and wondered if she could lift the material even higher so that she could feel him directly against her burning skin without anyone noticing. She forced her hand deeper into his trousers again and cupped his balls with her palm. Her fingers started to caress the soft, sensitive skin just behind them.

Justin's body shuddered violently and she felt his cock lurch against her arm. 'Oh Jesus. Let's get out of here,' he whispered urgently.

Maggie nodded silently, not trusting herself to say anything. She started to withdraw her hand, enjoying the feel of his burning erection as she ran her fingers slowly up him. When she reached the top, she started to tease the damp tip with tiny circular movements of her fingers. The trembling of his body and his ragged breathing in her ear told her how much he liked it, and his reaction fed her own passion so that they were both shaking as if consumed with a raging fever.

'Please Maggie. We have to go. I swear I can't take much more.'

His words were almost more than she could stand. Her clit was so hot and sensitive that she was half-afraid just the touch of her dress rubbing across it would be enough to bring her off. She knew that she would shout out loud when she came. Justin was right. They had to leave, fast.

Maggie pulled her hand out of his trousers and tried to force the zip back up. He was so hard that she couldn't close the material across him.

'Leave it. I'll do it.' Justin moved his hands up between their bodies. His knuckles pressed hard against her and she raised herself on tiptoe so that she could press her mound on to his hand. Her movements made his task even more difficult but, finally, she felt the zip close. Justin slipped his arm around her waist and, walking just behind her, began to guide her through the gyrating bodies surrounding them.

Maggie's legs felt weak and wobbly and she took small, careful steps; her hands were clasping his so hard that her knuckles whitened. We must look as if we're both drunk, she realised, as they weaved and swayed awkwardly across the dance floor. Justin was hunched over, trying to hide his obvious arousal and she could feel her dress sticking to the patches of damp sweat down her back and between her thighs. The soft material rubbed teasingly across her oversensitive clit, so that she could hardly think about anything else.

She had no idea where they were going. She didn't care. Just so long as he got them out before the heat, noise and excitement overcame her completely. She half-closed her eyes and allowed him to push her along in front of him until they were practically running. The tingling between her legs continued to torment her.

Justin steered her swiftly along a dim corridor that led

to an emergency exit at the back of the club. When he let her go to lift the bar handle, she swayed awkwardly and had to put her hand against the wall to steady herself. What was wrong with her? She had only had one glass of wine.

Maggie heard Justin sigh with relief as the door opened. He grabbed her arm almost roughly and pushed her through. As he slammed it closed behind them, he was already ripping at his tie. Dropping it to the ground, he unzipped his trousers and let them fall to his ankles.

She breathed in deeply. The air was sharp and cold after the intense heat of the dance floor and she felt the goose bumps rising on her skin. Apart from the faint boom of the disco music, the hotel grounds were quiet and deserted, save for a slight creaking of the branches in the surrounding trees.

Justin grabbed her again and pushed her round so that her back was up against the door. With one quick movement, he pulled her dress up over her head, trapping her arms and blinding her to the world. His strong hands began kneading her aching breasts and she felt his warm, damp tongue running across her stomach.

'Oh my God!' she cried out, as she felt one of her nipples sucked into his mouth. Another surge of animal lust tore through her. Almost unaware of what she was doing, she struggled one arm free and tugged her dress off her, leaving her naked but for her sandals. She reached out desperately to grab his pants. As she ripped them down, she felt his cock burst out and rub across her bare flesh. He groaned loudly. He grabbed her left leg and lifted it up round his hip, exposing her hot dampness.

Maggie dug her heel into his thigh and leaned back hard against the door to stop herself falling. She felt his arms lifting her up so that she was almost off the ground and she whimpered softly as his prick slipped effortlessly into her. Instinctively, she pushed her hips forward, pulling him in even deeper. She hooked her right leg round his other thigh so that she was totally impaled on him.

'God, woman. You've been asking for this all night.' Justin started to thrust roughly in and out of her and she felt her buttocks and thighs banging rhythmically against the door. Nearby, she heard the sound of another door opening and muffled voices carried clearly through the still night air as a couple of kitchen staff sneaked outside to enjoy a quick smoke. They sounded very close. What if they heard and came to investigate?

Maggie started to struggle, wiggling from side to side as she attempted to escape. Her movements only seemed to excite Justin further. She could sense that he was now so far gone that nothing would stop him. He probably wouldn't care if the entire kitchen staff stood round shouting encouragement.

Despite her fear, the thought of being caught only served to fuel her own passion. As she felt Justin lean forward and suck her nipple into his soft lips, Maggie gasped aloud and ground her clit desperately against him until she felt her long-overdue orgasm finally explode inside her. Sobbing almost incoherently, she sagged limply against him, then gasped again at the feel of his cock juddering violently as he, too, started to climax.

'Oh yes,' he groaned loudly, as the pleasure of his release overwhelmed him.

Totally spent, Maggie sank back against the wall and felt his cock slipping softly out of her. The kitchen door opened and closed again as the workers finished their cigarettes and returned to work. In the distance, through the heavy door behind them, Maggie could still hear the thumping rhythm of disco music. The cold night air caressed her naked body.

'I think that was probably worth at least four tickets, don't you?' she whispered huskily, as she reached out for her crumpled dress.

Chapter Two

Maggie struggled to appear nonchalant as she waved the coveted match tickets under her friend's nose. Jan's eyes widened when she realised what they were.

'Where the hell did you get those?' She snatched at the tickets. 'Four of them! I heard that there weren't any left to be had anywhere.' She grinned meaningfully. 'I said it was useful to have friends in high places, didn't I? Good ol' Justin. What did you have to do to get them?'

Maggie looked smug. 'Oh just be my normal, irresistible self,' she said, laughing.

Jan stared at the tickets again. 'It's a pity Marcus isn't going to be around. Mind you, I don't suppose he'd go. He's becoming so lazy, it's as much as I can do to get him to take me out for a meal these days.'

Maggie grinned to herself. No matter what Jan said, everyone knew who wore the pants in their relationship. If Jan really wanted Marcus to take her anywhere, then Marcus would take her. Secretly, Maggie found Marcus rather pathetic. She had always preferred her men to be a bit more forceful. Not too forceful, mind you. It was fun to take the dominant role sometimes, too.

'So, who else are you going to invite?' Jan questioned. 'You can't let these go to waste. They're like gold dust.'

'I've already asked Sara and Claire,' Maggie replied quickly. Jan and Claire did not always get on that well. They tended to argue pointlessly about the most stupid things while Sara and Maggie did their best to keep the peace. It was probably because Claire was even more flighty than Maggie was. Jan seemed to feel a kind of personal responsibility to set Claire straight on almost everything, from politics to fashion. Still, it couldn't be helped. She had four tickets and, if anything, Claire was a bigger Trojan fan than Jan was.

'What about accommodation? I don't fancy the idea of driving back afterwards and I can't afford anything too pricey. I've just paid out a small fortune to have the bedroom redecorated.' Jan was always redecorating one room or another. It was an obsession with her.

Maggie breathed a mental sigh of relief that Jan had not made a fuss about her inviting Claire. 'No problem,' she replied. 'Justin has promised to fix us up at a B&B he knows. It won't cost much.' Her smile broadened as she prepared to spring her other surprise. 'He's even hinted that he might be able to get us invited to dinner with the Trojans after the game.'

'You're kidding?' Jan grinned knowingly. 'That must have been some night.'

Maggie thought about what she had done to Justin in the Cellar. 'You could say that I found his weak spot,' she replied with a giggle.

The day of the match was dull and wet and the traffic on the motorway was even worse than Maggie had anticipated. Despite setting out mid-afternoon, by the time they reached Bristol and found the accommodation that Justin had arranged for them, it was already growing quite late.

Maggie was feeling tired and grumpy from the drive. No one had offered to help her navigate and the Saturday traffic through the centre of Bristol had been so heavy and erratic that she had had trouble finding her way. Several times she had missed a turning and been forced to double back.

While she had been concentrating on reading road names and dodging suicidal shoppers, the others had all been laughing and chatting excitedly as they discussed the match and the possibility of dinner afterwards. For once, even Jan and Claire seemed to be getting on, and as Maggie watched her three friends talking and joking together as they filed into the boarding house and began squabbling over who was going to sleep where, she felt a little excluded. She quickly dumped her overnight case on a bed by the window and then excused herself to go and freshen up.

As she stared at her flaming, angry face in the mirror above the basin, Maggie's bad temper melted away. Why spoil the weekend by sulking? The drive might have been awful but they were there now. In just over an hour they would be watching the game and, if Justin kept his word, afterwards they would actually get to meet the players in person.

Seeing that there was no shower attachment and deciding that she did not have time for a bath, Maggie stripped off to her lacy bra and matching thong and gave her body a quick sponge down. Then she splashed a little cool water on her cheeks and repaired her make up before hurrying back to the room to change.

The others were already unpacking their things. Maggie pulled on a long-sleeved jumper and wrapped her favourite calf-length tartan skirt around her slim waist. The players might be dripping with perspiration during the game, but it could be quite cold for the spectators. Normally, she would have worn trousers like the others, but the skirt was more flattering to her figure and she wanted to look her best.

* * *

The 'Birds' home rink was packed to capacity. Maggie was surprised at how many Trojan supporters were among the excited throng and delighted to find that the seats Justin had got for them were in the front row, right in the centre of the neutral zone. Maggie scanned the crowd, searching for Justin, but couldn't spot him anywhere. She could see the Trojans' coach talking earnestly with the team manager and another important-looking businessman, probably one of the sponsors. The coach's face looked strained and he seemed to be arguing with the manager about something.

The clock moved towards 7.30 p.m. and the four women quickly stocked up with popcorn and fizzy drinks from the kiosk. As they hurried to get seated before the face-off, Justin suddenly appeared, grinning excitedly.

'Hi Mags.' He kissed her cheek in an almost brotherly fashion. 'Sorry not to have caught up with you earlier. The coach was in a flap about something or other. Is your accommodation OK?'

Maggie smiled up at him. He was looking even smarter than usual in a beige-coloured suit and black silk shirt. His pale blue eyes were flashing with excitement.

'It's fine, thanks. And the seats are great.'

'Yes. Thanks Justin,' Jan added. 'I don't know what you made Maggie do for them, but whatever it was, it was worth it.' She gave them a sly grin.

Maggie glared at her friend, but Justin just chuckled. Sara smiled awkwardly and Claire giggled.

'Oh, by the way –' Justin gave Maggie one of his most dazzling smiles, '– the Trojans' manager hopes that you and your friends will join us for dinner afterwards.' He manoeuvred himself between Maggie and Jan as he ushered them towards their reserved seats. Maggie found herself on the end of the row, up against a partition, with Justin on her other side.

As they sat down there was an increased buzz of

excitement and the two ice hockey squads entered the rink, waving their sticks enthusiastically in the air to the delighted roaring of the fans. The first twelve players took up their positions and one of the referees held up the puck between the two centre ice players.

Justin leant forward and reached under his seat. 'We wouldn't want you to catch cold now, would we?' he explained cheerfully as he produced a quilted blanket and started to spread it out to cover their legs. It was just wide enough to cover Jan's knees as well.

'Thank you.' Maggie was touched by this unexpected consideration.

There was a yell from the crowd as the puck dropped to the ice in the centre of the face-off circle. The Trojan centre player was on it immediately. With an elegant and skilful flick of his stick, the puck went spinning across the ice into their attacking zone, with one of the Trojan's forwards in hot pursuit. It was difficult to see who was who under the helmets and heavy padding but Maggie had no trouble picking out Troy as he neatly intercepted the pass and spun round to try for a shot at goal.

The 'Birds' closest defender zoomed into action, barging full speed into Troy in an attempt to knock him off-balance. His stick passed in front of Troy's legs, just below the shins, and Troy went flying.

'Penalty,' screamed the Trojan supporters, as Troy struggled in vain to regain his balance and keep possession of the puck.

The whistle blew. 'Two minute hooking call against the 'Birds. Power-play to the Trojans.'

The crowd roared and Maggie's heart thumped with excitement. The 'Birds would be at a real disadvantage for the next couple of minutes while they were a defender down. She watched breathlessly as the two sides vied for possession of the elusive puck and the precious seconds ticked by. 'Come on, Trojans!' she muttered over and over. Suddenly, the puck shot across the ice, deep into the attacking zone, where it was neatly intercepted by Bri. With a deft flick of his wrist, the young Trojan forward sent the puck careering wildly towards Troy on the far side of the goal.

The 'Birds remaining defender sprang into the fray, skimming over the ice to barge heavily into Troy's broad back. Troy stumbled and the spectators gasped then cheered as he regained his balance and drove the puck relentlessly on towards the goal. Suddenly, the 'Birds' defender barged him again, whisking the puck away from under the blade of Troy's stick before he had time to react.

Maggie and her friends groaned in dismay as the puck flew back over the blue line and into the neutral zone. Maggie glanced at the clock. The power play was almost up. Another twenty seconds and the second defender would be back in play. The advantage was getting away from them. Justin's hand slipped on to her knee under the blanket and Maggie stiffened. She turned her head and saw that he was cheerfully discussing the 'Birds' checking skills with Jan. His hand crept up her leg.

Damn! She could be so naïve sometimes. The blanket wasn't meant to keep her warm at all: it was to hide what he was up to. She glanced nervously at Jan, wondering if her friend knew what was going on, but all three women seemed to be totally engrossed in what Justin was saying. She shifted her buttocks awkwardly, wishing that the seats were not so small and cramped.

'So, tell us more about some of the players,' Claire begged Justin. 'Like, what do they do when they're not skating? I mean, I've never seen any of them out clubbing or anything.'

Justin smiled indulgently. 'They don't have much time for clubs during the season. They have to train hard. Besides, a lot of them don't come from round here. When the season's over, they usually go home.'

'What about Pary?' asked Claire '– does he, like, have

a girlfriend or anything?' Maggie had been wondering how long it would take for her to get round to that question; she could be so transparent sometimes.

'I've no idea,' Justin replied. 'You can ask him yourself later.'

Claire reddened visibly.

'I've heard rumours that Pele is thinking of not renewing his contract next season,' Jan commented. 'Do you know why?'

Justin shrugged. 'There are always rumours at this time of year. It's all part of the game of negotiating new contracts for next season. I guess it depends if we win the cup or not. Pele's also a skilled mechanic. So far as I know, he plans to set up in business for himself when his hockey days are over.'

'Really?' Jan responded thoughtfully. 'Still, it would be a shame to lose him. He's the best goalkeeper we've ever had.'

'Net-minder, not goalkeeper,' Claire interjected scornfully. Maggie sighed, praying that she and Jan were not about to get into one of their stupid scraps. She felt Justin give her leg another gentle fondle and quickly squeezed her thighs together.

'At least you'd know where to take your car for servicing,' Maggie commented pointedly, knowing that it wasn't her car Jan was thinking about. Sometimes, Jan could be nearly as transparent as Claire.

There was another scream of anticipation from the fans and a sudden flurry of activity on the ice as the Trojan centre lunged madly to intercept the speeding puck. The crowd groaned as he overshot, crashed into the side of the rink and fell heavily. Immediately, a substitute rushed out on to the ice. It was the Trojans' newest recruit, Tor, and Maggie held her breath again as he expertly whisked the puck out from under his opponent's nose and sent it gliding back towards the Trojan attacking zone.

The penalty period came to an end and the 'Birds' second defender rushed back into the game. He was too late; Troy had timed the speeding puck perfectly. As it reached the blade of his stick, he whirled it round and sent it skimming straight into the goal. It was so fast and so precisely timed that the 'Birds' net-minder never stood a chance.

'One, nil!' Jan, Sara and Claire roared with delight as the scoreboard registered the Trojans' success and the fans all jumped to their feet to cheer and clap. Maggie took advantage of the situation to push Justin's hand away and leap up herself. Now that she was wise to him, she would be more careful when she sat back down.

Justin flashed her another beguiling smile. 'Enjoying yourself?' he whispered innocently as he helped her back into her seat and carefully rearranged the blanket over her legs before she could protest. Within seconds, his probing fingers had found the split in her wrap-around skirt and started pulling it clear of her clamped thighs. Maggie clenched her teeth as his hand began to slide higher and higher up her now bare thigh.

Out on the ice, the pace of the game intensified. The 'Birds' fans were screaming for blood and there were definite signs of panic in their ranks as their two forwards struggled to level the score. Substitute players were rushed on and off in a seemingly senseless frenzy, as if the 'Birds just couldn't settle on a coherent line up, and a vicious fight broke out between one of their burly defencemen and a Trojan winger. Inevitably, this resulted in both players being banished to the penalty box for roughing, and another exciting double power-play struggle ensued.

Maggie crossed her legs and tried her best to follow the frantic action. Without being too obvious about what she was doing, she tried to tuck the material of her skirt back between her thighs, while Justin remorselessly pulled it clear again with his fingers. Before she realised his intentions, she felt him fiddling with the skirt pin at her thigh. With a deft flick of his fingers, the pin came undone and Maggie tried to grab his hand before he could remove it. She was too slow. As he withdrew his hand, she felt her skirt falling away from her legs, so that all she was wearing under the blanket was her lacy thong and her stockings. Feeling incredibly exposed, she gripped the blanket tightly with both hands, holding it up over her nakedness.

Justin triumphantly examined the pin then slipped it into his far pocket, where she could not hope to reach it. 'Yes. Go for it!' he called excitedly, as Pary made a surprise attack on the goal that almost got past the skilful 'Birds' defence. His hand began to explore Maggie's legs once again, and she was surprised at the strength in his fingers as they forced their way between her tightly clenched thighs, obliging her to expose herself even further to his demanding caresses. Her knuckles had turned white with the effort she was putting into gripping the blanket up over her. If she had dared to let go of it, she would have slapped his face. Except, of course, she wouldn't really. If she did, then everyone would know what he was doing to her.

'Stop it!' she hissed at him as his probing fingers began gliding up her thigh towards her mound. His touch was now so light that she could barely feel it and goose bumps were making the little hairs on her thighs stand up. Another shiver of anticipation and longing trickled down her spine as his fingers drew ever closer to her tingling clit. She sighed with disappointment as he stopped and retraced his journey back down her leg and over her stocking top. Despite her discomfort at her predicament, her treacherous body was already responding enthusiastically to his caresses, and part of her was willing him to move back up.

Out on the ice, the battle continued. Despite their obvious panic to score, the 'Birds were not letting up on their relentless defending for one second. They were famous for having the best defensive play of any team and, no matter how hard they struggled, the Trojan's couldn't seem to get through their two defenders a second time.

Justin, on the other hand, was having a much easier time of it. As if sensing her growing arousal and wavering resistance, he intensified his assault. Maggie yelped softly as his hand glided up her leg and moved over to the other one, so that his knuckles skimmed lightly across her sex. She reddened and looked around quickly to see if anyone had heard her, but everyone seemed to be engrossed in the game, even Justin. She frowned at the innocent expression on his face and took a deep breath to calm her thudding pulse. As she struggled to return her concentration to the ice rink, she felt his knuckles return. She bit her lip to stop herself whimpering as his fingers started to grope under the elastic of her panties.

'Yes! Well played!' yelled Jan as Troy made another magnificent pass to Bri and the 'Birds' defenceman lost his balance and mistimed his attack. Maggie felt her panties starting to slip down her thighs.

'No!' She grasped his hand through the blanket.

'Yes!' Justin began to pull the blanket away with his other hand, so that Maggie was obliged to let go of him to pull it back over her. Immediately, she felt him resume his efforts. She pushed her bottom down hard on to the seat, but it was no use. Either the elastic was going to snap or her skirt was going to slide right off her with her panties. As she raised her buttocks in surrender, she glared angrily at his enigmatic smile and contemplated scratching his eyes out.

Justin's smile widened as he continued to lower her panties down her thighs. As soon as they were clear of her buttocks, Maggie sat back down quickly to stop her skirt disappearing as well. She could hide the fact that her knickers were missing, but she wouldn't be able to move out of her seat if her skirt fell right off too.

Out on the rink, another fight had broken out in the neutral zone between the two centre players, and the crowd was roaring and booing as the referee hurried to intervene. Justin had left Maggie's panties halfway down her thighs and was now using his fingers to prise her legs open even wider. She shivered and tried to wiggle her panties down further. Somehow, leaving them halfway down her legs seemed worse than if he had taken them right off. She shivered as he began to lightly caress her outer sex lips with his fingertips. She could feel the telltale dampness of her increasing arousal and was certain that he would notice it too.

'Popcorn?' Maggie jumped as Jan leant over Justin and waved the tub under her nose.

'No thank you,' she muttered stiffly, as she did her utmost to ignore Justin's insistent caresses. Part of her wanted to beg him to stop, part of her wanted to urge him on. She was growing more and more aroused by the second and was becoming desperate to feel his fingers inside her. Every time he touched her, she tensed her body and tried to hint what she wanted by pushing herself on to him. What was wrong with him? He wasn't usually so slow to catch on. Finally, it dawned on her.

Bastard! Maggie sank down on the seat and closed her eyes. He knew perfectly well what she wanted him to do. He was playing with her, trying to make her beg. This must be his revenge for what she had done to him in the Cellar. She opened her eyes again and stared determinedly at the game, fighting not to twitch as he parted her labia and started to tease her swollen clit. She shifted back in her seat to make it harder for him to reach her.

'Not too warm, are you?' he questioned innocently as he began to lower the blanket again.

'No! I'm fine.' Maggie grabbed the blanket quickly. Checkmate. If she didn't do exactly what he wanted, he would pull the blanket away and expose her. She watched without comment as he withdrew his hand and deliberately licked his fingers before slipping them back under the blanket.

Maggie glanced anxiously at the clock. There were only a few minutes to go before the end of the first period. She pushed her own hand under the blanket and tried to wriggle her panties down further. If she could just get them off, she could kick them under the seat before anyone noticed. Justin yanked at her arm.

'I'm taking them off,' she whispered, thinking that he had misunderstood her intentions.

Justin shook his head and resumed his relentless attack on her outer lips. Now what? Maggie sat there helplessly, watching the seconds tick by, while he continued to torture her; his caresses just enough to drive her mad but not enough to do any real good. She sighed with frustration and tried to tighten her thighs around his hand without him noticing. She almost jumped out of her skin when the hooter sounded. It was the end of the first period. Jan, Claire and Sara all stood up.

'I need another drink after all that shouting,' Jan announced, as she looked down at Justin and Maggie. 'Are you coming?' She started to pull the blanket off them.

Maggie slammed her arms down to cover herself. 'No!' she exclaimed loudly. Jan stared at her in surprise.

'Sorry. I only asked.'

'Shall I get you something Maggie?' Justin questioned as he slipped out from under the blanket and stood up.

Maggie nodded mutely.

'Pepsi?' he enquired. She nodded again.

'Come on then, Jan.' Justin took Jan's arm as they turned to follow after Claire and Sara who were already heading for the kiosk. 'Leave everything just as it is, Maggie,' he whispered, over his shoulder, as they left.

Maggie watched in silence as Justin and Jan moved off.

She glanced down at the blanket and realised that she could clearly see the ridge of her rolled-up panties underneath it. Quickly, she scrunched the blanket up so that it was not so obvious, then sat with her legs slightly apart so that she could feel the cold air from the rink rushing up between her naked thighs. Her legs kept twitching as if his fingers were still playing with her. She kept her face turned to the front, half-afraid to look round in case anyone had been watching what was happening.

Had anyone seen anything? Closing her eyes, Maggie started to imagine that the man sitting behind them had been watching it all. She pictured how excited he would have become. Was he still there, or had he rushed off somewhere private to relieve his frustrations? The idea of some strange man wanking in the loo because of her was so exciting that it was all she could do to stop herself from pushing her own hand down between her trembling thighs.

'Sorry to have been so long.' Justin's cheerful voice broke into her fantasy. 'The queues were awful.' He flopped down beside her and, before she could react, lifted the blanket up in the air to spread it back out over his and Jan's legs. Maggie felt the blood rushing to her cheeks again as she hastily yanked it back down over herself. She shot a quick glance out the corner of her eye to see if Jan or the others had noticed anything and was relieved to find that they were looking the other way.

Although she was anticipating Justin's hand under the blanket again, she wasn't prepared for the shock as he slipped a can of ice-cold Pepsi between her thighs and pushed it up hard on to her hot sex.

'Oh!' Maggie gasped aloud and doubled over, trying to push the can away. 'You bastard!' she hissed as the numbing cold began to spread over her mound and down her thighs.

Justin gave her a crooked smile and retrieved the can. Quite deliberately, he licked the side of it before handing it to her. 'Here's your juice,' he told her innocently. 'You taste better than what's inside it,' he added in a whisper as she snatched the can from him.

Her hands shaking, Maggie pulled the ring and took a long gulp of the fizzy liquid to ease her parched throat. She could still feel the numbing cold where it had rested against her and realised that she was tensed – ready for the warmth of his hand.

Jan, Claire and Sara were all chatting excitedly about the first period play, but Maggie refrained from joining in the discussion. Apart from being fairly certain that the Trojans were a goal up, she realised that she couldn't actually remember much of what had taken place. Although she clapped her hands enthusiastically as the players reappeared to start the second period, she remained firmly in her seat.

As the two teams started to race back and forth across the ice, Maggie fidgeted impatiently, longing to feel Justin's hand between her thighs again. What was he waiting for? She glanced round suspiciously to make sure that he wasn't doing anything with Jan and was relieved to see that Jan had not bothered to replace the blanket over herself when she had sat down.

From time to time, Justin patted Maggie's legs affectionately through the blanket, but she had the feeling that this was only to check that she hadn't pulled her clothes back on. For some perverse reason, his lack of attention seemed worse than his caresses had been. Her clit was still tingling and her preoccupation with her semi-nakedness made it extremely difficult to concentrate on anything else but her burning need to be fondled.

A roar from the fans directed her attention back to the ice, just in time to see their defenceman, Ean, expertly knocked off-balance by the burly 'Birds right winger. It was a superbly executed check. Before he could recover, the left winger has scooped up the lost puck and sent it spinning powerfully towards the Trojan net. Pele almost turned himself inside out trying to stop the shot but he was just not quick enough.

'One all!' screamed the ecstatic 'Birds supporters as the buzzer sounded to acknowledge the goal.

'Damn it!' Jan and Sara cursed in unison, while Claire groaned and wrung her hands together in despair. Maggie shifted awkwardly and pretended to look suitably upset. It was the first time she could ever remember being totally unaffected by a game.

Finally, with over half the second period gone, Justin seemed to remember her again. He slid his hand slowly down her back, neatly unclipping her bra on the way, then forced his fingers between the small of her back and the seat. Maggie leant forward so that his hand was resting on the top of her buttocks and Justin gave her a gentle push to tell her that he wanted her to lift herself up.

Maggie wriggled awkwardly, trying to cross her legs, but her panties were making it difficult to manoeuvre. She shifted her weight on to her left cheek, raising her right one, and gritted her teeth as she felt his hand slip underneath her. Without taking his eyes off the game, Justin began to casually caress, pat and even gently pinch her buttock between his fingers, causing little tremors of desire to race up and down her spine, and her pussy to grow damper and damper.

'Good, isn't it?' he murmured with a nod towards the ice rink. Before Maggie could respond, he slipped his hand further underneath her and she felt him deliberately collecting her juices with his fingertips. As he moved his hand back, Justin turned his head so that he could stare into her flushed face.

'Yes. Very good.' He ran one damp finger up her arse crack and round the hole. Maggie gasped and clenched her muscles, pushing him away. She tried to thrust herself back down on to the seat but that only seemed to make it easier for him. As she felt his fingertip beginning to slide in, she lifted up again so that he slipped back out.

'Two-minute slashing call penalty. Power-play to the 'Birds.' The jeers from the crowd quickly drowned out the rest of the announcement. Justin gave Maggie's hole another gentle probe and then withdrew his hand and winked at her.

'You've got a great arse, Maggie,' he told her. 'Very fuckable.' He watched her expression carefully. When she said nothing, he continued, 'Yeah, I think I might bend you over later and give you a good buggering. You'd like that, wouldn't you?'

Before Maggie could think of a suitable reply, Justin suddenly got up and, pushing past the other women, disappeared up the steps and out the exit tunnel. Maggie sat back on the seat and tried to stop her muscles twitching. She was very aware of the strange tingling in her back passage, as if his finger was still exploring her.

Jan moved across into Justin's vacated seat and gave Maggie a hard stare. 'Just what have you two been up to?' she whispered accusingly. 'Justin's cock was so hard when he left that I thought it was going to split his trousers.'

Maggie grinned feebly, not daring to answer. There was another yell from the crowd and Jan and Maggie turned back to the match. The 'Birds' wingers were making the most of their remaining advantage. As the left winger sent the puck gliding over the ice towards the goal, a Trojan defender was homing in to retrieve it. Before he reached it, however, the second winger knocked him flying, scooped up the puck and blasted it so hard at the Trojan net that Pele only just saved it. The crowd howled their approval as the teams repositioned themselves for the face off. Soon the desperate battle was once more in progress as both sides fought for supremacy.

Justin returned just as the hooter went for the end of

the second period. As Jan moved out to make way for him, he calmly sat down and began to rearrange the blanket.

'Where have you been?' Maggie demanded softly.

'Washing my hands,' he replied. 'Why? Did you miss me?'

'Liar,' she hissed. 'It doesn't take that long to wash your hands.' She was almost certain that she could smell his guilt. 'You've been wanking, haven't you?' she accused him.

'Tut, tut. Such language.' His grin seemed to grow to match her rising temper. Maggie wished that she had been able to relieve her own frustration while he was away but, with Jan sitting beside her, she had hardly dared to move. Even if Jan hadn't seen the way her clothing was rucked up under the blanket, she must have spotted that Maggie's bra was undone at the back. She'd certainly noticed the state Justin was in.

While they waited for the final period to start, the five of them remained in their seats, continuing their conversation about the players. Once again, Maggie took little part in the discussions, although her ears pricked up when Jan started to question Justin about Troy.

'He's a bit of an enigma, that one,' Justin told her. 'The coach once told me that he's got a first-class honours degree in maths or something. He's always been into sports of all kinds. Nearly chosen to swim for England in the Commonwealth games once, I believe. Anyway, he somehow got into ice hockey and here he is. I guess the money's better than teaching or whatever else he might have done.'

Maggie's heart sank. If Troy was such an intellectual he'd hardly be interested in her, would he? She'd only just scraped through her maths GCE at the second attempt. Jan was probably much more his type. It was a good thing that Jan had always seemed more interested in Pele. Besides, Jan already had Marcus, didn't she?

Maggie pretended to study a brochure about the teams while her mind raced. Every time she felt the blanket move she tensed her body, waiting for the feel of Justin's hands. The anticipation of what he might do was driving her crazy. By the time the players trooped back to resume play she was in such a state she couldn't think straight.

For a while, Justin took no further notice of her, directing all his attention to the game. Gradually, Maggie began to calm down and started to think about how she was going to make herself decent before she had to stand up.

'Drop your knickers to your ankles and open your legs wide,' Justin whispered suddenly, as if remembering how he had left her.

'No way,' Maggie responded coldly. He'd had more than enough fun at her expense already.

Justin tugged on the blanket, exposing the top of her thighs. Maggie grabbed it quickly. 'All right,' she agreed. After all, she had to do something about her knickers before the game finished. As casually as she could, she worked the offending garment down her legs and off over her ankles. Glancing round to make sure her friends were not watching, she pushed her hands up her sleeves and carefully removed her loosened bra, too.

'Very neat!' Justin grinned as he reached under the blanket to retrieve it. 'Give me your knickers as well,' he commanded, as he stuffed her bra into his pocket.

Maggie reached down and scooped up her panties from under the seat. She glanced at the clock and saw that there were only a couple of minutes of play remaining. The score was still even and, thankfully, everyone was riveted to the battle on the ice. Maggie did what she could to straighten out her skirt. She would have to try and hold it closed around her until she could get to the ladies room and do something about the missing pin. Sara might have something she could use. She was always prepared with a spare of everything.

As if reading her mind, Justin grinned and produced the skirt pin from his pocket. He waved it under her nose. 'Would you like this back?'

Maggie stared at him in silence.

'No? OK. I just thought I'd ask.' He went to put the pin back in his pocket.

'Yes, of course I want it,' Maggie snapped.

Justin held the pin up again. 'Only if you make me a promise.'

Maggie nodded mutely.

'I want you to promise me not to masturbate tonight. I want to think about you lying there, all hot and juicy and desperate, longing for me,' he told her.

Maggie frowned. It was all right for him, nipping off to the loo like that. She remembered that she was sharing a room that night anyway. 'All right,' she muttered. 'I promise, if it makes you happy. Now give me that pin.'

The clock moved into the final sixty-second countdown and the crowd leapt to its feet as the Trojans made one last, desperate bid for victory. Maggie thankfully pinned her skirt closed round her nakedness and, for the first time since the start of the game, stood up with the others to urge her heroes on.

As Troy scooped the puck from under the opposition's blade and bore down on the 'Birds' goal, Justin stood up beside her and she felt his hand creep in through the slit in her skirt. As he cupped her naked mound in his palm, she pushed herself down hard on to his hand, savouring the renewed tremors of passion rushing through her.

Troy seemed to move as if inspired. His stick flew over the ice and the opposition fell aside against his onslaught as though he was protected by an invisible force field. As he took his shot at goal, the whole rink fell silent, as everyone their breath. The puck skimmed effortlessly across the ice and into the net just as the hooter sounded for end of play. Two–one. The Trojans had won.

Maggie cheered with the others and then sighed with

regret as she felt Justin's fingers give her clit one final, lingering caress before it slipped away.

'Game over,' Justin whispered regretfully. 'And not a single interference penalty.'

She honestly couldn't decide whether to laugh or slap his smug face.

Maggie followed behind Justin's car to the restaurant the Trojans' manager had booked for their after-match celebrations. She drove silently, ignoring the conversation of her friends, with her thoughts in a whirl. Her body was still tingling from what Justin had done to her, and her imagination was fired-up by the realisation that she was finally about to meet the Trojans in person. She did her best to not even think about her lack of underwear.

By the time they arrived at the restaurant, the whole squad was already there, as well as their triumphant manager and the equally delighted coach, Stephen Jackson. There was also a pretty young brunette called Gemma, who was introduced to Maggie and the others as the Trojans' personal physiotherapist. Maggie instantly felt a pang of envy and admiration for the young woman. Now that was what she called a career! Imagine having a legitimate excuse to run your hands over all those divine bodies whenever you felt like it.

Maggie and her friends were introduced to everyone personally by Justin and her legs started to wobble when she finally found herself standing in front of Troy. She raised her head slowly, her eyes devouring his hard stomach and smooth, sleek chest. He had changed into an immaculate cream-coloured suit that fitted him to perfection. His neck was as thick and solid as a tree trunk and his chin was as square as if it had been carved from a block of solid granite. He was so close to her that she could see the gleam of perspiration on his brow and smell the strong masculine odour of his body.

Their eyes locked and, to her consternation, she

realised that he had been watching her careful appraisal of his assets. His eyes were jet-black and glistening like bullets. She blinked and tried to turn her head but his gaze was too commanding, almost hypnotic. She could not pull away. She felt her cheeks flame.

'Do you like it?' Troy murmured softly. His voice was almost as hypnotic as his eyes. She felt his warm breath across her burning cheeks and saw his gaze drop down on to his groin. She only just stopped herself from gasping.

'The suit. I've been told the colour compliments my skin.' His voice was filled with amusement and she was certain that he was playing with her. Maggie had the uncanny feeling that he could read her every thought and she remembered what she had just learned about him. Definitely not a man to be trifled with. She gulped hard and forced herself to find her voice.

'It does,' she croaked softly. Her eyes scanned his crotch again. Was it tighter than it had been a few seconds ago?

Troy laughed and put one huge hand on her arm. His touch burned like fire. 'I imagine you're thirsty after all that cheering and clapping. Can I get you a drink?'

Maggie nodded her head, not trusting herself to speak again. Her legs were now so wobbly that she was half-afraid she would fall over when he let go of her arm. She rolled her tongue around her mouth, trying to stimulate some moisture. It was ironic that her mouth should be so dry while the area between her legs was growing damper by the second.

By the time Troy reappeared with a glass of white wine in one hand, everyone was starting to move into the dining area to eat. In a daze, Maggie allowed herself to be guided to her place. She found herself sitting between Justin on one side and the physiotherapist, Gemma, on the other. She could just see Troy sitting down the far end of the table between one of the other forwards, Bri, and the Trojans' newly acquired Canadian centre, Tor.

Jan was sitting opposite her and Maggie noticed that her friend seemed to be watching the handsome new centre ice player with more than a passing interest. Tor was certainly worth looking at, with his close-cropped fair hair and big silver-grey eyes. Maggie grinned. Was Pele forgotten so soon? She realised that she felt a bit like a small child let loose in a sweet shop, surrounded as they were by so many desirable men.

As the first course was being served, Justin put his hand under the table and placed it casually on her thigh again. It occurred to her that he might be feeling a bit under threat with so much competition around. Perhaps he was subconsciously reminding her of his prior claim? She almost giggled aloud at that thought. It made her sound like a piece of real estate or something. She gave him an encouraging grin. A bird in the hand and all that. Still, if she were being completely honest with herself, should Troy indicate that he was interested all thoughts of Justin would be vanquished in a flash.

The Trojans' coach, Stephen, leant across the table and engaged Justin in a petty argument about the use of the ice resurfacing machine while Maggie supped her soup and tried to ignore the effect of Justin's hand burning into her leg. Hearing excited laughter on the other side of her, she turned her head to see what was going on.

Gemma was in full flow about something, and judging by the pink faces of her audience, her topic of conversation was nothing to do with the weather. Maggie leaned over slightly so that she could hear what Gemma was saying. She was talking to Claire and a couple of the younger players, and Maggie's ears pricked up when she realised just what the conversation was about.

'So, anyway,' Gemma continued her tale, 'it turned out that he was really into the S&M scene. You know: leather, rubber, whips, chains. The whole bit. He even had this special whipping stool back at his flat,' she continued enthusiastically, 'with a chain and handcuffs attached. I couldn't believe my eyes.'

One of the young ice hockey players turned red and squirmed uncomfortably in his seat and Claire looked stunned as if she couldn't believe her ears. Maggie suppressed another grin. Although she had never been all that actively involved, she had dabbled on the fringes of the scene once or twice and Gemma's tale, true or not, brought back some amusing and erotic memories that she had almost forgotten. She smiled cheekily at Justin and settled back to enjoy the rest of her meal.

After the final course had been cleared away, Maggie ordered a coffee while Jan and the others indulged in a colourful variety of liqueurs. She had never been fond of liqueurs, finding them much too sweet and sickly for her liking. Abandoning the remains of their feasting, the Trojans and their guests gradually began to wander back into the lounge area, where further drinks were being served.

The Trojans' smarmy-faced, middle-aged manager edged closer to her with his right hand outstretched eagerly. 'It's Maggie, isn't it? I've seen you around the rink. A real pleasure to meet you.' He took her hand in his own sticky paw and began shaking her arm up and down enthusiastically while his eyes devoured her breasts. 'As you probably know, I'm Roland Donaldson, the Trojans' manager. I do hope you enjoyed the match?'

'Yes, thank you.' She withdrew her hand and tried to resist the urge to wipe it down the side of her skirt. 'It was very kind of you to invite us.' Roland's pungent aftershave was turning her stomach and she tried to step back and away from him.

Her body bumped against a solid thigh and she looked round quickly. It was Troy. She hadn't even realised that he was anywhere nearby. Just for one delightful moment, she could actually feel his genitals pushed up against her, and a sudden pang of lust tore through her. Maggie casually put her hand down by her side and pretended not to notice as her fingers brushed against his crotch. She heard Troy's breathing deepen and was delighted as she felt him edging even closer to her.

Roland beamed at him. 'Here's our hero of the match.' He thumped Troy on the back. 'That was a splendid effort this evening. Really splendid. I expect you will sleep well tonight, eh?'

'I don't feel much like sleeping at the moment,' Troy muttered softly in Maggie's ear. Maggie felt herself tremble at his words and the touch of his breath on her neck. In her imagination, she could picture him guiding her away alone somewhere and taking her up against the wall the way Justin had. Her stomach started doing flip-flops at the idea of his huge hands caressing her burning flesh.

'A toast!' Roland yelled. 'Bring another tray of champers someone. Let's drink to the success of tonight's match and to the continued good health of all.'

A young waitress hurried into the room with a tray of drinks and Troy moved away from Maggie to reach for a glass. Maggie swayed slightly and steadied herself against Jan. When Troy handed her a drink she took a quick gulp and grimaced as the bubbles stung her nose.

The next twenty minutes passed in a blur of laughter and jokes, and an almost indescribable atmosphere of sexual tension. Although Maggie had now regained her composure, she was feeling hornier than ever. She glanced around the room and saw that her companions were all supping the champagne freely and becoming increasingly relaxed and abandoned as the time passed.

She noticed Roland was leaning back against one wall, ogling all the women intently. As she watched, he sidled up towards Claire and draped his arm around her shoulders. Claire leaned her body against him, her face flushed with too much champagne and excitement and, with a flash of insight, Maggie realised that Roland was using the Trojans to get the women worked up before he made his move on them.

Roland's hands started to paw Claire's breasts and Maggie grimaced. What a bastard. She moved quickly across the room and guided her friend from his embrace on the pretext of asking her something. Claire seemed too fuddled and bewildered to realise what was going on.

Troy had wandered over to stand beside Gemma and, as Maggie moved closer to them, she could hear Troy chatting to the pretty physiotherapist about water sports. Maggie felt a twinge of jealousy as she watched Gemma responding to Troy's deep sexy voice and natural charm. As she began searching for a way to interrupt them, she couldn't help wondering just how well they already knew each other.

'Sorry to spoil everyone's fun, but we really will have to be on our way soon. We have to be off the premises by midnight,' Roland announced suddenly. Maggie glared at him silently, wondering if that were true or if he just wanted to spoil everyone else's fun since he didn't seem to be getting anywhere with any of the women himself.

As Roland began to round up the squad, Maggie kept an eye on Troy who, with two other Trojans, was now busy talking to Justin. At least Gemma wasn't swooning all over him anymore. She glanced surreptitiously at Troy's fabulous body and felt more than a tinge of regret for what might have been.

Roland seized her arm and pulled her to one side. 'Perhaps I can arrange for you to join us again?' He ran his finger down her arm suggestively. 'I'd be delighted for you to be my personal guest sometime.' His eyes devoured her breasts, leaving no room for doubt about what he actually had in mind. Maggie turned away from him in disgust. For some reason, he really made her skin crawl.

Justin finished his conversation and came over to her. 'I have to get back to Fairwood tonight,' he told her. 'Stephen needs a lift back so that he can supervise the junior team's friendly match tomorrow afternoon.' He slipped his arm around her waist. 'If I were going back on my own, I'd take you with me,' he muttered.

She grinned. 'What, and abandon both my car and my friends? Thanks for arranging everything, Justin. I'll see you at work on Monday.'

'Dream of me?' he suggested.

'Of course.' Maggie saw Troy turning to leave and smiled to herself. Her dreams were already booked for the night.

'Don't forget your promise, though,' Justin added softly as he walked away.

Ten minutes later, with the noisy farewells and good wishes of the Trojans still ringing in her ears, Maggie unlocked the door of her car and slipped in behind the wheel. She was still feeling tense and excited. Over her shoulder, she could hear the exuberant chattering of the other women as they clambered inside. Although their jumbled conversations made Maggie smile, their words also served to remind her of her own thoughts about Troy.

She shifted her buttocks uncomfortably on the driving seat as she remembered the touch of his hand on her arm and the feel of his crotch pressed against her. She could smell the warm, sweet scent of perspiration and female arousal wafting through the car. There probably wasn't a dry pair of knickers among them!

'Fasten your seatbelts,' she called. 'If everyone's ready, we'll get on our way.' She put the vehicle into gear and let the clutch out slowly. Her fingers lingered on the gear stick, fondling the knob as another shiver of longing ran down her spine. She had been right about Troy. He was everything she had expected him to be. And some. She eased the car out the car park and turned left towards the B&B.

As the journey progressed, the others gradually stopped chattering and fell into a kind of dreamy silence, while Maggie found herself wide awake and restless. She drove the vehicle automatically, with all her spare concentration focused on Troy. Her thoughts did little to help her unwind.

To calm herself down she switched her mind back to the Trojan's creepy manager. He had made it more than clear that he fancied her. What a revolting thought! Not even the chance of free tickets to all the Trojan matches would induce her to hop into Roland's bed.

They arrived back at their accommodation just before 12.30 a.m. and crept up to their rooms, giggling foolishly at every creaking floorboard and squeaking door. As Maggie snuggled down under the duvet, her body was still tingling with excitement and pent-up desire. What with Justin fondling her all through the match and then her thoughts about Troy, she seemed to have been in a permanent state of semi-arousal all evening. Through the wall, she could hear Sara and Claire whispering to each other in the next room and guessed that they would be talking about the players. Maggie remembered Sara had once let slip that Ean reminded her of someone special from the past. Sara never spoke about her son Kevin's father, but Maggie was certain that was who she was thinking of when she looked at the handsome young defender. Across the room, Jan muttered softly to herself and rolled over restlessly.

'Are you still awake?' Maggie whispered. There was no reply. Lucky Jan. She must already be lost in her dreams. Maggie was feeling more wide awake than ever. She stared up at the dark shadows on the ceiling and listened to the sound of a dog barking somewhere in the distance. Gently, she ran her fingers over her breasts and felt her nipples spring up under her thin nightie. Her thighs prickled with renewed lust.

Maggie rolled on to her side and curled her legs up. As she tightened her thighs, she could feel the urgent tingling deep within her. She clamped her legs tighter together, savoured the pleasurable pressure on her sensitive clit, and thought about her stupid promise to Justin. Not that she would dare break it anyway: she had never mastered the art of coming quietly. If she masturbated now, she was bound to cry out when she came. What if she woke Jan?

Sighing with frustration, she rolled over on to her stomach and pummelled the pillow with her hands, trying to make herself more comfortable. She screwed her eyes up tightly and tried to picture Troy in his tight-fitting suit. A smile played across her lips as she remembered the way he had teased her about its colour.

She awoke later with a sudden start and stared around her, trying to remember where she was. Her body was damp and cold with perspiration and she could smell the harsh, musky odour of her arousal under the duvet.

She had been dreaming about Troy. They had been alone on the ice and Troy had been holding her tightly in his arms as he glided gracefully around the rink. She had been snuggled tightly against him, enjoying the warmth of his body and the pressure of his hard cock pushed into her stomach.

Somehow, she was suddenly naked and Troy had been rubbing his hands all over her body. He no longer seemed to be wearing any trousers and his erection had been caressing her bare flesh as he hugged her to him. Urgently, she had reached down to take his cock in her hands. She was going to impale herself on him; bury his hot shaft deep inside her.

Sod it! Maggie sat up and looked across the room. Jan still appeared to be fast asleep. Now what? She couldn't masturbate in case she disturbed Jan and she couldn't even manage to satisfy herself in her dreams. What a time to wake up! Just a few more seconds and she would have felt Troy rammed deep inside her dripping cunt. It was no good. She'd never get back to sleep now.

As quietly as she could, Maggie climbed out of bed and peeled her sodden nightie off her damp body. Shivering, she tugged on some underwear and slipped into a skirt and blouse. Pulling a jacket around her shoulders, she tiptoed silently out of the room. Maybe if she went out for a walk, the fresh air would help calm her down a bit.

Chapter Three

Maggie let herself out through the back door of the B&B and made her way down a narrow path. Clambering up on to a small gate, she sat astride it and surveyed her options. To the left, the pathway appeared to lead back on to the lane that passed round the front of the B&B. To the right, it disappeared into nearby woods. Maggie wiggled her buttocks; she was acutely aware of the hardness of the gate pressed up between her thighs. She remembered her promise to Justin and almost began to wish that she hadn't been so hasty in turning Roland down. The way she was feeling right now, any prick would do. She laughed to herself. Roland was definitely one of the biggest pricks she'd ever met – next to Justin! She didn't dare let herself think about what she'd like to do to Justin right now.

God, she was feeling horny. Although she normally prided herself on keeping her promises, she was beginning to admit to herself that this one might be the exception. She had the urge to do something totally daring and reckless. For once, her fantasies and her nerve were in perfect harmony. If it hadn't been so cold she would have ripped all her clothes off and run naked down the lane, yelling with frustration. She pushed herself harder on to the gate and savoured the tantalising pressure against her mound.

'Damn Justin!' Maggie ground her teeth together and slid off the gate on to the path. Hesitating momentarily as she gazed towards the dark privacy of the woods, she sighed heavily and started left towards the lane. With every step, she felt more wide awake than ever. She was very aware of the cold dampness between her thighs and thought longingly about her obliging vibrator lying alone at home, waiting for her.

Maybe she should just give in and take care of herself? Maggie stopped walking and felt a sudden shiver of excitement run down her spine as she glanced around. There was certainly no one about now to see or hear what she was doing. She shut her eyes and summoned up an image of Troy, naked but for a thong. She put her hand on her thigh and started to move her fingers slowly up under her skirt.

As her fingertips began to make slow, teasing movements around her already hardened sex bud, Maggie imagined herself peeling Troy's thong down over his rampant erection. Nearby, an owl hooted mournfully; she pictured herself lying naked on the grass with the moon shining down on her and Troy kneeling beside her with his cock in one hand, fondling her aching breasts. The image was so strong and powerful that she could almost smell the sweet scent of the grass. She wanted to feel the breeze on her bare skin. She was consumed with a crazy urge to pleasure herself naked with her body bathed in the moonlight like a Greek goddess.

Sod Justin and his stupid promises! How would he ever know anyway? Besides, a promise made under duress wasn't really a promise. Maggie peered down the lane ahead. Maybe there was a way into the field round the next bend? She started forward again eagerly.

As she walked, Maggie glanced around at the dark

shadows of the hedgerows on either side. The soft caress of the cool breeze on her damp underwear only added to her mounting arousal. Her whole body was tingling with anticipation. She increased her pace.

When she rounded the bend and saw a light ahead of her, she almost groaned aloud with shock and disappointment. There was some kind of van parked in a gateway just ahead. Images of a courting couple seeking privacy in the back of the van filled her mind and added to her fury. There was no way she could risk sneaking past them. What on earth would she say if anyone saw her? Her fantasy was disintegrating before her eyes.

As she stood, cursing her luck, the van door opened and a tall, dark shape climbed out and began to move towards her. Maggie froze as she was caught in the powerful beam of a torch, like a fly trapped in a web. She heard an exclamation of surprise and saw a second figure climb out of the front of the van.

'It's a woman.' The voice was deep and distinctly masculine. His words were as incredulous as if he had said: 'it's a Martian.' Maggie felt her temper flare. She put her hand up to protect her eyes.

'Would you mind pointing that somewhere else?' she called angrily. 'I can't see a damn thing.'

'Sorry.' The light moved to one side and Maggie blinked her eyes to clear the afterglare.

She couldn't decide whether to stand her ground or run away. She was acutely aware of her vulnerability but, at the same time, still keyed up enough to relish the titillation of this strange encounter. Perhaps this was the very opportunity she was seeking? She took a few steps forward and peered into the darkness. Two tall and heavily built men were standing just in front of the van, peering back at her. Through the windscreen, she could see several others moving about and realised that there was something familiar about them. No. Impossible. It couldn't be. She gasped as realisation dawned, then gasped again as her foot slipped on some loose gravel and she stumbled forward.

The man with the torch rushed forward and grabbed her arms to steady her. 'Hey. Take it easy. What's up? Have you been in an accident?'

Maggie gazed up wordlessly at the Trojans' new centre ice player, Tor. She blinked and shook her head to clear it. How could it possibly be him? Her overexcited imagination must be playing tricks on her. She heard the other men moving around inside the van and the side door began to slide open.

'What's happening? Who is it? What's going on?' Their questions were a confused jumble in her ears.

Tor stared at her in surprise. 'Wait a minute. Don't I know you?' Suddenly, he began to chuckle. 'Yeah. You were at the game tonight.' He grinned. 'Guess what guys?' he called over his shoulder. 'It's one of those babes that came to dinner with us after the match. The ones that gave us such a hard time,' he emphasised.

Maggie felt herself blushing from head to toe. 'What on earth are you doing here?' she stammered in confusion.

'We're supposed to be heading for our hotel,' he replied. 'Roland's got us booked into some fancy place way out in the country somewhere. But the stupid bastard put his foot down and left us behind.'

The dark shape in the night that was Troy stepped closer to them, so that Maggie could see his teeth and eyes gleaming with amusement in the light from the van. He always seemed to be smiling. She stared at him in shock. He was so close to her that she could feel the warmth of his body radiating from him. Her knees began to tremble.

'Hello Troy,' she muttered stupidly, as if there were nothing strange about her being out walking on her own at this time of night.

Troy stepped closer. He raised his hand and let his

finger trace the outline of her cheekbone. 'I think maybe you and I have some unfinished business,' he whispered suggestively.

Maggie's head started to swim. She felt remote and distant, as if she were in someone else's body, looking out. None of this was real. She was dreaming again, letting her fantasies run away with her. He couldn't possibly be out here, in the middle of nowhere. She felt the same as when she had unzipped Justin in the Cellar. Crazy and reckless. Horny. She lowered her eyes and stared hungrily at his groin. If it were only her imagination, it was the most realistic fantasy she'd ever had. Please God, don't let me wake up, she begged silently.

Tor followed her gaze. 'You know, I think she's curious to see just how big you really are without all the padding,' he sniggered. Maggie could smell the drink on his breath and realised that they were probably all slightly pissed.

Troy's grin widened. 'No problem.' His hand dropped from her cheek and started to explore the outline of her left breast. Apart from a sharp intake of breath, Maggie did not react. As he started to undo the buckle of his belt, she drew another deep breath. Casually, he flipped the button open and slid his zip down.

His trousers dropped to his ankles, revealing a pair of light-coloured boxer shorts. His legs were so dark that she could barely see their outline, so that his torso almost seemed to be floating in mid-air. Slowly, he put his hand between the opening of his shorts and peeled the material back. Maggie gulped and finally let her breath out.

'Well?'

She swallowed again and nodded her head. 'Very nice,' she croaked feebly without taking her eyes off his already expanding cock. Now she knew that she had to be dreaming.

'It gets bigger if you stroke it,' he promised crudely.

Maggie heard the sound of the van door opening

again. She glanced up at Tor, who was still holding her arm, then turned her head to look at four other Trojans who had now piled out of the van to gather round them. She could smell the alcohol on them too and wondered just how drunk they were. Obviously drunk enough to have got themselves lost in the middle of nowhere.

One of the other forwards, Bri, grinned at her and gave her an exaggerated wink.

'Go on, love. Make his day,' he encouraged her.

Make *his* day! Maggie remembered how desperately she had wanted him earlier and what she had been planning to do to herself before she had bumped into them.

Tor took her hand and guided it over Troy's groin. Although she could hardly believe what she was doing, she still made no effort to resist. She jumped as her fingertips made contact with his flesh. It seemed so hot in the cool night air. Totally unable to restrain herself, she closed her fist around his hardness and started to slide her hand up towards the tip.

He still wasn't fully erect and, as she began to move her hand back down towards the base, she could feel him expanding in response to her caress. She looked up into his face and noticed that his jaw was tightly clenched. Her stomach flipped and she felt a deep tingle of urgent arousal burning within her. Slowly, she slid her fingers down to the base of his stem and lightly caressed his balls. She felt his body stiffen as she pushed her fingers into the tight pubic curls and squeezed him gently.

'That's it, give him a good grope,' one of the other Trojans encouraged.

Maggie licked her dry lips and moved her hand back up to enclose his stem. At least he wasn't too drunk. His cock was now as hard as any vibrator and she could feel his pulse thudding as the blood surged through his swollen veins. Another stab of longing tore through her. She opened her fist and stepped back, straight into Tor.

'You know, Troy, you shouldn't go around exposing yourself like that. Should he lads?' Tor reprimanded him as he put his arms around Maggie's waist.

'You suggested it,' Troy protested.

'No I didn't. I just said that she was curious. I didn't mean for you to scare her like that. The poor girl's trembling with shock.' He squeezed her more tightly.

She was certainly trembling, but she wasn't sure shock was the most appropriate word to describe her emotions. Her whole body felt as if it was on fire and she was acutely aware of Tor's body pushed up hard against her.

'Get him guys. Troy needs to be taught a lesson,' Tor continued.

Two of the others grabbed Troy from behind and pushed him up against the side of the van. Chuckling sadistically, they whipped his boxer shorts down round his ankles. Maggie felt herself being herded up against his hard buttocks until she was pushed between the two men like the filling in a sandwich. Instinctively, she placed her hands on Troy's thighs and squeezed the taut flesh with her shaking fingers. It didn't matter what you did in a dream, did it? It wasn't real so it didn't count.

Troy grunted and began to roll his hips suggestively, pushing his cheeks back hard against her already over-sensitive mound and sending little tremors of pleasure coursing through her body. She squeezed him again and felt his muscles twitch in response. Tor thrust himself against her from behind and she could feel his own excitement hard and urgent through his clothing.

Suddenly, she felt herself being pulled back and she watched in silence as the other men continued to strip Troy's clothes off him. She almost giggled at the way he struggled and cursed furiously as he tried to break free. Three against one, it was hopeless. As soon as his shirt was removed, they spun him round and lifted him up as easily as one might lift a doll.

'Pull his trousers off,' one of them commanded her.

Needing no further urging, she bent down and ripped his trousers and shorts off his flailing ankles. Her eyes were fixed almost hypnotically on his massive penis and her fingers itched to stroke it again. Tremors of excitement and lust shot through her body and her mouth was so dry that no matter how often she licked her lips, no moisture seemed to stay on them.

'Shit! That's enough. A joke's a joke.' Troy strained against them so hard that his muscles bulged.

Tor chuckled. 'Bend him over,' he commanded mercilessly.

The two men spun Troy back round and pushed him over against the van. Maggie couldn't take her eyes off the sight of his buttocks twitching angrily as he struggled against their hold.

'Six of the best.' Tor took Maggie's hand and motioned for her to whack him. Troy twisted his head round to glare over his shoulder.

'Get off, you bastards!' he yelled and renewed his struggle as another of the players grabbed him and pushed his head back round. 'When I get free, I'll break your frigging necks.'

'Hang on. We don't want her to hurt her hand.' One of the defenders, whose name Maggie suddenly couldn't recall, climbed into the back of the van and rummaged around. A few seconds later he reappeared with a jubilant expression on his face. He was holding a hockey stick in his left hand.

'Here you go, love.' He handed her the stick. 'Six strokes. He has to learn more self-control or, next thing you know, he'll be getting a hard-on during a game. That would never do.'

'No, I can't.' Maggie's eyes were gleaming with anticipation as she slipped her jacket off and took hold of the stick.

'Yes you can,' Tor contradicted her. 'Otherwise, we'll let him whack you. After all, it's your fault he's got so excited.' He grinned. 'Not that I blame him. Hell, a sexy woman like you is enough to get anyone hot.'

Maggie was already moving into position. 'OK.' She gripped the stick firmly and lifted her arm. Thankfully, no one tried to stop her. She was so excited that it would probably have taken all of them to prevent her now.

'For fuck's sake, let me go. Ahh!' Troy's words were interrupted by the thud of the stick on his left buttock. He grunted with shock and renewed his attempts to wriggle free. 'Ow!' Her second hard whack was followed rapidly by two more on the other cheek.

'Bend him right over,' Maggie heard herself whisper, 'make him touch his toes.'

As Troy's buttocks were raised even higher into the air, Maggie dropped the stick and spat on her palm. 'I'll use my hand,' she added as she landed yet another resounding whack on his right buttock. Leaving her hand on his skin, she rubbed the flesh gently with her fingers then quickly raised her arm and planted another slap on his left cheek.

Tor laughed. 'Well, I guess that's taught you a lesson, eh, Troy?'

'Jesus, that stings,' Troy muttered softly as his three friends finally released their grip and allowed him to straighten up.

Rubbing his buttocks tenderly, Troy turned round to face her. His erection seemed bigger than ever and, without even stopping to think about it, Maggie wrapped her fingers round his cock and pulled him closer so that her body was rubbing against him. She slid her fist up and down, pumping him gently.

'You don't seem to have learned your lesson though, do you?' she whispered derisively.

'No ma'am,' he mocked her in return, 'and, since it's your fault you're gonna to have to take care of it.' He placed his hands on Maggie's shoulders and began to push her down in front of him. Excitement raced through her. He wanted her to suck him in front of everyone!

As she lowered her mouth over him, Tor put his hands round her and pulled her back, forcing her to bend at the waist to reach Troy. She slipped her hand between his legs and pushed against his thigh. Obligingly, Troy spread his legs further apart and Maggie placed her right hand on his prick to hold him still. The fingernails of her left hand started to trace soft patterns on his upper thigh.

As her tongue shot out to lick his swollen cock, Maggie felt his whole body shudder and saw his muscles tense. She could sense the other men gathering closer to watch. She turned her head slightly and saw one of them pulling at the front of his trousers to try and make himself more comfortable. Her smile widened as he gave up and pushed his hand down the waistband. She watched, fascinated, as he struggled under his clothing. When he finally pulled his hand back out, his cock was a hard bulge up the front of his fly.

Enflamed, Maggie started to run her tongue down Troy's shaft. She had no idea what was going to happen next. She had never sucked a man in front of an audience and the idea appealed to her more than she would ever have believed. She bent lower and wrapped her tongue around his balls. As she pulled them towards her, she slipped her hand further between his legs and used his buttocks to steady herself. She dug her nails into his flesh and felt him squirm in response.

Her body felt as if it were engulfed in flames. She was sensitive to every sound and every movement. She could feel the cold night air creeping up the back of her short skirt and caressing her thighs and she imagined the other men staring at her exposure. Were they all getting excited? Her mind filled with delightful images of them all stripped and wanking as they feasted their eyes on the curve of her buttocks. Maybe they hoped that she would take care of them all?

Exhilarated, she took Troy's full length into her mouth and sucked as hard as she could. Slowly, she slid her lips up his long thick shaft, allowing her teeth to graze lightly over the sensitive flesh. When she felt his muscles tensing still further, she put her hand between his buttocks and began to run her finger around his arsehole. He gasped with pleasure and her searching fingers felt his balls swelling and tightening.

Not wanting things to end too soon, Maggie took her hand away, pulled her head back and gripped him tightly between her fingers. Only when she felt him relax slightly did she replace her tongue on his hot tip.

Troy sighed and groaned with the agony and ecstasy of her deliberate teasing as, time and time again, Maggie brought him to the brink of his climax and then drew back, squeezing him with her fingers until his immediate urgency passed. His whole body was visibly trembling with the effort and his knees were shaking so much that he could barely stand. Each time she held him back it took longer to get him under control and each time she resumed her torment his desperate arousal seemed swifter.

Maggie could sense the other men moving in closer and closer. She could feel their body heat radiating from them and, when she swayed her hips, she felt her buttocks brush against a huge erection. Its owner placed his hand on the small of her back and gradually moved his fingers down over her bottom. As they moved back up under the hem of her skirt his fingertips caressed the bare flesh of her inner thighs so that it took all of her self-control not to clamp her teeth together. She parted her legs to encourage him further.

She began to knead Troy's cock even harder, trying to distract herself from the fingers creeping closer and closer to her sex. Gradually, she became aware of more hands touching her body. Sure fingers expertly unclipped her bra and she felt the ping of the elasticated straps springing open. A hand crept up the slit at the side of her knickers and started to caress her left buttock while another hand pulled her blouse free from her skirt.

Maggie shuddered again as a gentle kiss on the back of her knee drew her attention to the Trojan crouching behind her. His tongue ran down her leg and his hands guided her ankles further apart. She quickly smothered a groan of delight by sucking Troy back into her mouth. As she pumped him up and down with her lips, she watched the droplets of sweat running down his body. Unable to resist, she ran her tongue up his lean stomach muscles and licked the sweat from him.

Another sigh burst from her as someone opened her blouse. Her loosened bra had ridden right up and she felt a huge hand cup one of her breasts while another peeled the blouse back over her shoulders and halfway down her arms. Soft lips kissed her back and probing fingers flicked her rapidly hardening nipples. She gasped again and tightened her mouth round Troy's cock so that her teeth were pressed into his flesh.

There was a shuffling of feet as the other men moved back to stand behind her. She jumped as a hand lifted the hem of her skirt and started to lower her knickers. Maggie heard several sharp whistles as her buttocks came into view.

As soon as her knickers were down to her ankles one of the men lifted her foot and made her step out of them. Everyone cheered and she felt a hand slipping up between her thighs. Another shudder raced through her as she tightened her lips on Troy's cock and pumped him rapidly in and out. In her excitement, she misjudged his control and pushed him too far.

With a deep groan, Troy exploded. As his stream of hot spunk pumped out of him he grasped her head, forcing his prick further and further into her mouth and thrusting back and forth desperately until he was utterly spent.

Maggie heard his gentle sigh of release as he finally pulled back and leaned his drained body against the side of the van. Gradually, he slid down until he was resting on his heels. Still breathing heavily, Maggie stood up and watched silently as his cock gradually began to soften and relax.

A pair of hands snatched her from behind and began to slide up her stomach and on to her breasts. She felt her loosened blouse and bra slipping down over her arms and saw them drop to the ground beside her knickers. The man pulled her back hard against him, all the while squeezing and kneading her aching breasts. Her skirt began to drop over her hips and down her legs.

At the sound of a zip opening she glanced over her shoulder and saw Tor. He eased his cock free of his jock strap and Maggie bit back a moan as it sprang hard against her thigh. With a powerful thrust of his hips, she felt him nuzzling it deeper into her crack. Trembling with excitement, Maggie pushed back against him until she could feel his thick pubic hairs tickling her skin and the smooth tip of his cock was hard up against her anus. She looked down and saw Troy watching them silently.

'Bring me some oil,' Tor commanded hoarsely as he moved himself gently up and down her crack. He pushed her forward until she was balanced over Troy with her hands resting on the side of the van. Troy lifted his head and started to lick her breasts and, with a whimper of pleasure, Maggie lowered herself a little more so that he could suck her nipples into his mouth. His wide lips were as soft as silk, soothing her burning flesh.

Tor stepped back and tugged the remainder of his clothes off. He stood beside her, waiting for the oil and she turned her head to gaze hungrily at the massive erection standing out proudly from his groin. The glistening whiteness of his skin there was in sharp contrast to the darker area of his stomach and thighs.

She gritted her teeth against the teasing caress of Troy's soft lips and watched avidly as Tor took the baby oil from his friend's hand and carefully unscrewed the top. He stepped forward and she felt a few drops of the warm, sticky fluid dribbling down between her buttocks.

Tor smoothed the oil into her crack with his finger, passed the bottle down to Troy and slipped a condom over his cock. Troy tipped some of the oil into his hand and started to rub it gently into her breasts and stomach. Maggie moaned with pleasure at the unexpected massage then jumped as she felt Tor pushing his oil-covered finger gently into her back passage.

Dear God in heaven! Maggie shivered from head to foot as she watched Tor slowly and deliberately spread some of the oil down his shaft. He was intending to take her anally. She shivered again with a mixture of fear and excitement as he pushed her down until her hands were resting on Troy's shoulders. Tor moved round behind her and put his hand between her legs; he lifted her up until her toes only just touched the ground and her bottom was stuck up in the air.

She whimpered softly as she felt him opening her cheeks. She had never had anal sex before, although earlier Justin had made it clear he wanted it. Now, this man she had only just met, this virtual stranger, was about to take her virginity. Involuntarily, she clenched her buttocks. Should she tell him it was her first time and beg him to be gentle with her? She shivered again. Everyone was watching her. After what she had already done, how could she now simper like a teenage virgin? She bit her lips and tried to relax her muscles, giving herself up to the sensation of his finger slipping unresisting into her back passage.

Gradually, as she abandoned herself to the pleasure, she forgot her fear. Her clit was prickling as much as if he had been taking her from the front and she could already feel the little ripples of her building orgasm. She closed her eyes and pushed back against him.

'Go on. She's ready for it. Shove it in and fuck her.'

Maggie started at the words and opened her eyes. She had almost forgotten the other men. Now, she could feel them swarming round her, with their eyes and hands everywhere. How could all this possibly be happening? She took a long, deep breath then let it out again in a sharp whoosh as Tor pulled his finger out, yanked her backwards and thrust his slippery penis hard against her.

'Oh, Jesus!' she cried as his cock rammed into her and his hand slid round her thigh to squeeze her mound. She whimpered again as, with apparent ease, he lifted her bodily off the ground so that she was impaled on him. With the palm of his hand pressed hard on to her mound and his middle finger massaging her swollen sex bud, Tor swung her away from Troy and moved her closer to the van.

Maggie instinctively raised her arms to try and steady herself, but Tor used his other hand to brush them aside. Stepping forward, he pushed her breasts hard on to the side of the van. The metal felt as cold as ice on her burning flesh and a shiver ran through her body as another gasp burst from her lips. She felt his cock pull out slowly, then thrust back in again in time with his insistent caressing of her tortured clit.

'You should see the view from here,' a voice beside them muttered hoarsely.

The words seemed to enflame Tor. With a loud grunt, he thrust himself hard into her again, deeper and deeper; further than she would have ever dreamt possible. His thighs slapped against her buttocks and she moaned as she felt her tightness resisting him. She struggled to relax and felt a brief rush of surprise that what he was doing to her did not really hurt.

She relaxed further and felt the pleasure of the sensation increasing as her fears finally receded. Another tiny whimper escaped her lips as his hand pushed up between her and the van to squeeze her nipple. The combination of being simultaneously stimulated in three places at once was driving her wild, so that her breath was coming in short little pants and she could feel the perspiration dripping from her.

'I bet this is her first time,' another voice called.

'Nah. How could an arse like that escape for so long?'

'Is this your first time, love?'

Maggie had no voice to answer. Tor was pumping her harder and faster. His finger was pushed up inside her and his thumb was rhythmically massaging her clit. She was only seconds away from her climax. She pushed her body back against his chest and twisted her head round so that she could lick his ear.

Tor grunted and thrust into her again and Maggie cried out, biting his lobe in her overwhelming excitement. She leant back even harder against him, so that he was trapped inside her, then tightened her anal muscles round him as if trying to crush him. She could feel his sweat pouring down his body and mingling with her own. She bit his ear again and increased the pressure of her muscles.

'I'm coming,' he gasped. 'Oh Jesus, I can't . . .' He pushed her savagely forward, so that she almost lost her precarious balance. Quickly, she raised her hands and pressed her palms hard against the side of the van. Tor grabbed her round the waist and drew himself back for one final thrust. As he pushed into her, he pulled her body back on to him and they both cried out as she felt the urgent judder of his impending explosion. He moaned again.

'Oh yes,' Maggie whimpered as her own orgasm ripped through her body and they both collapsed forward against the van. With a final grunt, Tor climaxed, his whole body tensing as his fluid burst from him. He gradually began to pull back out of her.

When he released his grip on her waist, Maggie discovered that her legs were too weak to support her and she only just managed to catch herself with her arms before she fell. Dimly, she became aware of the other players cheering and whistling their performance.

'Phew!' Tor exclaimed as he wiped the sweat from his eyes. 'That was incredible.'

'I'm next,' cried a voice in her ear. 'You can go on top and I'll just lie back and let you fuck me.'

Two down and four to go, Maggie thought to herself with a shiver of anticipation. This was some fantasy!

'Nah, I'm next.'

Maggie looked round and saw Ean's huge dark eyes staring down at her. 'What she needs right now is a long, slow screw, don't you love?' He licked his lips. 'I'm just the man for that.'

'You'd better get in quick Pary,' Tor laughed. 'After Ean here has finished with her there won't be much left.'

Maggie leant back against the van and watched as Ean pulled his shirt over his head without undoing the buttons, slipped out of his shoes and whipped his trousers down. She was astonished at how casually she was taking all this. She wasn't normally quite so free and easy. But then, there was nothing normal about any of this. It wasn't even really happening. It was just some crazy, erotic dream. Any moment now the alarm clock would ring and she would wake up in her own bed, alone. She fixed her eyes on Ean's rampant cock and felt another shudder engulf her as he slipped a condom on and took her by the hand.

Ean led her over to the grass verge and gently helped her down on to her back. As before, the others gathered round to watch and Maggie was amazed to see that Troy was already beginning to recover. Ean lay down beside her and snatched a handful of her breasts.

'Come on, get on with it,' Pary moaned. 'I can't wait all night. You can play with her tits later.'

'OK, keep your pants on,' Ean laughed as he opened her legs and knelt between her thighs.

'That's just it. I don't want them on,' Pary complained as he massaged his groin. 'They're much too tight.'

Everyone roared with laughter as Ean pushed his hand between her legs and prised her sex lips apart. She quivered as she felt his fingers playing with her dampness. He shuffled closer and allowed his tip to rub against her teasingly. She immediately thrust herself against him, forcing him up into her. She lifted her legs and wrapped them round the back of his thighs, then pushed herself on to him. He groaned and pushed his hands under her. As he started to pump her, he used his strong arms to lift her up off the ground and on to his lap.

Maggie leaned forward and rested her hands on his shoulders, pushing herself up and down enthusiastically. She squealed as his finger slipped into her crack and penetrated her recently deflowered anus. Enflamed, she thrust her breasts forward on to his mouth, urging him to suck first one nipple then the other. All around them, the enthusiastic audience shouted encouragement and muttered obscenities.

'Do you think she'd do it with other women, too?' a voice questioned.

'Of course she would.' She recognised Troy's deep voice. 'She'd screw anything. Look at her go.'

Maggie found that their comments were only adding to her stimulation. Every word, every suggestion, seemed to push her closer and closer to the edge. Frantically, she matched Ean's movements thrust for thrust; her hands dug into his back as she tried to pull herself even harder and deeper on to him.

'What a goer. I'm beginning to wonder if we're enough for her.'

'Don't worry. I've got what she needs.'

Their words danced and swirled in her head. If there were any other women present she felt sure that she would do it with them, too, so that anal sex wouldn't be her only first of the night. She was beginning to understand just what a turn on it was for a man to watch two women together. She was starting to find the whole concept more and more intriguing.

Ean placed his hands back under her buttocks. He lifted her effortlessly up and down so that all she needed to do was to steady herself as he slid her up and down his hard shaft. She deliberately tightened her vaginal muscles around him so that she was squeezing him in time with his thrusts. She could hear his breath rasping urgently and imagined the thoughts of the other men as they watched his cock pumping in and out of her.

'Yes,' she cried as her climax engulfed her. 'Oh God, yes.' Another sob burst from her as she felt Ean start to come. She relaxed against him, hugging his chest as she savoured every burst of his own violent and powerful release.

Gradually, she became aware of the cold touch of the breeze against the dampness of her bare skin. Goose bumps covered her body. She could feel Ean shrinking away inside her. Someone took her arms and lifted her up off him and she could see the dumb smile of satisfaction on his face.

Tor produced a towel and started to dry her and one of the others handed her his can of lager, which she snatched gratefully and gulped from noisily. Tor finished wiping the sweat away and started kissing her breasts as he continued to rub her most private parts with the towel. Gradually, he turned her round and began to kiss her thighs and mound. She felt his probing tongue inching its way between her thighs. 'It's Pary next.'

Maggie saw that the brown-haired, green-eyed defender of Claire's fantasies was already stripping. It wasn't difficult to understand what Claire saw in him.

He had the most blatantly sensuous eyes Maggie had ever stared into.

'Bring her over here.' Pary lay back on the grass and took his cock in one hand. 'Stick her on this.' He ran his fingers up and down his erection.

Maggie put the can down and pushed herself free. Her earlier feeling of total recklessness returned and intensified. She had always sensed her potential to be good at domination. Very good. It was time to turn the tables on them. With an exaggerated roll of her hips, she strode across and stood astride him.

'You think you can satisfy me?' she questioned as she began to lower herself down on to his hard knob. 'Not quite right,' she complained. 'Move it back.' She warmed to her new role.

Pary did as requested and she felt his tip slide up between her sex lips. 'Good boy,' she encouraged him as she lowered herself down over him.

The others cheered approvingly. 'I reckon you've bitten off more than you can chew,' Troy goaded Pary. 'She's already beaten three of us, so far.'

Pary grinned confidently. 'No problem.' He gritted his teeth as she sank down to encompass him totally. 'I can take care of her,' he rasped hoarsely.

'Not before I fuck your brains out,' Maggie retorted in a voice similar to her own but using words she could hardly believe were coming from her mouth. She rolled her hips aggressively and squeezed her muscles. Pary groaned again.

Tor laughed. 'Now you're for it. We'll pick up the pieces after she's finished with you.'

'Yeah. We'll even give you a nice funeral,' Troy chuckled.

Maggie glanced down and realised that Pary wasn't listening to them anymore. His face was screwed up in total concentration and his breathing was already ragged. She grinned. She wasn't even moving up and down yet;

just massaging him with her inner muscles. She put her hands on his chest and increased her relentless pressure. She mouthed the ice hockey term for a ten-minute over-time session to determine the winner. 'Sudden death.'

'Ahh, Jesus!' Pary tightened his buttocks and tried to thrust up into her, but Maggie curled her fingers and dug her nails into his chest. 'Keep still,' she hissed, so softly none but he could hear.

Pary lowered himself back to the ground and gritted his teeth as she continued to squeeze him. He placed his hands on her buttocks and, with every movement of her muscles, he tightened his grip. One hand slid round to her mound and he started to finger her clit in time to the rhythm of her vaginal massage.

Maggie felt the perspiration starting to run down her again with the effort of maintaining her muscle contractions. Pary's finger had found its way up beside his cock and his fingertip seemed to have discovered her G-spot. She wriggled with pleasure at his relentless caress.

'Get on with it, for Christ's sake.' The voice of one of the others broke their desperate concentration, reminding Maggie of her audience. Pary pulled his finger out and seized her left breast. Taking a deep breath, he forced his buttocks up under her and thrust hard and fast inside her.

'No!' he cried desperately as he lost the fight.

As soon as she had squeezed him dry, Maggie stood up stared down at him. 'Not bad, but I think you need a little more self-control, too,' she said.

She swung round to face the onlookers. Her eyes lighted on the squad's baby-faced, golden-haired net-minder known as Pele. He looked like a young Greek god in the moonlight. He would make a fortune if he did open a garage. Women would bring their cars from miles around for the chance to see him in action. 'Well? What are you waiting for?' she demanded. 'Strip.'

Pele jumped at her words. One hand started to pull at

his shirt while the other struggled to undo his zip. As he pulled his trousers down, hopping on one foot, he staggered and nearly fell. Maggie suppressed a giggle and wondered how on earth a professional ice skater could manage to look so ungainly. Finally, he was naked. She examined his cock critically.

'Lie down and wank yourself while I have another beer,' she instructed. Was that what was affecting her, she wondered, marvelling at her total lack of inhibition? Or was it just the pheromone-laden night air? Whatever it was, she was burning for more.

Tor handed her a can of ice-cold beer and she rubbed it over her breasts, smiling as she remembered Justin's coke can. Her nipples puckered and doubled in size. She pulled the ring and felt the cold spray of froth across her chest. She gasped with delight, then glared at him.

'You shook the can,' she accused him. She stepped closer. 'Lick it off.'

Tor grinned and moved eagerly to obey. As his tongue played across her breasts, Maggie poured some of the beer over her pubes. 'There as well.' She looked at the others. 'Give him some help,' she demanded. 'Not you,' she added as Pele began to get up. 'You just carry on with what you're doing.' She ran her eyes greedily over his swollen cock, which was clutched tightly in his fist. She reached behind her and poured more beer down her buttocks.

By the time the men had finished their task, Maggie had polished off the last of the beer and recovered her energy. She tossed the can aside and moved closer to Pele. She stood across his chest, facing his groin, and looked round at the other men. Her confidence was growing by the second. She was in charge now.

'I want to see you all wanking,' she told them calmly. 'Even you,' she added, glaring at Ean, whose penis hadn't even started to recover yet. For a moment, she thought they were going to refuse but then Bri, the last of the six, unzipped his flies and whipped his cock out. Maggie smiled, remembering how he had been trying to rearrange himself earlier. After all this time watching, she thought, he must be fit to bust!

Maggie moved around, guiding the men into a straight line near Pele. She encouraged each of them in turn and smiled at the sight of Pary trying to coax some life back into his little willy. She gave him a couple of taps on the rump and ran her hand under his balls to help him along, then moved back over Pele. She lowered herself on to his chest so that her engorged sex lips were just above his mouth and her face was resting just inches from his cock.

By just moving her eyes she found she could see the other men quite clearly illuminated by the light from the van door. She felt Pele push his tongue up into her. Glancing down, she noticed his hand already sliding more rapidly up and down his shaft.

Maggie pushed back with her hips, forcing his tongue in deeper. A glance at the others told her that Pary was getting into it again, while Bri looked as if he was almost ready to let go. His hand was literally flying up and down his cock and his face had that urgent look of deep concentration as he fought to prolong his gratification.

She was so engrossed in watching him struggle that she almost missed Pele. A sudden, urgent thrust of his tongue and a loud grunt as his muscles tensed, just warned her. As she rolled herself clear of his body his cock exploded and a jet of spunk sprayed up into the air before splattering across his chest.

Pele groaned again as the first jet was followed by another, then another, until his chest was covered with his come. Maggie's eyes widened. He looked like a volcano erupting. She lifted her head. The other five were still engrossed in their play. How Bri was still holding on was a mystery. His face was beetroot and his chest was heaving with the exertion. She moved over to him and stood in front of him with her hands on her hips and her legs apart.

'Do you like what you see?' she taunted as she slipped a finger down over her mound and on to her clit.

Bri opened his eyes and stared longingly at her crotch. His hand stopped moving and she saw he was squeezing his tip tightly to hold himself back. He licked his lips and nodded silently.

'Then show me.' She put her other hand over his and forced his fist to resume pumping. Without moving her finger from her clit, she crouched down so that she could see his balls drawn tightly up against his body. She took her hand off his speeding fist and cupped them in her palm. Her fingers caressed the soft flesh and Bri cried out. A thick stream of come burst from his tip and ran down his fingers.

His cry was enough to set off Tor and Troy, too, so that Maggie felt as if she was standing under a waterfall of spunk. She moved over to the almost-recovered Ean and lowered her lips over his growing enthusiasm. As she began to suck him, she felt his stiffness increase further and heard him starting to pant. She sucked harder.

As Ean finally lost it again, she felt a gentle slap on her bottom. She spun round to face Troy. He slipped his arm round her waist and kissed her cheek. 'You're quite something, baby,' he told her as he handed her a towel. 'That was fantastic.' He kissed her cheek. 'Maybe we could have a one-on-one rematch sometime?' he added softly. 'Sometime soon.'

Tor took her by the arm. 'If we hadn't stopped to argue over which turning to take, none of this would have happened. For once, Roland actually did us a real favour.' He stared at her. 'You never did say what you're doing out here all alone.'

'I, er . . . I was just out for a walk,' Maggie told them.

'My friends and I are staying just up the road there and I needed some fresh air.' She pointed back down the lane.

Troy grinned. 'Lucky for us.' He put his arm round her waist again. 'Tell you what, sugar. Give us five minutes to put some clothes on and we'll give you a ride back.' He chuckled. 'A sweet thing like you shouldn't be out all on her own at this time of night. No telling what might happen to her.'

Chapter Four

On the short journey back to the B&B, Troy insisted that Maggie sit up in front with him. Maggie was surprised at just how easily she was able to sit and chat with him. It was almost as if her abandoned and wanton actions of the past hour had not taken place.

'So, how come you managed to get yourselves lost then?' she teased him.

'Roland drives like a maniac,' Troy explained ruefully. 'Besides, you can't really expect this old wreck to keep up with a brand new XK8,' he added.

Maggie was impressed. She had seen the car in the car park at the rink but hadn't realised who it belonged to. Thanks to Justin's obsession with fast cars, she had a pretty fair idea how much an XK8 was worth. She hadn't realised that the Trojans' manager did so well out of them. Still, it would take more than a fancy car to change her opinion of its owner. 'So, what will you do now?' she asked him.

Troy shrugged nonchalantly. 'Keep looking, I guess. If we don't find the hotel soon, we'll just curl up in the back of the van. Unless there's room for us in your bed?'

Maggie grinned at the idea of how her friends would

react if she sneaked back in with half a dozen of the Trojans in tow. Totally impractical, but very tempting.

Troy pulled up outside the B&B and turned to face her. 'There you go, Maggie. All safe and sound.' He kissed her cheek. 'Thanks again for an unreal time.'

Tor leant forward over the front seat and put his hand on her shoulder. 'We will be seeing you again real soon, won't we?'

Maggie twisted round and nodded. 'Probably.' She remembered that he was from Canada and had only been with the team a few weeks. 'I'm working the morning shift all next week.'

'Oh yeah, that's right. You work on reception, don't you?' He smiled warmly at her.

Maggie undid her seatbelt and opened the door. 'I might see you on Monday then?' She was flattered he had noticed her.

Tor grimaced. 'I've got to do a spot of house hunting first thing on Monday. Now I've signed on with the Trojans for next season I'm going to need somewhere better to live. The place I'm in at the moment is a real pigsty.'

Maggie stared at him thoughtfully. 'I've got a friend who's an estate agent,' she told him. 'You met her earlier this evening. Blonde hair and glasses?'

'Yeah. I remember her.' Tor said and nodded.

'She works for Hardy's in the High Street. I'll ask her if she can help you find something, shall I?' Just try to stop Jan from helping once she's heard about it, Maggie thought, remembering the way Jan had been eyeing Tor up earlier on.

'Great.' Tor smiled. 'Thank you.'

Boy oh boy, was Jan ever in for a big surprise, Maggie smiled to herself as she crept in the back door and tiptoed upstairs to the room.

* * *

Claire Patrick started her next shift at the rink at 7 a.m. the following Monday morning. She had had trouble getting off to sleep the night before and felt as if she had barely closed her eyes before the alarm clock jarred her back awake. When she had finally dozed off, her dreams had been haunted by muscular ice hockey players. It was hard to believe that she had really met them all in person.

In her exhausted daze, everything seemed to take twice as long as usual. Her eyes had dark shadows under them and her hair refused to obey the comb. She applied foundation and concealer to her face and rubbed a handful of mousse through her wayward locks. Still munching a piece of toast, she ran for the bus, catching it with only seconds to spare. By the time she slipped into the staff locker room to change out of her Gap jeans and into her crisp black and white uniform, she was already running very late.

There was a hastily scrawled note stuck on her locker door from the personnel manager informing her that she had been assigned to the players' changing rooms that morning. Claire read the note and then screwed it up angrily.

She hated it when she was reassigned from her normal work in the public locker rooms. It might be boring but at least she could get on in her own time and, usually, without anyone else interfering. The players' showers and changing area were always in such a mess after a match or a practice session. The women's junior ice hockey team had been playing a friendly match the previous afternoon and their changing rooms were bound to be in a right state. It was virtually guaranteed that she would end up wet and soggy before she was finished.

As she resentfully pushed her cleaning trolley along the corridor, Claire consoled herself with the thought that she might bump into Justin if he were on duty that morning. She had secretly lusted after him for ages but everyone knew that he and Maggie had a bit of a thing going, and she really liked Maggie.

Besides, if she was being completely honest with herself, Justin terrified her. He was so suave and sophisticated. If only she didn't always get tongue-tied at the wrong moment. If only she could be a bit more like Maggie or Jan. Even the quiet Sara seemed to find it easier to talk to men than she did.

'Good morning, Claire. You're late.' Justin had stepped out into the corridor in front of her. He glanced impatiently at his watch.

Claire jumped. Her pulse started to race as she realised who it was, and her face immediately reddened. 'I'm, I'm, er, sorry.'

'Well, you'd better get a move on,' Justin chided. 'I was promised you would be here by seven at the latest.'

'I'm sorry,' she said again, as her colour deepened. 'I overslept.' She wondered if he knew how good-looking he was in his dark suit and crisp white shirt, with his long blond hair tied back and his eyes sparkling against his tanned skin. Almost like one of the Trojans.

Justin put his hand on hers and flashed her one of his most dazzling smiles. 'Did you enjoy yourself on Saturday, by the way? We really slaughtered the 'Birds, didn't we?'

'Oh yes. It was wicked,' Claire replied nervously, thrilled that he was paying her so much attention. She remembered the way she had noticed him watching her once or twice while she was working and how some of his comments to her had seemed almost suggestive. After all, it wasn't as if he and Maggie were an item or anything. Maybe he really did fancy her? If only she could be sure.

Justin smiled again and his fingers tightened round hers. 'Perhaps I'll see you again when you've finished? You'd better start in the women's changing room first. I'll be in my office if you want anything.'

As he strolled off down the corridor, Claire watched his buttocks twitch up and down tantalisingly. Did he really mean for her to go and see him in his office later? Why else would he make a point of telling her where he would be? Maybe he was simply being a good manager or, then again, maybe he really did want her.

Shit. If only she could be certain. She would feel such a prat if he hadn't meant anything by his comments. Still, it wouldn't hurt to let him know she had finished, would it? Perhaps she could try to persuade him not to complain about her being late. It was not the first time she had overslept and she knew the personnel manager was unlikely to be sympathetic.

As she resumed pushing the trolley down the corridor, Claire pictured herself sitting on Justin's lap telling him how sorry she was for being late while he did wonderful things to her with his hands and lips. She sighed, already knowing that she would not dare to go and find him. If only she could learn to be a bit more assertive and confident, but she had always been too shy and reserved, even as a child. If only Justin had ordered her to his office so that she would have had no choice but to go. Maybe she could pretend that she thought he had.

Her mind still full of outrageous fantasies of herself and Justin making passionate love over his desk, Claire arrived at the women's home changing room and pushed her trolley through the door. She looked around and her heart sank. The place was an utter wreck. It looked as if it hadn't been cleaned properly for a week. It was going to take her ages to get this mess sorted out and she still had to do the men's room afterwards.

Claire scurried about frantically, picking up discarded paper towels and sweet wrappers. She even found a pair of knickers under one bench. Quite sexy but too big for her. She shoved them into the laundry bag with the damp towels. Let the laundry company worry about them.

She peered into the shower cubicles and grimaced when she saw the discarded shampoo bottles, the sticky globs of soap on the tiles and the strands of long hair blocking every drain. Talk about slobs. The women were far worse than the men. Angrily, she yanked at the cleaning hose, braced herself against the far wall and turned the tap full on. She had forgotten how much pressure it generated and before she could reach the tap to turn it down, she lost her footing. The nozzle slipped from her fingers and the hose began to writhe around on the floor like an angry python, spraying water in every direction.

'Bugger it!' Before she could regain her footing and scramble across the floor to the tap, she was soaked to the skin and the whole area was flooded. Justin would be livid if she didn't get this mopped up before anyone saw it. As she tried to brush the water off herself and wring out the hem of her sodden skirt she waded across the room to fetch the squeegee mop.

Maybe she could pretend that the drains had been blocked with paper towels. What if she lost her job? She wouldn't be able to afford her little bedsit if she was out of work. As she began frantically pushing the puddle of lying water towards the central drain, she pictured herself standing, dripping, in Justin's office and begging him not to report her.

'Please, Mr Edwards, I'm sorry. It was an accident. I'll do anything you want to make up for it.' Maybe she would undo her top button first so that he could see what she was offering. She could almost imagine his wolfish smile growing larger as he stared down her cleavage. She would have no choice but to do whatever he told her. Even her boyfriend would have to understand that she had had no choice. It was either that or move back home with her parents, and he would hate that even more, wouldn't he?

Having found an excuse to relieve the guilt of her

thoughts about Justin, she quickly warmed to her fantasies again. Her friend Sally said that if your boss took advantage of you, then it wasn't really a betrayal. Claire felt that if you deliberately flirted the way Sally did, it couldn't really be right, but she was coming round to her friend's way of thinking.

She must have been feeling like this because of Saturday. She was still excited from being with all the Trojans. She had been so turned on thinking about them all last night that, if her boyfriend had been there, she knew she would have let him. She hadn't been going out with Nick very long and, so far, she hadn't allowed more than heavy petting. Tonight, the two of them were going to try that new club in Guildford that she'd heard about. Claire adored clubbing. She could wear that brilliant new skirt she'd bought last week. Then again, maybe not. Nick only had a motorbike. She couldn't wear such a short, tight skirt on a bike.

Claire felt her cheeks start to glow as her thoughts drifted back to the Trojans and the way she had pleasured herself with her fingers under the bedclothes last night just thinking about them. Her mind had been so full of them that she couldn't get to sleep. Her fingers had been between her legs before she had even realised what she was doing. The Trojans were all so hot. They made Nick look like a skinny little boy. When she had come, her orgasm had been so intense she had cried out, then lay shivering in the darkness, hoping no one had heard her through the thin walls of her bedsit.

Claire pushed the last of the water into the drain, then wiped round the cubicles in record time. It wasn't a very good job, but it would have to do. She was running so late that she would never get finished otherwise. Hastily stuffing her cleaning things back on to her trolley, she hurried to the men's changing rooms.

In her rush, she forgot to hang the 'cleaning in progress' sign on the door. She didn't even stop to knock;

she just dashed inside and started gathering up the dirty towels and rubbish. Secretly, she often fantasised that she would walk in and catch a roomful of naked men prancing around, although, to be honest, if she ever had, she knew that she would probably die of embarrassment!

The room was empty and, thankfully, it was also fairly clean and tidy compared to the women's room. If she hurried she would be able to catch up on her work. As soon as she had mopped around, she unlocked the big walk-in storage cupboard and began sorting out a pile of freshly laundered towels.

She had just placed clean towels on the bench outside and returned to finish checking how many were left when she heard the outer door open and the sound of men's voices laughing and joking. In a blind panic, Claire reached out, pulled the cupboard door closed on her and switched off the light. So far as she could remember, the reserve team wasn't due to play again until Wednesday. Was there a practice session on this morning that no one had told her about? Holding her breath, she peered out awkwardly between the wooden slats in the door.

What if it was Justin coming to check up on her work? How would she explain what she was doing shut inside a dark cupboard with her clothes all wet? Why on earth had she panicked like that? She had every right to be in here. Then she remembered: the door! She had forgotten to put the cleaning sign on the door!

Four, no five men came into view, laughing and joking. Jesus! If she had only stayed where she was, she could have just said good morning and wheeled her trolley out. Now what was she going to do? Claire instinctively crouched down, making herself as small as possible, straining her ears to hear what was going on while she tried to remember whether she had left the key in the lock or not.

'That turned out to be quite a match on Saturday.'

'I thought we'd lost it when you nearly let that second one in.'

'Me let it in? It was your lousy checking that caused all the trouble.'

Claire heard the sounds of playful punches and raucous laughter, as if the men were scuffling with each other. She wiggled around and pushed her eye to the crack between two of the slats. As the room came back into focus, she put her hand over her mouth to stifle her gasp of shock. It couldn't be them! It just couldn't be. She was certain the Trojans weren't due to train again until tomorrow.

Pele, the golden-haired net-minder, was standing just in front of the door with his jeans unzipped so that she could clearly see the bulge of his penis under his pants. She swallowed her instinctive gasp and almost lost her balance.

Pele slipped his pants and trousers down his thighs and calves and stepped out of them. Claire could feel herself glowing from the tip of her toes to the roots of her hair as she stared at his nakedness. Her eyes began to sting and she realised that she had forgotten to blink. She rubbed them with one fingertip and twisted her head round to get a better view.

A second Trojan moved into range and Claire watched avidly as he, too, started to undo his trousers. She remembered that he was called Tor, and that he had just joined the team from Canada to play centre. She stifled another gasp. Jesus Christ! They were all stripping off!

Pele swung round so that his cock seemed to be pointing straight at her. He gave Tor a prod in the ribs.

'What about the lovely lady afterwards?' he chortled. We should have asked her who was the best. I bet she would have been more than happy to judge.'

'She was quite something wasn't she?' Tor responded. 'What a body.'

Claire wondered enviously who they were talking

about. She saw Troy turn round towards her so that his cock almost seemed to be dancing back and forth just for her benefit. She realised that she had involuntarily put her hand down between her clenched thighs and she quickly pulled it away. Supposing they heard her moving about? She could hardly bear the thought of being caught spying on them like this. She would die of shame. It didn't stop her moving her eyes from crack to crack trying to see all of them.

'This was all she really wanted,' Troy boasted, as he gave his genitals a loving caress. 'After me, she only took care of the rest of you to be polite.'

Pele snorted contemptuously.

'Truth is, if she hadn't been so polite, she would have been happier just to wait for me to recover,' Troy added softly.

'She would have grown old waiting for you,' Pele retorted.

'Look who's talking.' Pary slapped Pele on the back. 'If I remember correctly, you shot your wad without even getting your pencil-dick inside her.'

Claire swallowed hard. She had never heard men talking together like this. They were worse than women. She pushed her face even closer to the door and squinted her eyes so that she could examine the way Tor's cock was nestled up against his soft blond pubes. She could almost imagine herself gently coaxing him to respond to her body. The idea both shocked and excited her. She knew she was blushing but she didn't care.

Tor looked around the room and then began walking towards the cupboard. Claire watched, mesmerised at the way his balls bounced up and down in time with each step and how his cock flopped from side to side. As he drew closer, she shrank back away from the door, terrified that he was about to discover her. Her head twisted back and forth, seeking an escape route. What could she say? What possible excuse could she give for being in here like this?

Just a few steps short of the door, Tor stopped and leant over to pick up a towel from the bench. Claire released her breath again and peered out at him. His movements seemed so graceful yet so powerful as his muscles rippled under his tanned skin. Poised on one leg, with the other raised to provide a counter-balance, he looked just like one of those erotic sculptures Sara had once taken her to see. His penis was only inches from her face and she could see the individual hairs covering his balls.

She opened her lips. Her tongue slipped out towards him as if eager to taste his manhood. Tor turned his head towards the door and she froze, certain that he must have caught a glimpse of her movements. She sighed with a mixture of relief and regret as he suddenly turned round and leant his body against the door. His buttocks were pressed up into the wooden slats, and she had an almost irresistible urge to reach through and pinch him, just to prove this wasn't all a dream. She raised her hand up towards the door and ran her fingertips gently along the slats. Her heart was hammering so loudly in her chest that she was half-afraid he would hear it.

She leaned forward and peered up through the gaps until she could see the line of curly hairs under his legs, leading her eyes on up towards the curve of his scrotum. Overcome with guilt, she strained harder, twisting her head awkwardly, until she could make out the root of his penis. She longed to wrap her fingers around it and slide her hand slowly and teasingly up towards the smooth tip.

Tor stepped away and Claire remembered to breathe again. She could feel the cold dampness of her wet panties pressing against her sex and a trickle of perspiration ran down between her breasts. Her face was burning with a flush so deep that she felt almost faint with the heat.

As Pele moved back into view, Claire fastened her gaze on his groin. She could feel her bra cutting into her and she reached behind her to undo the catch. As her breasts flopped forward against her still-damp blouse, she put her hand under the bottom of the blouse and pushed the cups right up. She ran her fingers over her tiny breasts and was surprised at how hard her normally small nipples had become.

She pinched one of her super-hard nipples between her thumb and forefinger and felt a deep burning sensation between her legs. If only Nick were here with her now. She wouldn't mind him looking at her breasts like this. In fact, she was aching for him to fondle her. She couldn't remember ever feeling so hot. Was it because it was so unusual to see men like this? Or was it just the fear of being caught spying? Whatever the reason, she was burning all over with excitement and desire.

She pulled her skirt up her thighs as far as she could get it and ran her fingers over her mound and on to her sex lips. She was so aroused that it was all she could do to stop herself from pulling her knickers down and rubbing herself.

She couldn't do it. Not here. What if she cried out, like she had last night? Her clit burned and she closed her legs tightly together, squeezing her mound urgently as she continued to fondle her breasts with her fingers. She imagined the feel of Nick's hand probing urgently between her clamped thighs, forcing his way through her defences so that there was nothing she could do but surrender to him.

A bare leg banged against the door, making it rattle, and Claire jumped and almost toppled over backwards. She peered out again. Troy had snatched Pary's jock strap and was holding it up above his head teasingly. Pary was leaping naked about the changing room as he tried to retrieve it. His genitals bounced and flopped around in front of him, taunting her. His hip banged against the cupboard door again and Claire jumped, praying that it would not spring open and give her away. Quickly, she straightened her skirt. Her fingers were much too shaky to do her bra up again so she slipped her arms out of her sleeves and removed it completely. Before she could get her blouse back on there was another heavy crash and she had to cover her mouth to stifle her scream.

As she crouched back deeper into the cupboard, struggling with the sleeves of her blouse, she was practically sobbing with fear. She could feel her chest heaving in and out as she gulped lungfuls of stale air and fought to calm herself. Another pair of naked buttocks pressed against the slats and she shrank back until she was pushed up against the far wall. As her fingers fiddled desperately with the buttons she was certain that the door would spring open at any moment.

The shouting outside seemed to be growing fainter. What were they doing now? Claire leaned forward again and peered out. The men were heading for the showers. She could hear their laughter echoing down the tiled corridor as they continued to tease Pary.

What now? Should she creep out quickly before they returned? Supposing they came back in before she could gather up her cleaning things? Maybe she could just leave them where they were until later. Claire dithered, undecided, trying not to think about them all naked and covered in soap. She knew that she ought to get out, fast, but she was scared to move.

Before she had pulled herself together, it was too late. Claire heard damp footsteps approaching and realised that the men were returning to dress. She peeped out through the slats and watched in fascination as they finished drying themselves and donned their padded hockey gear. Thank God she had put enough fresh towels out or they might have opened the cupboard to fetch more!

After what seemed like forever, they were finally ready. Claire waited as they laced up their skates and picked up their hockey sticks before heading out to the rink. She hesitated another few minutes to make sure that she was quite alone, then stuffed her bra into her pocket and peered out at the wall clock. Just after eight: she had no time to lose. Quickly, she pushed the door open and stepped out.

As she moved towards her trolley, she realised that her panties were still rolled down round her thighs. She began pulling them up with one hand while she reached for her cleaning tools with the other. The broom slipped from her shaking fingers and crashed to the floor. She snatched it up again and quickly ran her eyes round the room to make quite sure she hadn't forgotten anything.

'Oh!' Her hands flew to cover her face and her eyes opened wide in shock.

Pele was standing on the far side of the changing room with an amused grin on his lips. She peered out at him between her fingers.

'You've tucked your skirt into your knickers,' he told her calmly. He started to walk towards her. The skimpy towel around his waist would have left little to the imagination, even if she hadn't already seen him without it. Claire stood as if made of stone, too shocked and horrified to speak or move. Where on earth had he come from? Hadn't he dressed and left with the rest of them? She couldn't remember.

Pele reached out and pulled her fingers from her face. She stared at him in silence, acutely aware of the way her breasts were heaving as she struggled to catch her breath. Pele took her arm and stepped backwards towards the bench, tugging her along with him. Claire moved her feet woodenly in his wake.

'You were in the cupboard just now watching us, weren't you?' he accused her softly. 'Naughty girl.'

As the back of his thighs made contact with the bench, Claire lowered her eyes and stared down at his crotch. The towel seemed to have pulled even tighter across him so that she could clearly see the outline of his cock. She glanced back up at his face and shuddered with shame at his words and at the knowing smile on his lips.

'It's lucky I like to take my time over my morning shower,' he continued with a wide grin. 'Or I might not have caught you.'

Her heart skipped a beat. God, he had a gorgeous smile. Despite her humiliation, she found herself smiling back. His grin was infectious, like when someone starts giggling helplessly and everyone else finds themselves joining in without really knowing why.

He sat down on the bench with his legs spread wide. He pulled her nearer to him and closed his thighs around hers. She flinched at the contact.

'Don't worry. I'm not gonna tell on you,' he reassured her. 'But, I couldn't let you go like this, could I?' He let go of her arm and moved his hand round to the back of her rucked-up skirt. Claire overbalanced and fell forward so that her breasts brushed across his face. She quickly put her hands up on the wall behind him and arched her back, pulling her body away from him. She could feel the warmth of his breath caressing the skin at her cleavage.

Pele slid his hands up her thighs and gently lowered her panties enough to free the hem of her skirt. Every touch of his skin against hers made Claire shudder with longing. Every shudder caused her breasts to brush against his face again. She twisted her head to try and see what he was doing and spotted their reflection in the mirrored tiles on the far wall. A small sigh dropped from her lips.

Pele had draped the hem of her skirt around her waist. As she watched, he slid his hands down over the curve of her hips and on to the top of her panties. Claire stared in silence as his fingers slid under the elastic. She felt and saw them lowering. Another shiver of fear and longing tore through her and her sweaty palms started to slip down the wall. He immediately let go of her panties and grabbed her round the waist to steady her.

Claire put her left hand on his shoulder and tried to push herself upright. He grinned and moved his head forward to suck one of her buttons into his mouth. If she kept struggling, the button would probably come open, revealing her naked breasts. She stood perfectly still and tried not to notice his fingers caressing her buttocks and thighs. She was almost afraid to look at their reflection again, yet at the same time she desperately wanted to watch.

Slowly and carefully, Pele pulled her knickers back up over her buttocks and ran his fingers over the material, smoothing it into place. His fingertips slipped round to the front and lightly caressed the swell of her mound. A sharp tingle of longing surged through her trembling body. With a soft whimper, Claire slumped forward and sank her teeth into his shoulder. Her head felt dizzy, and her whole being was shaking with a mixture of fear, shame and uncontrollable passion. She had never experienced anything quite like this.

As if oblivious to her reactions, Pele calmly released the hem of her skirt and tugged it back down over her knickers. Realising that she still had her teeth buried in his skin, Claire relaxed her jaws and raised her head again. She could see the reddened imprint of her teeth marks quite clearly. Her eyes travelled down his body and she stared in fascination at the shiny smooth tip of his engorged penis now peeping hungrily over the top of the towel.

Pele used his hands to guide her upright, although his legs were still holding her tightly in front of him. Uncontrollable shivers wracked her body and her mouth was so dry that she would not have been able to speak even if she could have thought of anything to say.

'Do you know what happens to naughty girls who hide in the men's changing rooms?' he questioned her teasingly.

Claire just shook her head helplessly. Her terror of public exposure flooded back.

'Yeah you do. They get their bottoms spanked,' he threatened her.

She shook her head again, already picturing one of his huge hands whacking her tiny buttocks red raw.

'Good and hard.'

She could see the lust on his face as he turned her sideways and flicked her hem back up before pulling her down so that she was sitting on his right knee. As her buttocks made contact with his bare flesh, Claire felt a jolt like an electric shock race through her body. There was a desperate, almost painful, ache deep inside her, growing stronger and stronger until she felt as if she were about to explode. What was wrong with her? She had never felt like this with anyone. Every touch of his body against hers seemed to burn her skin and she just couldn't stop herself from shaking. She had to get away.

Mustering all her strength and willpower, she leant forward and tried to pull herself back up on to her feet. Pele laughed and held her down as easily as if she were a small child. As soon as she stopped struggling, he pushed her face forward over his left thigh with her buttocks in the air. His crotch was hard up against her left hip so that she could feel his cock burning into her side as he thrust himself on to her. She could hear his breath coming in rapid, shallow gasps.

'Please stop,' she begged him. 'Please.'

Her words seemed to steady him. She heard his breathing quieten and he stopped thrusting himself against her. Claire turned her head sideways to look up at him and experienced another little shiver of lust when she saw his hungry smile.

'Oh no, missy,' he informed her loudly. 'You've got to be punished.' His voice sounded strange, as if he were having trouble speaking and Claire realised that he was no longer totally in control of himself. Instead of frightening her, this realisation caused another rush of desire that made her whole body feel weak. She felt her panties slipping down her thighs again and his fingers began stroking and squeezing her naked cheeks.

Claire bit her bottom lip and tried to stop herself from twitching. She wanted to beg him not to touch her between her legs. She knew what would happen if he did. She was so close to climaxing that his touch there would be all it would take. As inexperienced as she was, Claire hadn't realised that it was possible to get so close to coming without doing so.

Oh shit. Would he be able to tell? What would he think of her if she came that easily? Even the thought of her humiliation did not seem to help. She had never known such intense feelings of arousal as those she was now experiencing. It was all she could do to stop herself groaning aloud with the desperation of her passion.

'What a delightful little arse,' Pele growled softly as he tucked the hem of her skirt securely into its waistband. 'I don't know whether to smack it, kiss it or just eat it. It's gorgeous.' She felt his tongue caressing her left cheek, and another shudder of desire coursed through her.

'I bet your boyfriend can't stop fucking this, can he?' Pele's fingertip prodded the opening of her anus. Claire gasped and clenched her buttocks against his probing. No one had ever touched her there before. Her fear overcame her excitement.

'Please don't,' she mumbled. 'Please stop. I can't . . .'

'What's the matter? You're not afraid to let yourself go, are you? I've seen plenty of women climax.' Pele told her calmly. 'I love watching them wank. Watching them really letting themselves go.'

The lust in his voice made his words sound hard and Claire shivered with fear at how far he might be intending to go. She felt him deliberately pull her up against his cock again.

'Do you wank for your boyfriend?' he demanded hoarsely. 'I bet you do. Would you wank for me?'

Claire was unable to stifle a small squeal as he thrust his hand underneath her and she felt his fingers brushing insistently back and forth over her clit. 'Oh! No!' she clenched her teeth as she came. Wave after wave of pleasure rushed through her, leaving her breathless and trembling. Pele was seemingly unaware of what had happened; his finger continued to gently rub her, while his other hand caressed her buttocks and teased her anus.

As the last tremors of her orgasm died away, Claire struggled upright and sat shaking helplessly on his knee with her head resting on his chest. She could still feel his erection pushing against her thigh and knew that he wasn't finished with her yet. Was he planning to fuck her? She shuddered as she imagined him lowering her down on to his massive cock. What if someone walked in on them? Justin might come looking for her at any moment.

She trembled as Pele began to undo the buttons on the front of her blouse. She moved her thigh gently against his penis and savoured the feel of him twitching in response. She really should put a stop to this. She couldn't let him take her there in such a public place. She didn't want him to stop. He pulled the two sides of her blouse back and ran his tongue across her naked breasts. She flinched but he seemed not to notice. His tongue circled one nipple while his fingers began gently teasing the other.

'You have the loveliest tits I've ever seen,' he whispered. 'So tiny and firm.'

Claire flushed at the unexpected compliment and tried to decide if she should finish removing her blouse or wait for him. She wished she was sitting the other way round so that she could see herself reflected in the tiles. What must she look like? Christ, this was the men's changing room! Claire almost giggled. What did it matter? She wouldn't be any better off if it were the women's. Just, please God, don't let anyone come in and catch them.

Pele slid one hand back down between her legs and his finger started to fondle her clit again. Claire was amazed at the renewed rush of excitement pulsing through her. She felt his fingertips parting her engorged lips and tried to open her thighs wider for him but her panties stopped her.

Pele tugged her knickers down over her knees to her ankles. 'Lift up.'

Claire lifted one foot to kick them free and Pele immediately pushed her legs as wide as possible, clamping her with his thighs. She could see that he was staring hungrily at her exposure and the thought of his desire for her sent little shivers of delight up and down her spine. She found herself twitching helplessly as his hands explored her sex and his tongue devoured her nipples.

Pele finished undoing her blouse and began to slip the sleeves from her arms. 'Close your eyes,' he instructed her. She felt him placing something around her head and realised that he had bound her eyes with her rolled-up blouse. He lifted her into his arms and moved her along the bench.

'That's not fair,' she complained, amazed at her own daring. 'You can see everything and I can't.' She lifted her hands up towards her face, but he caught her wrists gently and moved them back into her lap. She felt herself being shifted around so that she was sitting on his lap with her back against his chest.

Claire could feel his cock pushed up into her crack and

realised that his towel must either have fallen off or he had removed it. The tip of his cock was pushed up against her arsehole. Maybe she would let him put just the tip of it up into her, she told herself. She whimpered as he pulled her legs wider apart and his finger slipped back between her sex lips. His other hand cupped her left breast and resumed teasing her nipple. She sensed her passion building up again and shuddered all over at the feel of his lips nuzzling the back of her neck.

The blindfold seemed to be heightening all her senses so that his every caress drove her wild. It was as if not being able to see somehow alleviated the guilt and fear of what was happening. All her inhibitions seemed to be melting away and she began to relax, giving herself up to the pleasure of his touch. She felt him take her hands and push the flattened palms down on her thighs, just inches from her mound.

'You do it.' His fingers guided hers towards her pussy while his tongue and teeth continued to lick and nibble her neck and ears.

Claire hesitated. Her clit was on fire from the touch of his knowing fingers, but she'd never played with herself in front of anyone else. She was scared to do it and scared not to. What if he got angry with her?

Timidly, Claire ran her fingertips over her tiny bud, trying not to squirm with the pleasure of it. Pele stopped kissing her neck and sat perfectly still. She knew that he was staring at her and she could feel his cock juddering excitedly under her. She stopped moving her finger and took a deep, shuddering breath.

'Don't stop,' he pleaded urgently. His words were faint and breathless and Claire licked her lips excitedly at the note of desperation she detected in his voice. She tried to assume a look of total submission as she lifted her hand slightly. She was automatically clenching her buttocks against his erection and she could feel him thrusting rhythmically back and forth in his excitement.

With a deep breath, Claire raised her finger to her lips and sucked it into her mouth. She heard the whoosh of his breath as she lowered her hand back between her thighs and ran the dampened fingertip over herself. A thrill of excitement raced up inside her and, for a second, she thought she was going to come again. Quickly, she pulled her finger back, breathing deeply to try to control her lust.

'Oh yeah! Don't stop, baby.' His voice was hoarse with need and the sound of it drove her crazy. She had always enjoyed teasing Nick and watching him getting all horny and breathless, but she had never experienced this sort of power over a man before. Careful not to actually touch her sensitive little bud, Claire returned her fingers to her pussy, rubbing the soft, damp flesh and savouring the feel of his bursting cock grinding relentlessly into her crack. She felt her orgasm rushing to overwhelm her again. What would he think of her lack of self-control if she came again so soon?

Quickly, Claire twisted away from him and lifted her leg over his. She heard him groan loudly as she pushed herself down between his thighs until she was kneeling, facing him. Blindly, she reached out, searching for his cock. She ran her hands up towards his groin. Pele groaned again.

'Sorry. Did I hurt you?' she questioned anxiously, pulling her fingers back.

'No. It's OK,' he assured her softly, as her questing fingers caressed his balls and started to inch their way back up his rigid shaft. She felt him raise his buttocks, thrusting his cock towards her. Her fingers tugged the towel away from his waist, exposing him totally.

'My turn,' she gloated as she felt her way down on to his thighs. Her fingers found their way back on to his cock and she ran them inquisitively all over it, trying to picture it in her mind from touch alone. It felt so huge and swollen that a momentary panic engulfed her at the idea of him pushing such a monster up inside her.

Remembering the sound of his voice and breathing when she had done it before, Claire put her fingers to her mouth and licked them again, before gently sliding her clenched palm down his length from tip to base. She could feel the thick bush of his hair at the base, but his cock seemed silky smooth to her touch. She wondered if he had deliberately shaved it.

Nervously, she raised her buttocks and leaned forward so that she could suck him into her mouth. She had only ever done this once before and had been excited by the reaction. When she had made him as desperate as she herself had been, she would stop and start to play with herself again. Maybe she could make him come too, so that he would know how it felt to lose it like that.

Pele groaned with pleasure and put his hands on her shoulders. She could already taste his spunk, warm and salty. She pushed one hand underneath him, fingering the skin behind his balls and trying to push her fingertip up into his crack the way he had done to her.

'Jesus!' She felt a rush of triumph at his desperate whisper, and smiled to herself at the way he was lifting his buttocks up so that she could push deeper and deeper into him. She could feel his cock jerking up and down in her mouth and knew that he was close.

Her own excitement was getting the better of her again, too. Claire ran her other hand down her body and between her legs, rubbing urgently to relieve the pressure. Suddenly, he seized her by the hair and pulled her lips off his cock.

'Not yet, baby,' he told her softly. 'I've got other plans for you first. After what you did, you won't get away with just sucking me off.' She felt his fingers pushing into her anus again.

Claire shivered all over at his words. She knew what he wanted. He wanted to fuck her. Fuck her in the arse.

Despite her fear, part of her wanted him to. Yet part of her wanted him inside her cunt too. She wanted to feel him come as she came.

'Jesus Christ! Will you look at that? Trust Pele. We leave him playing with his dick in the shower and he finds himself some juicy pussy!' The unknown male voice chuckled with delight.

Claire shot upright and ripped the blindfold from her eyes. She spun round and blinked in horror at the sight of three of the other Trojans lined up by the far door. How long had they been there? How much had they seen? She felt the colour flooding to her cheeks as she remembered what she had been doing. Pele must have known they were watching. She turned back to him.

'You bastard! You, you wanker!' she yelled furiously.

'Not guilty,' Pele grinned. 'I'm not so sure about them, though.'

Claire suddenly realised that the other Trojans were all openly fondling themselves through their clothing as they stared at her. She shook her head in disbelief, then squealed as she felt herself being lifted up from behind.

'What are you doing?' she cried as Pele stood her on the bench and raised her leg up over his shoulder. 'Stop it! Oh!' She sagged back against the wall as he leaned down and pushed his tongue into her pussy. His hands tightened around her buttocks, pulling her harder on to his mouth and she felt her passion growing again as his tongue probed deeper and deeper into her warm dampness.

She could hear herself making little mewing noises in the back of her throat as his relentless tongue rapidly carried her towards climax. A slight grunt caused her to lift her head, and her eyes widened as she saw that the other Trojans had unzipped themselves and were now caressing their swollen cocks while they watched Pele devour her. Claire gulped and closed her eyes. None of this could possibly be happening. Not here. Not to her.

Her hips writhed urgently as her inevitable orgasm burst inside her.

'There now. All nice and dry.' She opened her eyes again and saw that Pele had already used a paper towel to wipe her thighs. She allowed him to help her climb down from the bench. Glancing down, she saw his still-urgent erection thrust out in front of him like a sword. It was so gorgeous, she felt a desperate compulsion to take him back into her mouth and give him as much pleasure as he had given her.

Before she could move, however, one of the other Trojans stepped closer and knelt down behind her. She had almost forgotten about them. Panic engulfed her as his hands started to pull her thighs apart.

'No!' she screamed. She couldn't take anymore. She just couldn't. What if they all wanted her? She pulled the hem of her skirt back down and snatched her blouse up from the floor. Before anyone could react she fled out, across the corridor and into the women's changing room.

Claire perched breathlessly on the seat of one of the loos, breathing deeply as she struggled to regain her composure. Her mind was full of images of naked Trojans with enormous erections, and her whole body was still tingling from Pele's caresses. She stared out of the partially open door at the clock on the wall. Incredibly, it was still barely 8.30 a.m. Nick probably wasn't even awake yet.

Chapter Five

When Maggie awoke on Monday morning, for a moment she couldn't think where she was. She had been living in a kind of exhausted daze ever since the events of Saturday night and couldn't remember much of what had happened on Sunday. For reasons that she couldn't explain even to herself, she had said nothing to her friends about her adventure. Considering that any one of them would have given a week's pay for such an opportunity, her reluctance to even speak about it was peculiar. Was it because she felt she had gone too far, or because she was not sure they would believe her anyway? She was no longer certain that it had ever really happened.

She climbed out of her bed, emitting a small groan, and tottered into her bathroom. Five minutes under an almost cold shower cleared her head sufficiently to allow her to function as a human being again. She patted herself dry and slipped into an old pink robe before heading into the kitchen for several cups of strong black coffee.

As she sipped the steaming liquid, her mind filled with memories of Saturday. The whole episode seemed so incredible. Could it have been nothing more than a figment of her overstimulated imagination? It had seemed so real. What if it wasn't a dream? If it had really happened?

She thumped her coffee cup down on the work surface and moved across the room to pick up the phone. As she dialled the number her fingers trembled slightly. Her call was answered on the fifth ring.

'Jan. It's Maggie.'

'Maggie! Hi. Shit. Hang on a sec. Try the top drawer on the left.' Maggie heard her friend's muffled voice yelling. 'No. The left one.' There were a few bumping noises and Jan's voice returned. 'Men, honestly. Are they really all that helpless or is it just something about me? Do you have any idea what time it is, Mags?'

'Yes. Sorry. I figured you would be gone if I didn't catch you first.'

'I would be if everything wasn't going haywire this morning. When I got back yesterday I found Marcus had arrived back early from his trip. I had a hell of a job explaining where I had been. He was convinced that I'd been out with someone else behind his back.' Jan paused to take a breath and Maggie jumped in quickly.

'Talking about Saturday . . .' she began.

'Yes. If Marcus says anything to you, you will confirm I was in Bristol with you, won't you?' Jan pleaded.

'What's with you all of a sudden? I thought you and Marcus had an understanding?' Considering how Jan usually totally dominated Marcus, Maggie was feeling more than a little confused by this conversation. It was doing little to help clear her own muddled thoughts.

'We do,' Jan replied. 'It's just that I don't like him assuming I've been up to something when I haven't. Besides, the poor thing was in a real state about it. It took me ages to soothe him.'

I bet, Maggie thought to herself, picturing what Jan had probably done to soothe him. No wonder she sounded nearly as tired and ratty as Maggie felt. 'OK. No problem. I'll tell him you were with me. Now, shut up and listen for a minute, will you? I didn't get a chance to say anything to you yesterday, but there's something you need to know about.'

Jan practically dropped the phone back into its cradle. As she rushed into the bedroom to dress she was already planning her strategy. Christ Almighty. Her boss would be delirious if she managed to get one of the Trojans as a client. Just think of the publicity. Just think about the chance to see Tor again.

Maggie had sounded really strange on the phone, Jan mused to herself as she carefully applied her favourite lipstick. It was almost as if she were hiding something. Come to think of it, she had been acting funny all day yesterday. Sort of quiet and moody, as if her mind had been elsewhere. When had she had the chance to discuss house hunting with Tor? And, why hadn't she said anything about it sooner? She and Maggie obviously needed to have serious chat.

As soon as Jan was ready, she picked up her bag, grabbed her car keys and gave Marcus a cheery wave. 'Sorry, I've got to go. I've got a great chance of making a real coup if I hurry.'

'Who was that on the 'phone?' Marcus glared at her suspiciously.

'Only Maggie.' Sod it, she really didn't need another of his sulks right now. She had to get hold of Tor before one of their competitors got wind of him. Marcus would just have to get on and sulk. She could make it up to him later, once the deal was in the bag.

'How about dinner at Francesco's tonight? My treat.' she bribed him. It was their favourite restaurant.

'Well. OK.' His lips curled into a slight smile. 'How about giving me a proper goodbye?' He ran his eyes over her body suggestively.

'I can't now, Marcus.' Jan was certainly tempted. Whatever else you might say about Marcus, he was a great lover. She saw his mouth start to pout again. 'Look. I'll make it up to you tonight. Promise.' She blew him a kiss and hurried out the door before he could argue.

After grabbing himself some breakfast in the small hotel dining room, Tor returned to his room. If he left it up to Roland there was no telling how long he would be stuck in this sleazy hotel. Knowing from bitter experience what it was like to live out of a suitcase for weeks on end, he felt that it would be a good idea if he found himself somewhere to rent as soon as possible. He checked the 'phone book for local estate agents and then took a taxi to the address of the agents that Maggie had mentioned.

He wondered if she had remembered to speak to her friend about it, then shrugged. It didn't matter. One advantage of being a bit of a local celebrity was that people were always eager to drop everything once they realised who you were. He might not have been with the Trojans for very long, but long enough to know that they were pretty popular around there. He was quite sure that Jan would recognise him.

Tor leant back in the seat of the taxi and stared out the window. He liked being back in England. Most people assumed that he was Canadian and he was content to let them. It made him seem more interesting. There was nothing very glamorous about being born in the eastend of London. Besides, he had been living in Montreal since he was a child and had practically come to think of it as his home. The Trojans were a good career move for him, though. A few more years and, who knows, maybe he could return to Canada and sign with one of the top nationals.

'Here you go, mate.' The taxi driver's voice broke into his thoughts as the car pulled up outside the estate agents. 'That'll be £6.50 please.'

Tor climbed out of the car and handed the driver the money. 'Cheers.' The half-forgotten English expressions from his childhood had come back to him easily, although he was not sorry to have swapped his harsh London accent for the softer, gentler Canadian tones. As the car pulled off, he looked around him with interest. Fairwood was a nice little town. Small and friendly. The sort of place where everybody knew everybody else.

As Tor pushed the door open and stepped inside, a bell jangled insistently. He studied the interior carefully. The door led straight into the large front room of what had clearly once been an old house. The room was fitted out as an office, with three large desks. It seemed to be deserted and Tor wondered if they were even open for business yet.

'Hello. Anybody there?' he called out in his deep baritone voice. 'Am I too early?'

'Too early for what?' A tall, slim woman with blond hair and glasses walked through from a back corridor on the far side of the room. Tor recognised her immediately from the dinner on Saturday. He had forgotten just how attractive she was.

'Hi. Your friend, Maggie, said you might be able to help me find a place to rent.' He examined her critically. Very nice. Firm breasts, long shapely legs. Yeah. Very nice. He would enjoy her company this morning. Then, maybe lunch and . . .

'Finished?' Her voice sounded slightly harsh and Tor started guiltily. He lifted his eyes back to her face and laughed uneasily when he saw the way she was looking at him.

'I'm sorry, I . . .' his voice dried up. He hadn't realised that his stare had been quite so blatant. But, hell, she was an attractive woman. She must have been used to men looking at her.

'It's not a problem. Just so long as you know it's only

property we rent out. I'm Jan Nichols.' She held out a slim, well-manicured hand.

Although the tone of voice was still hard, there was a twinkle in her eye and a slight smile at the corners of her mouth as she spoke and Tor breathed a little more easily as he shook her hand. He had been afraid that he had put his foot in it. You could never be sure anymore. Some career women seemed to get totally pissed off at the slightest hint of anything that might be taken as sexist. 'Tor,' he responded softly.

He risked giving her another admiring look and grinned as she immediately twirled around for his benefit. Her skirt had a wide, flared hem so that it floated up away from her body as she moved, giving him a tantalising glimpse of her legs and the lacy tops of her stockings. God, she was sexy.

When she had finished her twirl Jan stared into his face and raised a sardonic eyebrow. 'Well?'

Tor swallowed hard. 'Perfect,' he murmured.

Jan's eyes seemed to focus on his crotch and he was certain that the bulge there was already expanding. He resisted the urge to cover himself and was relieved when she returned her gaze to his eyes. There was a slight flush on her cheeks that had not been there before, but he was not sure whether it was from excitement, embarrassment, or both.

'Well?' he mimicked her earlier question and Jan laughed and nodded.

'Just fine,' she agreed. 'So, now that we know we both come up to spec, perhaps we should get down to business,' she added suggestively. 'Considering who you are, I assume you are looking for something secluded and private? Something a bit out of town, perhaps?'

Tor nodded. Had she and Maggie been chatting about him? Would Maggie have told her friend what had happened on Saturday night? Guys would boast about that sort of thing, but he wasn't so sure about women.

'Did you come by car?' Jan questioned.

Tor shook his head. 'Taxi.'

'That's OK. We'll use mine. I've got three places that I think might be suitable for you.'

Jan walked over to one of the desks and bent over to open the bottom drawer. Tor watched the curve of her legs and buttocks through the soft material of the skirt and decided that she must be wearing a thong. He made a pretence of tucking the front of his shirt back in, and did his best to rearrange his ever-hardening cock.

Jan pulled out a folder and opened it on the desk. She picked up some advertising leaflets and spread them out side by side. Tor moved closer to look at them so that he was standing right beside her. He could just catch a subtle whiff of her perfume. He hated those strong body sprays some women wore so that you could smell them coming ten feet away. Jan's scent was just right. Sexy and suggestive – just like the lady who was wearing it.

Tor shifted closer so that he could study the information on one of the houses. His hip brushed against hers and he was pleased to notice that she did not move away. She didn't move any closer either. The warmth of her body aroused him even more. Did she realise the effect she was having on him? He glanced at her nipples. Yeah. They were definitely hard but then, they had been earlier too.

'This is probably the most suitable.' Jan tapped a long, varnished fingernail on one of the leaflets and turned her head to smile into his eyes. Her lips were only inches away from his.

'Well, OK.' His voice was a high-pitched squeak. He turned his head and coughed to clear his throat. 'Let's get started then.' He still sounded more like a soprano than a baritone. Unable to resist touching her, her put his arm loosely around her waist as if to guide her.

'Where's your car?' He felt suddenly foolish, steering

her across the office without knowing where they were headed.

'Out the back. I have to lock up first. I'm on my own this morning.' Jan slipped easily from his grasp and walked across to fasten the lock on the front door.

Tor watched her move, enjoying the way her skirt swirled round her legs and moulded itself to her thighs. The light seemed to shine straight through it and the view was definitely worth looking at. His pants were feeling extremely tight and uncomfortable. He shifted his hips and moved his hand round towards his waistband to try to adjust himself again. The bolt shot across and Jan started to turn round.

Tor whipped his hand away and thought quickly. 'I, um, I need to use the bathroom first if that's OK?'

'Sure. I'll show you the way.' He was almost certain that she deliberately brushed against him as she walked passed. His cock was showing its predictable lack of good timing. Instead of shrinking in response to his discomfort, the damned thing was actually so hard that it was difficult to walk.

Tor gritted his teeth and shuffled awkwardly in her wake. One day he was going to actually ask a woman like Jan if she realised what she could do to a man without seeming to even try, or if it was just accidental. Either way, it was a relief to get out of sight and slam the door behind him.

Tor unzipped himself and put his hand down inside his pants. His prick was as hard as a rock. He dropped his trousers to his ankles and bent awkwardly over the bowl. It was bloody difficult to piss straight when you had a hard-on. As he finished, his cock started to soften. He redressed himself carefully, adjusting his prick inside his pants so that if, or rather when, he expanded again, he would be more comfortable.

As he rejoined her, Jan glanced pointedly at his crotch

and Tor was certain that the look on her face was far less innocent than it seemed. Did she know?

'Better?'

He saw the way her lips were crinkling with suppressed laughter. Well, that answered his question. She obviously knew exactly why he needed to get out of sight. Thank God, he had resisted the temptation to jerk off.

'Yes thank you,' he answered and nodded awkwardly.

'Good. My car's through here.' Jan led the way along a dark narrow corridor leading to the rear entrance. Tor trouped after her like a lost sheep following the shepherd girl; his eyes were mesmerised by the way her buttocks swayed so seductively.

As soon as they were outside, Jan stopped to lock the back door and then slipped the key into her bag. Tor took her arm to help guide her down the narrow brick steps. Not that she needed any help, but it was an opportunity to get closer to her and she didn't seem to object. When they reached the bottom step, she pressed the remote button on her keyring and unlocked a white BMW.

'Nice wheels,' said Tor.

'Thank you.'

He steered her towards the car and opened the driver's door for her. As she slid gracefully in under the wheel, he caught a quick glimpse of her lacy white bra and bronzed skin through the buttons of her blouse. It was only a flash but it was more than enough to cause another surge of blood to his groin.

As he closed the door and walked round the front, Tor pondered over why he always seemed to turn into a tongue-tied, clumsy moron whenever he was alone with a beautiful woman. Considering what he and the other guys had got up to with Maggie the other night, it seemed unbelievable that he could be so unsure of himself now. Funny how he always knew what to do when opportunities like that presented themselves or when he was with the others, yet on his own, with a lady like Jan in a situation like this, he was reduced to a stammering idiot. It was almost as if he were two separate people: Tor the Trojan on the outside, yet still hapless old Andy Robbins underneath. Drink helped, but he could hardly walk around permanently drunk.

He climbed into the passenger seat and gave Jan another quick stare. How far was she prepared to let things go? He leaned forward and slipped his jacket off so that he could put it on his lap to cover himself. Now, at least, he could sit back and enjoy the view. He should have thought of it before.

'Safety beat, please.' Jan's voice snapped him out of his daydreams. Tor yanked at the belt, tugged it across his broad chest and plugged the end in with a sharp click. He twisted his body slightly so that he could just see the tops of her stockings and enjoyed the way the soft material of her skirt had moulded itself around her thighs again. She had wonderful legs. His fingers tingled with the urge to caress them but he resisted the temptation; instead he made do with imagining how soft and smooth her flesh would feel if he ran his hand up over the top of the nylon and on to her bare skin.

He pictured his fingers gliding up over her thigh and on to her hips and stomach. He was fairly certain that she was only wearing a tiny thong. Was it cotton or silk? His fingers would slip down over it and feel the outline of her mound. Would she have shaved? She had a good suntan, so she was bound to have at least shaved to the bikini line. His fingers would rub gently over her, exploring the slight sponginess of her remaining pubes. His cock twitched impatiently. Perhaps his other hand could slip in between the buttons and fondle those luscious breasts.

His thoughts were interrupted again as Jan suddenly slammed on the brakes. His jacket slipped off his lap on to the floor. Oh Jesus. Had she guessed what he was thinking? He reached down and grabbed the jacket quickly before she saw the evidence of his fantasy.

'Sorry about that.' Jan blasted the horn and glared out the windscreen. 'That stupid sod needs to take driving lessons.' She pulled round the car in front of them.

Tor slipped his hand under his jacket to try and make himself more comfortable. Zips might be convenient but they could certainly be a pain at times. He winced at his sudden memory of the first time he had ever been with a girl when he was fifteen.

He had just finished removing his clothes when her older sister had walked in on them. In his panic, he had jumped off – what was her name? Oh yeah, Charlotte. He had jumped up off Charlotte and whipped his jeans up without bothering about his pants. As he had tugged the zip up, he had caught himself. Shit, that had been painful. He never did know the name of Charlotte's sister, but he would never forget her cruel smile at the way he was doubled over in his agony.

'Forget something?' she had sniggered, holding his underpants out on the end of her finger. She had stood in front of the door and watched while he removed his jeans and dressed himself properly. He had never been so embarrassed, especially when she'd caught sight of his, by then, shrivelled cock. Her final words were permanently etched into his subconscious: 'Well, little sis, I don't think he could have done much damage with that!'

Tor frowned in disbelief. Normally, the memory of that incident was more than enough. Today, it wasn't working. His cock seemed to be as hard and desperate as ever. Carefully, so Jan wouldn't see, he pushed it sideways away from the zip. He tried staring out the window to distract himself but he could see the reflection of her face in the glass. It was a very lovely face, full of character as well as classic English beauty. Although he couldn't see the colour of her eyes, he was very aware of the way they kept flicking from the road ahead to glance at him. There was something almost regal about her features but he could detect no emotion, just concentration. It made her seem even more beautiful and desirable.

'You don't sound very Canadian,' Jan said, breaking into his thoughts. 'Where abouts do you come from?'

'Montreal. Although actually I was born in London.'

'Really? I guess that explains it.'

'It was a long time ago.' He wasn't entirely sure if he was talking about living in London or his humiliating first attempt to lose his virginity. He wanted to continue the conversation, but was becoming tongue-tied again.

Five minutes later she turned the car into a driveway and stopped at the closed gates. She released her seatbelt.

'No, I'll get them.' Tor opened the door.

'Thank you, but don't you think it would be easier if you undid your safety belt first?'

In his rush to be helpful, Tor had forgotten about the belt. Her words were spoken kindly, and he had a feeling that she was more than used to men making total arses of themselves around her. He unclipped the belt sheepishly, then had to laugh at the warmth of her smile. It was worth playing the fool just for that.

After he had opened one gate, he had to scrabble around looking for something to prop it open with while he held the other. As he moved an old brick into place and walked across to the other gate he could feel her eyes appraising his every move.

As soon as Jan had driven inside, Tor closed the gates and climbed back into the passenger seat. It didn't take him long to realise that one of her blouse buttons had come undone. He smiled to himself. If she thought that he wouldn't spot something like that, then she had seriously underestimated him. He might be having trouble remembering his own name, but there wasn't much about her he hadn't noticed. He knew exactly how many buttons she had on the front of her blouse and which side of her skirt the zip was on. He even knew that her bra did up at the back with two hooks.

The car reached the end of the drive and stopped. As Jan switched off the engine, Tor jumped out and practically ran round to hold the door for her. As she turned to climb out, he again took the opportunity to look down the top of her blouse. He thought he could just catch a glimpse of the pinkish outline of her nipples and the idea of them was enough to set the blood boiling in his veins. He took her arm and helped her out, doing his best to make it difficult for her to straighten her skirt.

'Well, this would be my choice.' Jan stood by the side of the car and let her eyes roam around the house and grounds. He could see now that her eyes were blue: a deep almost violet-blue, enhanced by the magnifying properties of her glasses so that they made the sky pale into insignificance.

'Rather large grounds, but there's a gardener who comes in once a week so you won't have to worry about that,' she told him.

She had turned slightly so that the sun was shining straight through the front of her blouse. The material seemed to have become almost transparent and Tor could not take his eyes off the clearly defined outline of her breasts. Was she posing like that deliberately, or was she totally unaware of the effect she had created? His cock certainly wasn't unaware. Somehow, his single-minded friend had managed to get itself into an even more uncomfortable position; his zip was really cutting into him.

Tor realised that Jan was staring at him again, waiting for some reaction to the house. He forced his eyes from her breasts and glanced round swiftly. 'Yeah. I like the idea of large grounds. What's the back like?' His eyes locked on to her cleavage again.

'Let's go and see, shall we? I think you'll find it even better.' She was glancing at the advertising blurb again.

'Very private and mostly south facing. Although I guess it's a little early in the year for that to matter much.'

As they started round the back Tor took her arm again. The pathway was narrow and winding so that they were forced to walk quite close together and Tor caught another heady whiff of her perfume. He slipped his arm round her waist and pulled her gently towards him.

'Careful –' he nodded down at the moss-covered paving slabs '– those look very slippery.'

'Oh yes. Thank you.' Jan made no attempt to escape his embrace. In fact, to his delight, she put her arm round him. 'Just in case I slip. You don't mind, do you?' She looked up at him and raised one eyebrow inquisitively.

Tor struggled to resist the urge to place his lips on hers. 'Just make sure that if you fall, you fall on me,' he muttered.

Jan laughed. 'It's a promise,' she responded huskily.

Thigh to thigh, they continued walking along the narrow path. Tor's hand slid down on to her hip so that he could feel her muscles tightening and loosening with each step she took. His cock jerked violently against his zip and he had to bite his bottom lip to stop himself from groaning at the exquisite pain of it. He looked around, trying to distract himself.

'What's that over there?' He pointed to a small building, partly hidden under the branches of a huge weeping willow tree, which was already beginning to bud.

'I'm not sure,' Jan admitted. 'I don't remember anything about it in the write-up. Let's take a look.' She took a step off the pathway and then pulled a face. 'Maybe not. The ground's so soft that my heels are sinking in to it.'

'No problem. I'll carry you.' Tor swept her up into his strong arms before she had time to protest.

Jan looked startled and then smiled. 'Well, if you don't mind?' She wrapped her arms around his neck and snuggled more comfortably against his muscular chest.

Tor could feel the softness of her breasts pushed against him and the scent of her perfume grew stronger, making his head feel light and fuzzy.

With one arm under her legs and the other wrapped around her back, Tor began to stride confidently across the lawn towards the small building. He could feel her skirt slipping against the nylon of her stockings and he shifted his hand higher up her thigh so that he could feel the lacy top. It was all he could do to keep the triumphant grin off his face. His fingers felt as if they had been charged with electricity where he was touching her and, impossibly, his cock seemed to be looking for room to expand further. He shifted his other arm further round her so that his fingers were just touching the curve of her left breast. Jan snuggled so close against him that he was sure she would hear his heart racing. Thank God she couldn't see his crotch. Nothing could hide his obvious arousal now.

As they drew closer he could see that the building was some kind of old summerhouse, clearly disused and badly neglected. He mounted the wooden steps warily, uncertain that they were strong enough to take their combined weights.

'You can put me down now.' Jan's words cleared his fuzzy brain.

'Of course.' Tor reluctantly lowered her legs to the ground, turning her body into him. As she slid down, her skirt slid up. He held her at the waist, pulling her stomach against his rock-hard erection. He couldn't really see much, but his imagination was running riot. Lust rippled through his body as he pulled her closer. If she would just give him a sign, do something. He caught the knowing smile on her face. Quite obviously, she was not only aware of the effect she was having, but was also revelling in his clumsy attempts to get closer to her. He gritted his teeth and felt the familiar rush of anger he always experienced when he sensed he was being teased.

He had always hated the idea of being toyed with. It drove him mad with desire. He wanted to see Jan squirming helplessly in his grasp, hear her sighing and moaning with her uncontrollable passion and desperate need. Shit! He released her so quickly that she stumbled slightly before regaining her balance.

'Thank you for the lift,' she said with an innocent smile that was so endearing that Tor felt his heart skip. She could melt an iceberg with that smile. He noticed the laughter dancing playfully in her eyes and felt his own mouth grin in response. She was so beautiful. He wanted her so much.

Jan stepped away, bending forward to brush down her skirt. Tor caught a quick glimpse of her panties – an image that would remain in his mind for a long time. God, he just wanted to drop to his knees and beg her to let him fuck her.

Walking across the outer veranda, he peered inside the filthy windows and took several deep breaths to calm himself down. The adrenalin was still rushing through his veins, making his hands shake. He made a fist with one hand and slammed it into the other one, then gripped it tightly, trying to physically stem the trembling. Dimly outlined in the dirty windowpane, he could see Jan standing just behind him. Even without looking up, he could feel her eyes boring into his back. He was determined not to turn around until he got himself back under control.

Tor twisted his head to the left and let his eyes roam over the gardens. He hoped to have a place like this of his own one day. Not that he was an avid gardener or anything, but he could learn. It would be a while before he could afford something quite so grand, unless his income improved dramatically. There always seemed to be so many expenses.

'The garden extends to those trees beyond the bushes,' Jan's voice broke his meditation. 'There's a vegetable plot behind the bushes, though I doubt there are any vegetables in it.'

Tor realised that she had moved closer to him. He could feel the warmth of her body and he sniffed the air to catch another hint of her alluring scent.

'Do you want to see?' she questioned. 'That is, if you don't mind carrying me again?'

It was tempting, very tempting. The feel of her lithe body in his arms, those pert little breasts pressed against his chest . . . 'No.' His voice sounded a bit harsh, even to his own ears. Jesus, she made him so randy! 'No, I'll take your word for it.' He made a show of tucking his shirt in and surreptitiously slipped a bit more material between his cock and the zip. Much better!

Jan moved closer still and took his arm. 'Would you like to see the house now then?'

Tor turned and looked at her. He nodded silently and Jan raised one arm up round his neck.

'Well?' she challenged him. He was trapped. House or vegetable garden. It made no difference. Either way, he would have her in his arms once more. His heart began to race as another surge of adrenalin coursed through his burning veins.

'OK.' This time, as her lifted her, he deliberately put his fingers under her skirt and allowed his other hand to slide even further round than before, so that he was cupping her breast. He was having trouble keeping his breathing steady and, as he began to move, his trousers tightened over his groin, rubbing his tormented cock. All his efforts to calm himself were completely wasted. He was shaking all over with passion. Although he could not see, he could vividly imagine the way her skirt was rucked up so that the tops of her thighs were visible.

'I'm not too heavy am I?' Even her voice drove him wild.

'No. You're perfect. I mean, perfect weight for me to carry.'

Jan twisted round to smile up at him and his hand moved even further on to her breast. He struggled to resist the urge to squeeze it between his fingers as he felt the outline of her lacy bra and the soft warmth of her flesh underneath. His fingertip made contact with the small rise of her nipple and a surge of lust caused him to stumble. His fingers instinctively tightened and her nipple became more distinct to his trembling fingers.

Jan turned slightly and pointed to a small rose garden. Her other breast pushed hard against him and his cock spasmed. Her skirt had ridden up over the top of her stockings so that his eyes were mesmerised by the soft whiteness of her bare thighs. He was almost overwhelmed by a surge of panic at the realisation of how close he was to losing it. He quickened his pace, feeling the sweat trickling down his body as he raced towards the path. As he lowered her to the ground again, he pulled his body back away from her. He didn't dare even so much as let her touch him until he had calmed down a little.

'This way.' Jan took his arm. 'The alarm can be switched off from the front or the back. It's linked to the local police station. If you set if off by mistake remember to call them or you'll have the local plod swarming all over you.' She stopped outside the back door.

Tor just nodded. He wasn't thinking about alarms. He was certain that she knew exactly what she was doing to him. The only question was how far she was willing to go. Shit, she had him shaking like a leaf. He'd never been so expertly teased in his life. He couldn't stop now. If she wouldn't go all the way, he was going to take his cock out and wank right in front of her. The idea excited him even more. It was a favourite fantasy. If she said no, he would do it. He would lie her on the floor, sit astride her and wank all over her breasts while he told her all the things he wanted to do to her.

'Are you all right? You look a bit pale.' Jan's question brought him back to earth.

'No, I'm fine.' Stop fantasising, he told himself sternly. She's running rings around you and you're making it worse. Don't let her get the better of you. He took a long, deep breath.

'Let's look inside, shall we?' he suggested in his deepest, strongest voice. 'After you.' He pushed the door open and stood back to let her go first. He followed after her, only just avoiding walking straight into her when she stopped to reset the alarm before it went off. He watched her breasts move tantalisingly under her blouse as she reached up to key in the numbers.

'Man of stone,' he muttered to himself.

'Sorry? Did you say something?'

'No, nothing.' He couldn't take his eyes off her. 'Just thinking aloud.'

'The number can be changed to whatever you choose if you decide to take the place,' Jan informed him as she began to move on down the corridor. 'Now, let's see. I think this must be the kitchen.' Jan pushed a door open and peered in. 'Freezer, microwave, gas oven and hob, plenty of cupboards and workspace.' She moved into the room while he stood by the door and watched as she pointed out the various utilities. 'It's fully fitted and complete with all the cutlery and crockery you'll need.'

Tor swallowed hard as she stood on tiptoe to peer in a wall cupboard, then bent over from the waist to pry under the sink. The sun poured through the large window so that he could clearly see the outline of her buttocks through her skirt.

'Washing machine and tumble dryer through here.' Jan moved towards another door. 'Whenever you need to wash something.'

'Any second now if you keep doing that,' Tor mumbled to himself.

'I'm sorry?' Jan looked confused.

'Nothing,' Tor grunted softly. Christ. He was going to have to be careful. He had never actually lost it in his pants before but he couldn't stop fantasising about her. He shifted his weight from one foot to the other, trying to relieve the almost unbearable pressure.

'Do you cook?'

'I'm sorry. What was that?' She had obviously asked him a question. His thoughts had been elsewhere.

'I was just wondering if you enjoy cooking. It's such a beautiful kitchen.'

'Why not come round one evening and find out?' His question took him by surprise. Better, much better, he congratulated himself. That had sounded very suave and sophisticated. He was tired of making such a fool of himself in front of her.

'Perhaps I will,' Jan replied. 'What's your speciality?'

'Um, well I can turn my hand to most things, though I don't get much chance during the season.' There was no way he was going to admit that he couldn't boil an egg to save his life. He always ate out or bought take-away.

Jan smiled again and headed back into the passage-way. Tor followed her around each room in turn, doing his best to look at what the house had to offer and not what her body was tempting him with. He kept his hands behind his back and leaned forward slightly as he walked to conceal the obvious outline of his groin. It had got to such a state that every move provoked him more, so that he was having one long fantasy about her. He had already imagined her begging for it at least three times. As they started up the stairs, Tor tried not to look at the back of her legs or the way her skirt was tightening across her buttocks.

'Oh.' Suddenly Jan stumbled and lost her footing. Tor's reactions were lightning fast: he leapt forward and wrapped an arm around her waist while reaching out with his other hand to grasp the banister.

'Thank you.' Her voice was genuinely shaky. 'I must

have caught my heel. If you hadn't caught me, I would have fallen.' Her lips were so close to his that he just couldn't resist. Her mouth tasted as sweet as honey. Although she wasn't kissing him back, she wasn't trying to pull away either.

He lifted her effortlessly into his arms and carried her to the top of the stairs. She said nothing. He stood with her like that, then gently kissed her again. This time, he felt the pressure of her own lips returning the kiss. She parted them slightly and he pushed his tongue eagerly on to hers.

Jan pulled her head back and smiled sweetly. 'It seems my knight in shining armour is claiming his reward.' She wriggled out of his arms and then stood on tiptoe to wrap her own arms around his neck. Pulling his head down towards her, she started to kiss him passionately.

Tor responded with equal ardour. He wrapped his arms around her slim body and pulled her tight on to him. He could feel her body warmth radiating from her and sending a blaze of heat all through him. His aching cock jerked and juddered against his clothing and he groaned helplessly as he savoured the feel of her soft, slippery tongue probing his.

As she pulled back from him and turned away, Tor grabbed her and pulled her back hard on to his body. Slowly, he slid his hands up her waist to cup both breasts, while his lips began to kiss her neck and ears. He could definitely feel her hardened nipples pushed against his eager fingers and he moaned softly as he began to undo the buttons of her blouse. Her skin was so soft and smooth. Gently, he slipped one hand up under her bra to caress the tender flesh of her breasts while his other hand tugged his zip open to relieve the pressure.

Jan whimpered softly and the sound drove him crazy. His pulse was racing and his cock felt as if it was about to split wide open with the pressure of his ever-increasing excitement. With shaking fingers, Tor tugged the sleeves of her blouse down her arms and over her wrists.

As the blouse fell from his fingertips, Tor bent forward and ran his tongue and lips down her back. His fingers fumbled with the catch on her bra. They both sighed as it came undone and Tor continued his journey down her back to her waist. He slid his hands round over her flat stomach and back up to caress her breasts. Moving more quickly now in his excitement, he peeled her bra straps off her arms and dropped it on the floor beside her blouse. He could feel her whole body trembling at his touch and see the goose bumps rising up on her soft white flesh.

Consumed with his burning passion, Tor ripped his own shirt off and pulled her back hard against his chest. His fingers started to toy with her engorged nipples as he savoured the thrill of her burning skin pressed against his own.

'You're so beautiful,' he whispered softly in her ear. 'So very desirable. I have to have you.' He felt her body tremble in response to his words and a fierce pang of longing coursed through him, setting his loins on fire. He felt as if he had never wanted any woman as much as he wanted Jan at that moment.

Tor's heart stopped as she pulled away from him, but then she took hold of his hand and started to lead him into one of the bedrooms. She guided him over to the large double bed, pushed him down on to the bare mattress and stepped back to undo the zip on her skirt. As it fell down her body, she stepped out of it and swung her leg over him so that she was straddling his thighs. With a tiny smile, she ran her fingers across his hard stomach and opened the catch at his waistband.

Tor shuddered with pleasure at her touch and held his breath as her sure fingers discovered that his zip was already open. He writhed from side to side, gritting his teeth in his effort to contain his excitement. He was too close again. Much too close. It was only sheer willpower holding himself back. Dear God, when she touched him there, he wouldn't be able to help himself.

Her burning fingers started to peel his pants down off him. His cock leapt out into the air as if loaded on springs with its swollen, purple head damp and ready. So ready. Just one touch was going to be all it would take. Tor closed his eyes and gave himself up to the inevitable.

He felt her pull his pants down as far as she could, then put her hands back on to his stomach and slide them round under his buttocks. He jumped at the pressure of her fingers pulling him up and realised that she wanted him to raise himself. Totally under her spell, he lifted himself off the bed, gritting his teeth and ready to feel his cock make contact with her breasts. As soon as he touched her, he would lose it. He knew he would. He needed to take control, to play with her until his overexcited body had a chance to calm down a bit.

Jan slipped his clothing down over his buttocks and thighs then bent forward and pushed him back on to the bed while she kissed his nipples. His cock rubbed against one of her breasts and Tor groaned in desperation and despair as he exploded. His penis juddered uncontrollably, spitting and spurting urgently as all the pent-up pressure and longing of the morning finally burst from him.

As the first hot spurt splattered her breast, Jan sat up and watched silently. Dimly, through the almost excruciatingly pleasurable sensation of his release, Tor could see the tiny smile of amusement on her lips as she witnessed his complete loss of control. He moaned incoherently, vaguely aware of just how humiliated he was going to feel, once the pleasure was over. As the final burst of his orgasm died away and his still-rigid cock ceased its jerking, Jan's smile seemed to widen.

'Hmm. A bit sensitive aren't we?' she mocked.

His eyes fell from her grinning lips to the sight of his dripping cock finally beginning to shrivel back to size, and he felt the first wave of utter shame sweep through him. He could actually feel the tears of humiliation burning in the back of his eyes. He closed them tightly so that he couldn't see her face, but the image of her amused expression was burnt on to his memory. He lay silently as she stood up and walked across the room. A door opened and he heard the sound of water running in the adjoining bathroom.

What was going through her mind? The smile on her face had seemed to indicate that she had enjoyed what she had done to him. Had she? Is that what she had intended all along? To push him so far so that he finally lost all self-control? If so, she must be very pleased with herself. The trouble was, he was still feeling incredibly randy. His explosion had done little to relieve his overwhelming passion, just taken away his immediate ability to do anything about it.

Tor stood up and finished stripping his clothing off. Naked, he walked through into the bathroom. Jan moved over to him and gently wiped the sweat from his broad chest.

'You know, in a way that was probably one of the most flattering things that has ever happened to me.' She smiled sympathetically.

Tor tried a weak smile in return. Well, it was a hell of a lot better than anger. After all, it had shown her just how much she turned him on, hadn't it? He stepped under the shower and started feeling a lot better.

When he had washed the sweat and semen from his body, he took a towel from the rail and wrapped it around his waist. Jan had already returned to the bedroom and replaced her skirt. She started towards the door, presumably to fetch her bra and blouse from the landing.

'Wait.' Tor grabbed her arm. 'Aren't you going to finish showing me around?'

Jan looked surprised and then stared around the room as if looking for something else to show him. 'Well, there are some built-in cupboards over there but I think you've seen the rest.'

Tor shook his head. 'No, I haven't seen everything, yet.' He was looking at her, not at the room. The sight of her naked breasts was already having a positive effect on his treacherous organ.

'Well, there are two other, smaller bedrooms and a separate bathroom.' Jan shrugged her shoulders. 'Don't you want to get dressed first?'

Tor shook his head. 'I'm still a bit damp. Come on.' He led her out the door and down the landing, not giving her time to stop for her clothing. As they walked, he watched the way her breasts bounced up and down.

'This is the second-largest bedroom,' she told him as they opened another door. 'If I remember correctly, this one has got a lovely view of the back garden.' She jumped at his touch. 'What are you doing?' she questioned as he quickly opened the zip on her skirt and tugged it back down her legs.

Tor turned her to face him. The towel dropped from his waist and fell to the floor. He saw her eyes glance down and then widen slightly. He leant forward and ran his tongue across her breasts while his hands glided over her waist and on to her tummy. He slipped his fingers under the elastic of her thong and started to pull it down, gradually revealing her mound.

Jan's lips parted slightly and he could hear the soft sigh of her breath as his lips wandered down her body. The feel of her trembling at the touch of his hands and tongue excited him further, so that his cock sprang back to full size and its shiny head joined his fingers, teasing her willing flesh.

'Oh yes,' Jan moaned and writhed in pleasure as his

tongue reached her partially shaved mound and its soft tip found her tiny pink clit. Her body spasmed and the air rushed from her lungs in a sudden whoosh as he sucked her swollen bud up into his lips. Tor felt her straining against the elastic of her thong as she tried to pull her legs wider apart. She grabbed his head, pushing him harder against her and he felt her fingers winding and tugging his hair as her passion mounted.

Tor felt the elation washing over him, adding to his own increasing excitement. This was much better. After his earlier loss of control, his total humiliation, now he was calling the shots. He was pushing her. Already, her little squeals of delight were becoming louder and more urgent. He could feel her clit swelling and hardening even more as he teased and licked her. The dampness on her sex lips and thighs was increasing by the second as her arousal intensified.

Soon, very soon now, he would push her just a little further. Then a little further still. He was going to give her the fuck of her life. Before he was finished, she would be begging him to stop. His cock jerked as his tongue slipped effortlessly into her and her whole body shuddered yet again. He wouldn't stop, no matter how hard she begged. He would drive her mad with passion as he explored every inch of her body. He was much calmer now; he had plenty of time.

'Oh my God,' Jan whimpered as Tor lost himself in his fantasies. 'Oh, yes . . .'

Chapter Six

Sara Williams was humming contentedly to herself as she bustled around the huge kitchen. She actually enjoyed her work, although the kind of fast food they served in the ice rink's café certainly didn't challenge her skills as a cook.

For the past few days, however, Sara had been somewhat preoccupied with her own thoughts to give more than passing attention to beefburgers and chips. Ever since the away match in Bristol, and the dinner afterwards, her mind had been filled with amorous thoughts about the dark-haired Trojan defender, Ean.

She had only spoken with him for a few minutes. In fact, she had spent more time talking with the big, blond centre player, Tor. Nevertheless, those few minutes, during which her body had brushed against his, had been enough to set more than her imagination on fire. As she had always suspected, Ean was the image of Mark twenty years ago. Well, almost, if you overlooked the muscles.

Sara finished stacking the dishwasher from the early morning breakfasts for the staff and looked around the kitchen critically. Everything was done except for restocking the freezer and preparing for the first coffee and snacks when the rink opened to the public at 10 a.m.

As she started buttering the rolls, Sara found herself worrying about why the Office Services Manager at the catering agency wanted to see her when she clocked off at noon. Ms Jamison's voice had given nothing away, but then it was always difficult to fathom out what was going through the woman's mind. She was super-efficient and friendly enough, but impossible to read. Neither her face nor her voice ever gave an inkling of what she was actually thinking. A week or so back, Sara had asked if she could work some extra shifts: with her son at college, money was always a bit tight. Hopefully that was all Ms Jamison wanted to see her about.

An hour and a half after their meeting, Sara was on the far side of town, standing outside the gates of a long winding driveway leading to a big old house. She double-checked the address written on the piece of paper in her hand and then stared apprehensively at the inter-com system fitted on to one gatepost.

At least Ms Jamison had not kept her in suspense for long.

'Hello Sara. Sit down. I'll be with you in a minute.'

While the Office Services Manager had flicked through Sara's file, Sara had watched nervously, wondering if someone at the rink had complained about her work. She couldn't think of any reason why they should have done.

'Some of our clients are feeling the pinch of the rising interest rates and strong pound,' Ms Jamison had begun. 'They are tightening up on expenditure wherever they can and, as a result, our own business is suffering.'

Sara had felt her heart sink; suddenly she was afraid that she was about to be laid off. But that didn't make any sense. The rink was doing really well. She had heard Justin telling Maggie that the Trojans' successful season had made skating more popular than ever.

'Here, at Butterflies, we've decided that we need to make a few changes of our own in order to survive. So, we've decided to branch out and cater for a wider clientele.' Ms Jamison had looked up at Sara thoughtfully. 'I believe you said you would be interested in some additional work?'

Sara wrapped in the misery of imminent redundancy, was taken by surprise by the woman's words.

'Well, yes,' she had stammered. 'Things are a bit tight at the moment, what with my son . . .' Sara had stopped herself. Normally, she was a very private person, but she had always had a habit of talking too much when she was nervous and later regretting her hasty revelations.

'Well, I have a new client who is looking for a housekeeper for a few months. Someone who is both efficient and discrete. I see from our records that you have done this kind of work before.' She had looked up expectantly. 'Can I take it that you would be interested? It'll mean giving up the ice rink for a while, but it will be easier to replace you there than it is to find a good housekeeper. It will pay extremely well.'

When Ms Jamison had gone on to explain just what she meant by 'pays well', Sara had not hesitated. With Kevin away at college much of the time there was nothing to keep her at home anyway.

'Of course, you will have to attend an interview, but I'm sure that will only be a formality.'

As Sara smoothed her dress down and reached up to press the intercom button, her mind was already busy running over various recipes. Ms Jamison had said that she would probably have to contend with quite a lot of entertaining. It had been years since she had catered for dinner parties. What if she had forgotten how to cope on her own?

'Yes.' The voice sounded both cold and suspicious.

Sara reminded herself that this was a client who valued his privacy.

'Good afternoon. My name is Sara Williams. I was sent by Butterflies, the catering services group.'

The only reply she received was a short buzz, followed by a sharp click as the gates started to swing open.

Sara scowled. 'Please come in. I've been expecting you,' she muttered sourly to herself as she began walking down the long gravel driveway. Obviously, her prospective new boss was not a man given to wasting words.

'Sara Williams?' The man standing on the front step of the imposing redbrick house was middle-aged and overweight. There was something very familiar about him. Was he someone famous or had she seen or met him somewhere before? She racked her brains. If he was famous he might be offended if she didn't recognise him.

'Welcome, my dear. I've been so looking forward to your arrival.'

His words took her by surprise and she found herself swiftly re-evaluating her first impressions. Perhaps he wasn't unfriendly, just cautious with strangers? Where had she seen him before? She was certain that they had met quite recently.

The man hurried down the steps and shook her hand. 'Roland Donaldson. Call me Roland.' He took her arm. 'Please, come inside and let me show you around.' He glanced down in apparent surprise. 'You don't seem to have any suitcases with you? Are your things being sent on?'

'Well, um, no.' His hand felt damp and clammy on her skin and his body odour was not entirely masked by the heavy aftershave he appeared to have bathed in. Who was he? Suddenly she remembered. Roland Donaldson. Of course. He was the Trojans' manager! How could she have not recognised his name straight away?

'I was just told to come for an interview,' she added

quickly as she stared at him. She was certain that it was him.

'Interview? No need for that. You come highly recommended, Sara. I am delighted to take you on. Now, in you come. I can arrange for your things to be collected later.'

'Haven't we met?' she asked quickly.

'Met?' Roland looked puzzled.

'Yes. You're the Trojans' manager aren't you? I work, have been working, at the rink café. And, thanks to Justin, I was at their away match in Bristol last week.'

'Ah yes, of course. That's why you seem familiar. You were one of the lovely ladies who joined us for dinner after the game, weren't you?'

Sara nodded and felt her cheeks colour slightly. Her head was in a whirl of confusion.

'And a fan, too?' He raised his eyebrows in a questioning way. 'You are a fan?'

Sara nodded again.

'Splendid!' Roland started to guide her up the steps and through the wide oak doorway. 'How nice that we've all already met,' Roland continued. 'Some of the lads spend so much time here that it's practically their second home. I'm sure they'll all be delighted to see you again. Besides,' he gave her a sly wink and tightened his grip on her arm. 'None of them are what you might call domesticated. Prepare them a good home-cooked meal, Sara, and the boys will all become your instant and willing slaves. Ah, talk of the devil.'

Sara's eyes widened as several of the Trojans filed into the room. She was tempted to pinch herself to make sure that she wasn't dreaming. She almost laughed at the idea of Roland calling them 'boys'. Her stare found Ean, and her legs started to tremble.

'Lads, this is Sara. She has just agreed to move in and take care of me.'

Sara was too shocked to mention that she had agreed

to no such thing. She just stared at the ice hockey players and felt a flush of colour flow up her neck and on to her cheeks as they returned the compliment.

'In case you've forgotten, this is Tor, Troy, Ean, Pele, Pary and my little brother, Bri.' Roland pointed to each of the men in turn then put his arm across Bri's shoulders. 'Or, rather, ex-little brother,' he added.

Sara stared at him in bemusement.

'Roland used to be married to my sister,' Bri explained as he pulled away from Ronald's clasp and held out his right hand. 'Welcome aboard.'

Sara shook hands with each of them. When she took Ean's hand, she felt her blush deepen even more and a tingle like an electric shock run down her arm. His dark eyes twinkled at her cheerfully. He was the image of Mark.

'I know you from somewhere, don't I?' Tor questioned her as he shook her hand briefly. Sara nodded. 'I was at your game down in Bristol the other week,' she responded softly.

Tor grinned. 'How flattering,' he laughed. 'Everywhere I go, I seem to keep bumping into loyal female fans. I had no idea we were so popular.'

'Justin managed to get Maggie some complimentary tickets,' Sara explained. 'You know, Maggie. She works on reception at the rink. I work, used to work, as a cook in the café,' she added, wondering who else he had come across and where.

'Ah, um, yes. We know Maggie,' Tor agreed quickly and Sara could have sworn the men exchanged a highly meaningful glance at the mention of her friend's name. How curious. Had she missed something?

'A cook. Great.' Pele broke into her thoughts. 'What's for dinner?' he questioned. 'I'm famished.'

Roland laughed. 'Always thinking about your stomach. Don't scare her off.' He put his arm around

Sara's shoulders and gave her a friendly squeeze. 'She hasn't even seen her room yet.'

Sara pulled away from him and tried to think. Things were moving much too fast for her. 'I couldn't possibly start before tomorrow,' she told him firmly.

Ean pulled a face. 'Tomorrow? Take pity on us, Sara. I can't face another meal cooked by Roland and I'm sick to death of take-away.'

Pele took her hand. 'We'll waste away if we don't get some decent food soon. How can we possibly win matches if we don't eat a balanced diet?'

'Yeah. Please, Sara. There's only one thing worse than Roland's cooking,' Tor added pitifully as he dropped down on one knee in front of her.

Sara grinned. 'What's that?'

'Eating it,' Tor responded mournfully.

Sara shook her head and gave in. 'OK. I'll look around and see if I can rustle you up something.' She looked at Roland. 'If that's all right with you?'

Ean held her playfully by the waist. 'You angel of mercy.' He kissed her cheek and took her hand. 'You can feel me wasting away,' he complained as he placed her fingers on his hard stomach.

Sara shivered and ran her fingers lightly up his chest. 'I think you're exaggerating just a little,' she chided him softly, although she certainly couldn't feel an ounce of fat on his gorgeous body.

'Well, that's settled then.' Roland sounded extremely happy. 'As for the menu, just cook whatever is easiest for you. Right. Come on lads. We have some work to do. Especially in defence.' He glared at Pary and Ean. 'Your checking in the second period was pathetic. Sara here could do a better job of taking control.'

'It's because we never eat properly,' Pary muttered.

Sara laughed and felt another little tremor of excitement at the fun to come. Who would ever have thought she would end up playing 'mum' to the Trojans and their manager? Although, to be honest, she wasn't feeling the least bit maternal. Far from it!

Later, as she bustled around the beautifully equipped kitchen, Sara could feel the beads of perspiration gathering between her breasts. Not surprisingly, from what the men had said, she had found Roland's kitchen cupboards virtually bare and had been forced to make a trip to the supermarket to purchase what she needed. Roland had thrust a generous fistful of notes into her hands, assuring her that there was no need to worry about expense and that they would sort the finances out properly later.

The room was hot and steamy with a roast sizzling in one of huge ovens and three kinds of green vegetables simmering gently on the gas hob. Sara could feel her pulse hammering at her temples and her hands were trembling slightly when she removed the meat tray from the oven to drain the succulent beef juices into the gravy boat. She kept trying to tell herself that there was nothing to worry about. She often prepared a roast at the weekend for herself and her son Kevin. This was no different; there was just more of it.

Sara prodded the huge baron of beef with a long fork. The juices ran slightly pink, just the way she liked it. With a small grunt of satisfaction, she wrapped the joint in foil and bent down to check on her Yorkshires. They were perfect: the raised edges golden brown and crispy and the shallow centres soft and spongy – just waiting for a lavish helping of her rich dark gravy. Her stomach rumbled at the delightful combination of savoury aromas filling the air.

'Something smells wonderful.' The masculine voice behind her almost made her drop the pan of roast potatoes. She quickly put it back on to the shelf and stood up, closing the oven door and spinning round nervously. Ean was standing just behind her and the room suddenly seemed to grow even hotter.

'It will be ready in about five minutes,' she stuttered as she hastily wiped the steam off her brow and pushed her silvery-blonde curls back behind her ears.

'Great. I'm so hungry I could eat a horse.'

She noticed that his eyes were appraising her with interest and she wished that she'd had time to remove her cooking apron.

She tried to lighten the atmosphere with a weak joke. 'Well, you'll have to make do with half a cow.' When he didn't respond, she turned her back on him and gave the gravy an extra stir.

'The smell reminds me of home.' Ean had moved closer to her. 'My mother always does a roast at the weekends.'

Sara stiffened. With the thoughts she had been having about him lately, this untimely reminder of their age difference was the last thing she wanted to hear. 'Let's hope I can come up to her standards,' she muttered.

Ean grinned. 'Tough challenge. She is pretty good,' he replied and Sara felt her heart sink. 'Mind you, she's had a lot more practice at it than you. She and dad have been married almost twenty-five years.'

Sara felt her burning face flush even deeper at the compliment. She was grateful for the steamy atmosphere to hide her blushes. 'I'm just about ready to start serving up.' Sara reached for the colander to begin straining the vegetables. 'Do you think you could round everyone up for me?'

'Sure.' Ean gave her another cheeky grin and casually brushed a strand of his soft dark hair out of his eyes. 'Believe me, they're not far away.' His stomach rumbled noisily. 'Whoops.' He patted it. 'Excuse me.'

His face was now glowing pink from the heat and steam, and she could see herself reflected in the depths of his huge, almond-coloured eyes. The skin on his cheeks looked as soft and smooth as buttermilk, contrasting starkly with the dark shadow of stubble over his lip and chin. Sara lowered her gaze and took in his wide shoulders, the swell of his biceps and the narrowing waist above his almost concave stomach. His casual grey trousers were thin and tight and the slight bulge of his manhood drew her eyes like a magnet.

'Then I'll come back and give you a hand, shall I?'

She pulled her thoughts away from her fantasises and nodded dumbly. As he left the room, her eyes followed every wiggle of his hips and buttocks and a lump began to form in her throat. If only he were not so much like Mark. She turned quickly and forced her attention to serving the food.

Five minutes later, as Sara and Ean loaded up the dining table with plates and dishes, Tor examined the place settings in surprise. 'Where's your plate?' he questioned her.

'I'm not really all that hungry,' Sara replied quickly. 'I'll just have a small plate in the kitchen.'

'What? A cook who won't eat her own food?' Roland grinned. 'What are you trying to tell me?'

'Another time, maybe. I've still got a lot to do.'

Pele and Troy childishly started to bang the table with their spoons. 'Join us. Join us,' they chanted in unison. Sara laughed.

'Behave yourselves, or you won't get any pudding,' she threatened.

'Pudding?' Tor's eyes lit up. 'What's for pudding?'

'Blackcurrant pie and cream,' she replied.

'You know, I think we should let Sara return to her work after all.'

'Seconded,' Ean agreed. 'But only this once,' he added, almost as an afterthought.

Back in the kitchen, Sara smiled to herself as she sipped a glass of red wine and pushed her portion of blackcurrant pie around her plate. She still couldn't believe how much fun the Trojans were to be with. She had barely stopped laughing at their antics all afternoon. Roland had made her feel so welcome too. More like an old friend come to stay than a hired help.

She raised her hand and massaged her aching neck and shoulders. It was much more tiring than she had anticipated though, cooking for such a large number all on her own. She looked around ruefully at the huge pile of dirty dishes. She would have to make a start on stacking the dishwasher or she'd never get finished.

'Let me do that.' Ean's voice took her by surprise. She had thought that they had all retired to Roland's big living room to watch a film and polish off a few beers.

Sara jumped as she felt his large hands push hers aside before his fingers started to massage her shoulders. She rolled her head, luxuriating in the feel of his strong fingers easing her knotted muscles.

'You're as tense as a coiled spring,' he chided her softly, as he moved his hands down her back. 'What you need is something to relax you completely.'

Yes please, Sara thought to herself dreamily. She imagined his hands running all over her body and her stomach suddenly felt as if it was full of butterflies. This couldn't be happening, could it?

'I think I should give you a proper massage,' he continued. 'After all, if you are going to cook regularly for us we don't want you off work with a bad back, do we?'

Before she could pinch herself to see if she was already asleep, Ean had pulled her chair out from under the table and twisted it round so that she was facing him. Crouching in front of her, he lifted her left leg and gently slipped one of her shoes off.

'From the bottom up,' he told her as his fingers started doing delightful things to the soles of her foot. Her thighs prickled at the implication of his words and her imagination was already running wild. She sighed softly and leant back against the chair with her eyes closed.

Ean lifted her foot on to his thigh and began to caress

each of her toes in turn. Through the softness of her stocking, his fingers felt incredibly smooth and their caress unexpectedly erotic. Sara felt her nipples hardening in response and the muscles at the top of her legs spasmed. His fingers slid under the sole of her foot and encircled her slim ankle. Sara shivered from head to toe and opened her eyes again to stare at him.

'We need to get you somewhere more comfortable,' he told her. He looked thoughtful for a moment, then nodded. 'I know. There's a big soft couch in Roland's library.'

Before she had a chance to protest, to insist that she still had work to do, Ean stood up and swung her up into his arms as easily as if he was lifting a small child. Cradling her against his broad chest, he carried her gently out the door, along the hall and into the large, deserted library. Sara snuggled guiltily against him, enjoying the feel of his muscles rippling under his shirt as he moved.

Ean placed her on a long, velvet-covered couch in front of the fireplace and stood in front of her. Sara looked around the room. A huge cabinet behind Roland's desk was filled with ice hockey trophies.

'Did you win all those?' she asked him nervously.

Ean nodded without taking his eyes off her. 'Well not all of them. At least, not personally. Some of them are from before I joined the squad. Now, slip off your dress and lie down on your stomach,' he commanded. 'I won't look, I promise,' he added when he saw her hesitation. 'It's OK, Sara. I know what I'm doing,' he assured her softly.

His words seemed full of double meaning. Or was it just that she wanted them to? Maybe he knew what he was doing, but did she? All the things Sara knew she should say fled from her mind. She forgot that she was a hired housekeeper with duties to attend to, forgot that he was a Trojan. It was as if she was a client at some exclusive clinic and he the concerned therapist.

Sara stood up slowly with her back to him. She lifted her dress up over her head and tried not to think about him standing there. She breathed a quick, silent prayer of thanks that she was wearing her most expensive undies and tried not to remember that she had been thinking of him that morning when she had put them on. As she turned back, she saw him watching her avidly.

'I thought you promised not to look,' she reprimanded him.

Ean grinned and put his head on one side. 'I had my fingers crossed,' he confessed and helped her down on to the couch.

Sara lay face down and rested her forehead on her arms. Almost immediately, she felt his firm fingers caressing her smooth calves. Another shiver of desire raced through her body and she felt the quick rush of moisture aound her pussy. She pushed her thighs as tightly together as his hands would allow, and raised her chest slightly so that her engorged nipples were not chaffing against the lace of her bra.

'Relax,' he chided her. 'I can't massage you properly while you keep tensing your muscles like that.'

'Sorry.' Sara tried hard to comply. It wasn't easy. His hands were slowly but gradually working their way up her leg, squeezing and kneading every inch of her. She stifled a gasp as his fingers reached the top of her stocking and slipped on to the bare skin of her upper thigh. His touch felt hot, even to her already burning flesh.

'Where did you learn to do that so well?' she asked him.

'I once did a course in remedial massage,' he replied. 'I was thinking about doing it for a living, before I got my break with the Trojans. Maybe I will still, later.'

'You'd never be short of clients,' Sara assured him with a gentle sigh.

'You know, you have a really sexy body,' he complimented her in return. 'I bet you work out regularly.'

Sara failed to stop another tiny sigh of pleasure as his knowing fingers slid over the curve of her left buttock and began to knead the knotted muscles at the base of her spine.

'Does that feel better?' he questioned in response to her sigh.

'It feels wonderful,' she mumbled softly.

His hands moved on up her body and she felt his fingers release the catch at the back of her bra. Her aching breasts flopped forward on to the couch. Her nipples felt as hard as marbles. He pulled her bra straps out of the way and she felt his hands making large sweeping motions all over her back.

'Why are you doing this?' she questioned sharply.

Ean's hands stopped in the centre of her back. 'Don't you like it?'

'Yes. Of course. It feels incredible. I just wondered why. I mean, wouldn't you rather be with the others?' She wanted to ask why he, of all of them, should have singled her out. Was it just a coincidence or had he sensed her special attraction to him, even if he didn't know the reason for it.

'We threw dice,' he admitted. 'And I won.'

It was the first time a man had ever gambled over her. Sara wasn't sure how she felt.

'Look at it from my point of view,' he told her, as if sensing her confusion. 'A few beers with the lads or get my hands on your beautiful, sexy body. I don't believe that's a serious question.'

Sara twisted her head slightly and peered up at him curiously. Did he mean that? Did he really think of her as a beautiful woman? She felt beautiful. Young, beautiful and desirable. He was beautiful too. And desirable. So very, very desirable.

'You know, you've got incredible skin. It's like massaging

silk or ivory.' Ean patted her buttocks. 'You've also got a really sexy arse.' He pulled the sides of her panties up into her crack.

Sara had been about to protest but closed her mouth quickly. The tingling sensation in her buttocks was not entirely due to his slap. 'Flattery will get you everywhere,' she whispered huskily.

Ean was crouched over the couch, level with her breasts. The zip of his trousers was unsettlingly close to her face. His penis was pushed across to the left and, from the way the material was stretched so tightly, there could be little doubt that he was at least partially aroused. Sara felt another trickle of lubrication dampen the crotch of her panties and her head began to spin as the faint but unmistakably masculine odour of his body teased her nostrils.

'I can't believe how stiff you are.' His hands started to squeeze her neck and shoulder muscles. He leaned even closer over her, so that his crotch and thighs were resting lightly against her upper torso and she felt the unmistakable hardness of his erection expanding through his trousers.

'So are you,' she murmured softly. 'Perhaps you should massage yourself?' Christ! What a thing to say! What had come over her? She buried her blushing face in the cushion and gave herself up to the exquisite sensations of pleasure and arousal coursing through her whole body.

'Roll over,' he instructed her suddenly.

She responded without hesitation and heard the slight catch in his breathing as she turned herself on to her back. Ean slipped her bra straps down her arms and pulled the loose material off her breasts. Sara automatically crossed her arms to cover herself, but Ean gently lifted them back out of the way. His lips were opened slightly and his eyes seemed to grow even bigger as he stared down at the soft swell of her naked breasts and dark swollen nipples. Almost reverently, he placed his hands on the front of her shoulders and began massaging her upper chest muscles.

Sara tried to hold herself rigid. She could feel the way her breasts were wobbling gently up and down in time with his movements. Her panties were now so damp that he could be in no doubt as to the extent of her arousal. She shivered as his hands glided down either side of her body and his fingertips brushed the edges of her aching breasts. She felt his hands coming together over her navel and was powerless to stop the little tremors in her stomach and thigh muscles. His fingers met in the middle and began to move outwards again, retracing their path.

Sara moaned and clenched her thighs tightly together. Her clit was tingling with the rapidly building rhythm of her passion and it was all she could do to stop herself pushing her fingers between her legs to satisfy her desperate longing.

She turned her head and stared up at his groin again. His zip was now bulging so tightly that she could see the stitches straining. It seemed impossible that the material could continue to resist the pressure. She half-expected it to burst open so that his rampant manhood might spring out and ravish her. His fingers reached her neck again and started on a new journey down over her breasts. Sara cried out when he cupped them lightly in his hands. The deep tingle between her legs turned into an urgent ache and she arched her back, instinctively pushing her nipples hard on to his huge palms.

'Relax,' he murmured again, 'just let yourself go.'

Let herself go! Jesus. It was all she could do to stop herself from letting go. She couldn't remember when she had last been this excited. Yes she could. The first time Mark had made love to her. Every time Mark had made love to her. She felt one of Ean's hands wander down her stomach and trace the outline of her navel before moving on over the lace of her panties. She bit her bottom lip and tried to keep her hips still as his feather-light touch caressed her mound and ventured on down between her dripping thighs.

'Please,' she sobbed. She wasn't sure whether she meant please stop or please keep going. She was too confused to think straight. What if one of the other Trojans walked in on them like this? What if Roland found them? She would probably get the sack. She'd have one hell of a time explaining that to the super-efficient Ms Jamison!

Ean's right hand had begun to squeeze and knead the soft flesh of her inner thigh. His other hand was still playing with her right breast and she could feel his fingertips gently teasing the hardness of her nipple. Every inch of her flesh in between his two hands was glowing. Her clit was on fire and she was desperate to feel his lips kissing her there.

Before she had time to think about what she was going to do, Sara lifted her hands and took hold of the waist-band of his trousers. She fumbled awkwardly with the button and then took hold of the zip with her forefinger and thumb. She could almost of sworn that she heard the material heave a sigh of relief as she tugged it open and released the tension.

She lifted her head to stare at him. His underpants were bulging out of the opening and she could just see the shiny tip of his engorged penis over the elastic waistband. She ran her fingertip over it and felt him shudder. She put her finger to her mouth and licked it, then moved it back to rub him again.

Ean sighed heavily and his fingers stopped all pretence of massaging her thighs. She felt him tugging urgently on her panties and she whimpered when his finger started exploring her hot damp sex.

'Take these off.' Sara tugged at his trousers. 'I want to see you.' She slid her hand down his shaft as she started to pull his pants down.

Ean stood up quickly and pulled his trousers and pants off in one smooth movement. His cock was as hard as granite and swollen dark purple-red with his lust. As she stared at it, a single drop of moisture bubbled out of the tip and trickled down his length. She reached out for him greedily, catching the liquid on her finger and smearing it over him. His cock bobbed excitedly and, suddenly, she just couldn't wait any longer.

'Please,' she whispered again. This time, neither of them could be in any doubt what she wanted.

Ean kicked his clothing free from his ankles and knelt over her on the couch. He took his cock in one hand and leant forward to guide himself into her. Sara spread her thighs and eagerly lifted her buttocks up to meet him.

Instead of penetrating her, Ean held the tip of his cock against her sex lips and used his hand to rub himself gently up and down over her hard little bud. She groaned loudly with a mixture of enjoyment and impatience. It felt so good. Her pussy was so damp and slippery with her juices that his cock seemed to glide over her effortlessly. She was only moments away from her climax. She had to have him inside her.

Sara reached out and seized his buttocks, pulling him down on to her. Her fingernails raked across his skin, gouging red deep welts in his flesh. Ean grunted with the shock and pain of her attack and thrust himself hard into her waiting dampness. The force of his penetration was so strong that she felt his balls slapping hard against her thighs.

'Oh Mark. I've missed you so much,' she cried helplessly. She ground her clit against his pelvis and a powerful orgasm rippled through her as she felt him draw back ready to thrust in to her again.

Outside, across the hall in the living room, the TV was blaring loudly. Somebody yelled something and others began to cheer and whistle enthusiastically. Totally oblivious, Ean continued to pump urgently in and out of her. Sara responded eagerly, her desire rapidly building up towards another climax as their lovemaking gradually massaged all her pent-up tensions and longings away.

Chapter Seven

'Good morning, Maggie.'

Maggie looked up from the reception desk in surprise. She had thought that she was the only one around. Her spirits sank when she saw who it was.

'Mr Donaldson. Good morning.' She forced herself to be polite. 'Is there something I can do for you?' She rather hoped that there wasn't. She didn't much like the idea of having anything to do with Roland Donaldson. He was such an unpleasant man.

'Several things spring to mind,' Roland responded suggestively, as he placed a hand on her arm. Maggie repressed a shudder. 'You can start by calling me Roland. Then, perhaps you would like to join me for a cup of coffee . . .'

'I can't. Sorry. I'm on duty until twelve o'clock,' Maggie interrupted him quickly.

'So late? I thought you finished sooner.' Roland looked at his watch. 'In that case, shall we make it lunch? What do you say to a quick drink and a bite to eat in the Royal Standard?'

'Well, that's very kind of you, but I already have plans for this afternoon.' This was actually true. After what she had said to the little girl with the sprained ankle, Maggie had been thinking seriously about her own lack of skills and qualifications. Or was it because of what she had learned about Troy? Either way, she had been wondering if there was something she could do about it. Jan had been attending business studies evening classes for some time now and Maggie had talked herself into a visit to the local library, just to see what courses were on offer.

'I won't take much of your time, I promise,' Roland persisted. 'But there is something I want to discuss with you. Something I'm sure will interest you.'

'Such as?' Despite herself, Maggie was intrigued. She might dislike Roland, but he was the Trojans' manager. Besides, she hated secrets. Roland grinned.

He repeated his invitation: 'Lunch?'

'I'll have to be away by two at the latest.' Maggie gave in to her curiosity.

'I'll see you at twelve, then.' Roland removed his sweaty palm from her arm and she breathed a sigh of relief. She was already half-regretting her haste. What could he possibly have to discuss with her that was worth spending at least an hour in his company for? Oh well, too late now. At least she'd get a free meal.

The Royal Standard was a popular local and it was already filling up when they arrived. Roland found a place by the window and held the back of Maggie's chair for her while she sat down. She had to admit that he had good – if somewhat old-fashioned – manners. She had enjoyed the ride in his flashy red XK8 too – even though, as Troy had said, he drove it like a maniac.

'What will you have to drink?'

'Vodka and tonic, please.'

'I'll order the food before it gets too busy, shall I?' he suggested. 'The Ploughman's here is excellent. Unless you'd prefer something from the menu?'

'Yes, I know. A Ploughman's will be fine, thank you.'

Maybe she had been a bit too hasty in her assessment of Roland? He wasn't that bad, after all. Quite distinguished-looking too, with his short, dark hair shot through with silver and his deep brown eyes. A bit plump maybe, and definitely too fond of himself, but he wasn't the only man she knew with that particular fault! She smiled as she thought immediately of Justin.

When Roland returned with their drinks he took the chair opposite and smiled across the table at her. 'Cheers.' He took a long swig of his beer. Maggie returned the smile and took a small sip of her vodka.

'You seem to be a number one fan of ours, Maggie. Do you reckon we're in with a chance for the Championship this season?'

Maggie was surprised. It seemed a strange question for the Trojans' manager to be asking her. 'You tell me,' she retorted brightly. 'I'd say it's looking good.'

'Providing the players keep their minds on their game and don't allow themselves to become distracted by anything,' Roland agreed. 'Or anyone.'

So, that was it. Don't say he had asked her out just to tell her to keep away from Troy and the others? Like some overprotective, Victorian father! Maggie was having trouble keeping a straight face.

'I'm sure the players all want to win as much as you do,' she told him.

'They'd better, if they all want to keep their places next season,' Roland replied. 'Ah, here's the food. Thank you.' He beamed at the pretty young waitress who had brought their meal over to the table. 'Do you think I could have some French mustard, please?'

They ate in silence for a few minutes before Roland spoke. 'Incidentally, are you planning to be at the match this weekend?'

Maggie frowned. Was he trying to tell her to stay away? Who the hell did he think he was? If she wasn't so broke she would buy a ticket just to spite him. 'I haven't decided yet,' she told him stiffly. 'Why?' Go on, say it, she thought. Just try to tell me not to go and see what happens.

'Oh, it's just that I need someone to act as the official hostess for the squad. The young lady who usually takes care of it has broken her leg skiing.' He looked almost put out, as if the girl had done it deliberately, just to spite him.

Maggie stared at him in astonishment. After his earlier comments this was the last thing she expected.

'I just thought that as you work for the rink anyway, and since you're obviously such a huge fan, you might be interested in filling in. Free accommodation and a top seat at the game, of course.' He stared at her. 'I realise that it's very short notice,' he added, when she remained silent. 'Perhaps you have other plans for the weekend?'

'No. Nothing important,' Maggie assured him, her mind racing. 'Thank you, Roland. I'd love to do it.' She had seriously misjudged him, she decided. He was really rather nice, once you got to know him. Not only would she get a free ticket to the match, but she was going to spend the whole weekend with the Trojans! She felt like jumping up and giving him a big hug.

'Good,' he said and beamed. 'That's settled then. I'll let you have all the details later in the week. I've hired a coach to take everyone this time. I don't want another farce like we had in Bristol, with half the lads getting lost after the match.' Fortunately, he didn't seem to notice her sudden, guilty flush. He reached out and patted her hand. His eyes locked on to her cleavage with a lecherous glint.

Maggie felt a tingle of apprehension. Had she just made a bad mistake? Did he think that she was now in his debt? He certainly wasn't that attractive! Oh well, what the hell! With a hotel full of Trojans, she wasn't going to have much time for anyone else. If Roland thought that he had just bought himself a cosy little liaison with her in Nottingham, he was in for a big disappointment.

Maggie was outside the ice rink just after 2 p.m. on Friday, with her suitcase packed and ready. She hadn't been able to find anyone to take over her morning shift, but fortunately the rink had been fairly quiet and she had managed to get away on time at 12 p.m. to change and pack.

A small luxury coach was waiting in the main car park and a few of the squad were already milling around aimlessly, laughing and joking. Stephen Jackson, the squad coach, and their physiotherapist, Gemma Sullivan, were also there. Gemma looked calm and relaxed as she bantered with the players, while Stephen was rushing around like a headless chicken, clutching a large clipboard.

'Maggie. Good.' As soon as he saw her, Stephen rushed over. 'Here's a list of everyone who should be on the coach. Make very sure we don't leave any of the equipment behind. Check and double check. These lads can be worse than a bunch of naughty kids on a school outing.'

Maggie took the list and nodded gravely.

'When we arrive, the hotel will give you a room list. See everyone gets to the right place and make certain no one leaves anything on the coach. Somebody is always losing something.' Stephen grinned ruefully. 'I hope you know what you've let yourself in for, Maggie. Playing nursemaid to this bunch of *prima donnas* is hard work!'

She grinned confidently, far too excited to allow Stephen's warnings to daunt her. 'No problem. I'm great with naughty kids,' she informed him.

'Just as well. Excuse me, I need to have a quick word with the driver.' Stephen dashed off towards the coach and Maggie glanced down at the checklist.

Gemma ambled over to stand beside her. 'Hi Maggie. Welcome to the mad house,' she said.

Maggie looked up and smiled at the pretty young woman. Although she was still the tiniest bit jealous of Gemma's position with the squad, she realised that it might be good to have some female company. Besides, Gemma must have been on dozens of away matches and would know the score. 'Hello. How are you?' asked Maggie.

Gemma pulled a face. 'Bloody exhausted, to be perfectly honest. I was clubbing until the early hours and I've been at the rink since first thing this morning, packing everything the boys conceivably might need: from aspirin to spare jock straps!' She pushed a strand of long brown hair behind her ear and reached into her shoulder bag for some gum. She held out the packet. 'Want some?'

'No thanks.' Maggie wasn't all that fond of gum. It made her feel a bit like a cow chewing the cud.

Gemma rolled up a wad and popped it into her mouth. Maggie watched without comment, trying not to smile at the thought of the gum getting stuck around Gemma's tongue stud. She had often tried to imagine what it would be like trying to eat with a stud through your tongue, and was almost tempted to ask Gemma whether she had ever swallowed the stud by mistake. She had also wondered what it would be like to kiss someone with a stud. Gemma would have to be very careful giving head or the passion could easily turn sour! Maggie's smile broadened but, fortunately, Gemma didn't seem to notice.

'As soon as we get on board, I'm going to sprawl out and catch up on my beauty sleep,' she informed Maggie. 'Unless any of them get hurt or sick, they're all yours. Good luck.' She headed back towards the coach just as Stephen reappeared, looking, if anything, even more harassed than before.

'Start getting everyone on board will you, Maggie,' he

called. 'I'd like to get on the road as soon as possible. The driver says there are major roadworks on the motorway.'

She looked around again and noticed that most of the squad seemed to have arrived. She spotted Tor and Troy stowing their gear in the baggage compartment under the coach and her heart began to race. She was burning to know how Tor had got on with his house hunting with Jan. She had been meaning to call Jan and find out. She felt the colour rushing to her cheeks at the memory of what Tor had done to her. Jan should be so lucky!

Troy stood up and turned around. When he spotted Maggie a wide grin appeared on his sensual lips. He nudged Tor and then swaggered over towards her.

'Hi babes. I heard you were coming along to take care of us. Nice. Real nice.' He winked suggestively.

'Hi yourself,' Maggie muttered awkwardly. 'I hope you and the others aren't going to give me any trouble. I hear you can be a bit of a handful at times.'

Troy flashed her another lecherous grin. 'You'd better believe it, sugar,' he drawled teasingly.

'Right then, let's get everyone on the coach.' Maggie tried her best to look and sound businesslike and professional. 'Is everybody here?' She moved over to the door of the coach and began checking names on the list as the players piled in beside her.

'Come and sit at the back with us, Maggie,' Tor told her, as he swung himself up into the coach. 'We'll keep a seat warm for you.'

By the time the last member of the squad was safely inside and Maggie had assured Stephen that everyone was present and accounted for, she could already hear some sniggering coming from the back seats and wondered what they could possibly be up to already.

'OK. Listen up everyone.' Stephen leapt on board and held up his hand for silence. 'Keep the noise down and remember that any damage comes out of your pay packet. No obscene gestures or bare arses out of the windows and absolutely no alcohol. Try to remember that you've got a crucial match to play tomorrow.' He sank down wearily in the front seat and looked up at Maggie. 'Ready?'

She nodded.

'OK,' he told the driver, 'let's get going.'

'I'm just going to check everyone's all right,' Maggie told Stephen. The noise from the back was becoming more raucous and her curiosity was getting the better of her.

'Sure. Whatever,' Stephen responded. 'If you don't come back, I'll send a search party.'

Maggie made her way down the centre isle of the moving coach, smiling at the soft whistles and suggestive whispers as she passed. Stephen had been right. It was just like taking a bunch of kids on a school outing – extremely attractive and well-endowed kids, mind you.

Several of the men were leaning over their seats, facing the back. Everyone was laughing.

'Look out! Here comes trouble,' Pary yelled as she approached. Troy turned around and grinned up at her innocently. Maggie smiled back and moved past them to the back seat. Gemma was spread out on the seat, sleeping peacefully. Lying beside her with one arm across her pert breasts and the other under the hem of her skirt was a full-sized blow-up doll, stark naked and anatomically correct in every detail.

'Meet Anna,' Bri chuckled.

'She's sort of our unofficial mascot,' Troy told her. 'The perfect woman: mouth always open, but never says a word,' he added cheekily.

'Hey, watch it you,' Maggie scolded. 'We'll have no sexist comments while I'm in charge.'

'Yeah, shove it, black boy,' Bri chided.

'Hey, whitey! Watch who you're calling black or I'll set Maggie on to you.'

Before Maggie could think up a witty reply to this,

Gemma stirred and opened her eyes. 'What the fuck . . .' She sat up quickly and pushed the doll on to the floor. 'OK. Very funny.' She glared round at her laughing audience. 'Just wait till I get you on my massage table, that's all,' she threatened them.

'But, you and Anna make such a lovely couple,' Ean insisted. He ducked quickly as Gemma took an angry swipe at him.

'In your dreams,' she retorted.

'OK. Settle down everyone,' Maggie told them. 'If you don't cool it, Stephen will blow a fuse and I'll never get asked to play hostess again.'

Troy shifted over in his seat to make room for her. 'Come and sit by me,' he suggested. 'I'll show you what your duties are.'

Now, there's an offer no girl could refuse, Maggie thought to herself as she wriggled in next to Troy and snuggled herself up against him amidst the raucous catcalls. As she had anticipated, it was promising to be quite a weekend.

Roland caught Maggie just as she was coming out of her room later that afternoon.

'Ah, there you are, Maggie. I thought you might like to join me for dinner tonight. Not here. Somewhere where we can be alone.' He pulled a face. 'It's not that they're not a great bunch of lads, but, with an average age of around twenty-five, I do find some of their antics a bit childish at times, don't you?'

She smiled. Childish was not the word that immediately sprang to her mind. Demanding might be more apt. At least she now knew why Gemma always wore trousers when she was on duty. So far, she had been unable to come up with any threat of punishment that didn't encourage them all the more.

'I've already agreed to eat with them,' she told Roland. 'After all, I am working this weekend.'

'Your hostess duties don't require you to spend the evening with the squad. On the contrary, you should be helping the coach and me make sure that the lads restrain themselves. Remember that they have an important match tomorrow,' Roland told her stuffily.

'In that case, shouldn't you have dinner with them yourself?' Maggie suggested cheekily.

'I'm their manager, not their babysitter,' Roland retorted. He put his hand on her arm. 'I was rather hoping that you would want to show your appreciation. After all, if not for me you wouldn't be here.'

Maggie shook his hand off impatiently, annoyed but not totally surprised by his words; she had been half-expecting something like this. 'I'm here to do a job. I wasn't aware it involved any obligation to you. I appreciate your invitation, Roland, but I already have plans this evening.'

Roland's eyes narrowed. 'I see. My mistake. I shan't make it again. Excuse me.' He turned on his heels and briskly strode away.

Damn! Maggie watched his retreating back with dismay. Not the best of starts to the weekend. Oh well, it couldn't be helped. She had already known that Roland's interest in her went beyond her interest in him. The sooner he realised that he was wasting his time the better. Still, she might as well make the most of this opportunity. It seemed unlikely now that Roland would ask her to act as hostess for the squad again.

Later that night, Gemma stood in front of the mirror and turned her head from side to side as she admired the new silver-blonde highlights in her shoulder-length brown hair. Although she had been a bit taken aback by the cost, she was delighted with the results. Under the flashing lights of a nightclub they would look really wicked.

She twirled round slowly, critically examining her short lycra skirt and tight-fitting red top. Her breasts were firm and round under the thin crop top and her nipples stood out clearly. She pushed a diamond stud into her nose and added two more sets of earrings in each of her multi-pierced ears, then pulled on some stay-ups, buckled her feet into her favourite ankle boots and picked up her suede jacket. Pausing only to apply another quick burst of body spray, she dashed out of her room and hurried down to the reception area. If Roland thought she was going to hang around here all night, he had another think coming. The squad might be in training, but she certainly wasn't.

The club she was heading for apparently had a bit of a reputation as a gay haven but, according to the cute young hotel waiter who had told her about it, it also had the best music and cheapest drinks. She hurried out of the hotel and hailed a passing cab.

After she bought herself a drink at the bar, Gemma headed upstairs to where dozens of hot, sweaty punters – men and women – were already dancing energetically under the strobe lights. She found herself a tiny table against the wall and sat down to watch the dancers; most of them were male, and some were obviously trying hard to attract attention to themselves. The hotel waiter had obviously been correct. She would be hard-pressed to find any talent here. By the look of it, most of the men only had other men on their minds.

Gemma's eyes brightened as she spotted a group of young women dancing together in a ragged line. Despite her protests about being partnered with Anna, she had nothing against gay sex, under the right circumstances. With her blood already boiling from the combination of the loud music and the strong alcohol, Gemma jumped up and made her way over to join the women. Soon, she was lost in the excitement and stimulation of gyrating her body to the compelling beat, while the overhead lights flashed hypnotically across their colourful outfits.

Gradually, a kind of sensual feeling of peace and

wellbeing flowed through her whole body, making her skin tingle as if it was electrified. There was almost nothing Gemma enjoyed more than a good night out. She smiled at the pretty blond dancing next to her and felt a small shiver of lust between her thighs as the blonde parted her lips and ran her tongue invitingly over her full, red lips. Almost nothing except a suitable partner to end the night with.

Gemma had been dancing for about ten minutes when her attention was captured by the arrival of two men who, even in the low rippling lights, quite obviously had bodies to die for. Given where they were, Gemma assumed that the two of them were probably together and could not help reflecting on what a waste that was.

The two men leaned up against one wall to sip their drinks, and Gemma grinned as she moved closer and saw who they were. She had assumed that Stephen and Roland would have the squad all safely tucked up in bed by this time, as they usually did. How in the world had these two managed to slip away?

'Pary! Bri! I see you managed to escape? I ought to report you both you know.' She had secretly lusted after Pary for ages but, until now, had never found the opportunity to do more than massage his aching body after a game. She kept her hips swaying seductively in time with the beat as she moved over to stand just in front of them.

'So, what are you doing here?' she questioned, wondering if they knew what kind of a reputation this place had. Maybe they were gay? Several of their fellow players were quite open about it. She hoped they weren't.

Pary shrugged. 'It was the first place we came across that looked worth trying. This town is really dead, you know.'

'Not as dead as that crummy hotel,' Bri added. 'We were bored stiff with sitting around listening to Stephen rabbiting on about tactics. The way he's acting, anyone would think we've never played an away match before.'

'We sort of sneaked out when he and Roland got into an argument about something,' Pary confessed. 'They probably think we're safely asleep by now and dreaming about winning the game. You won't tell on us, will you?'

'Depends,' Gemma giggled. 'I doubt if they would approve of me being here either, so I guess we'll just have to trust each other.'

'It's a good job you are here,' Pary told her. 'The local talent doesn't seem much to get excited about. Most of the women look a bit suss, if you get my drift.'

Gemma giggled again. 'Hardly surprising. You do realise that this is considered to be *the* spot for gays around here, don't you?'

'I thought the bartender was giving us a funny smile,' Pary joked. He stared at her thoughtfully. 'So, what brings you here?' he questioned. 'Don't ruin my evening and tell me I'm wasting my time.'

Gemma grinned. 'I heard it was a great place to dance and that the drinks are cheap,' she explained quickly. 'Besides, you never know who you might come across.'

'Maybe we'd better move on somewhere else,' Bri suggested somewhat nervously.

'I've only just got here,' Gemma protested. 'Don't you want to dance?' She began to sway her hips seductively.

'I don't suppose Maggie's with you, is she?' Pary questioned hopefully.

Gemma felt a surge of jealousy. What was his interest in Maggie? She must be heaps older than him. It had never even occurred to her to ask Maggie if she wanted to come. 'You're kidding!' she replied scornfully. 'Miss Goody-goody didn't think Roland would like it if we went out without asking him,' she lied. 'She's probably already asleep.' She was tempted to add that Maggie probably needed the rest, but she bit her tongue. She didn't want to sound bitchy.

Pary looked disappointed, then shrugged. 'Why don't

you go down and get us another round of drinks,' he suggested to Bri. 'What are you drinking, Gemma?'

'Oh, I'll have a Campari and soda, please.'

'Off you go, Bri. I'll have another Scotch.' He drained his glass and handed it over. Bri took it grudgingly and headed off towards the stairs. Gemma suspected that it was a deliberate ploy to get rid of him. She was still a bit miffed about Pary's interest in Maggie, but was willing to forgive him.

'You do realise we'll probably never see Bri again, don't you?' she chuckled as she reached up to put her arms around Pary's neck. 'Wandering around on his own like that, he's bound to attract attention.'

'I was sort of thinking that the bartender might keep him busy for a while,' Pary admitted as he put his arms around her waist and pulled her tightly against his body.

'If he gets that far,' Gemma replied. She had seen several men watching with more than a passing interest as Bri walked across the dance floor. Poor guy.

'Forget about Bri.' Pary pulled her even tighter against him so that she could feel his cock pressed into her navel. She wriggled her hips, deliberately rubbing herself against him until she felt his trousers growing tighter. It always turned her on to feel a cock stiffening against her body.

'One–nil to me,' Pary muttered softly.

'You what?'

'Nothing.' Pary lowered his head and put his lips over hers. She felt his tongue probing her mouth and she quickly swallowed her gum and opened her lips. His tongue slid in, hot and slippery, and wrapped itself around hers like a hungry snake. His mouth tasted of Scotch and his chin was prickly with the day's growth. His skin smelt warm and musky.

The music changed to something much faster and Gemma reluctantly released her arms from his neck and stepped back. Her lips were tingling from his kiss and her tongue felt too big for her mouth. Her panties were dripping and her whole body was covered in a fine sheen of perspiration.

Pary began to dance alone in front of her. His every move was filled with the grace and beauty of an athlete; his limbs seemed to flow like liquid and his muscles rippled under his clothes as if they had a life of their own. She couldn't take her eyes off him.

Neither could anyone else. She gradually became aware that most of the people nearby had stopped dancing to watch him. She could see the admiration and lust burning in several pairs of eyes, male and female alike. She grabbed his arm and pulled him back into her embrace.

'That's probably not such a good idea,' she whispered in his left ear.

'Sorry?' He stared down at her with a puzzled look on his face.

'Your dancing. If you value your backside, you had better stop wiggling it like that,' she sniggered. 'Maybe Bri was right. Maybe we should go somewhere else before it's too late.'

'I was just getting going,' Pary protested.

'So are they.' She nodded towards a group of men nearby who were all openly fingering their crotches as they watched him. 'Come on, let's go and rescue Bri and get the hell out of here.'

As she led Pary by the hand across the dance floor, Gemma could feel every eye following them: willing him to stay, willing her to disappear. She held on to him possessively and ignored the stares.

At first, she could see no sign of Bri at the bar. They were probably already too late. Someone would have snapped him up by now, with or without his consent. Well, he was a big boy – no doubt about that – he would just have to take care of himself. She tugged Pary towards the door, wondering where they could go to be alone. Somewhere close. She couldn't wait much longer.

They found Bri just inside the main doorway, talking with a couple of attractive women who were holding on to each other possessively. Boy, was he going to be in for a shock if he thought he was getting anywhere with them! Gemma grinned to herself.

Bri was in full flow, explaining something to them that had both women in fits of giggles. He said something else and they doubled over, clutching each other for support as their tears of mirth mingled with their mascara. Gemma could see that Bri appeared to be quite drunk. His babyface was flushed and his dark eyes were hooded and reddened. She hoped it was only drink. Trying anything else on sale in a place like this would be sheer madness. Either way, Stephen would kill him if he found out. He'd probably kill her too, for not taking better care of him.

Pary stepped forward and grasped Bri firmly by the elbow. 'Time to go,' he announced firmly as he steered his fellow Trojan away from the two near-hysterical women.

'What were those two dykes cracking up about?' Gemma asked him as they headed out the door.

'Dykes?' Bri's cheeks grew even pinker. 'You're kidding? I thought I was well-in there.' He glowered angrily as Gemma and Pary both started to snigger. 'Well? How was I to know?'

Pary shook his head. 'Only you . . .' he muttered. 'Come on, let's go.' He took Gemma's hand.

As they walked through the deserted town centre, Gemma flicked her eyes from one to the other trying to decide which of her two dark-haired escorts she fancied most. Truth was, she wanted them both. Where could they go? She didn't know Nottingham at all. Shame she was sharing with Maggie, or they could have tried to sneak back into the hotel without being seen. Did Pary and Bri have a room together, or were they sharing with any of the others?

Pary's hand slipped off her arm and slid down round her waist. She felt his fingers caressing the top of her buttocks. She wondered if he would try to send Bri packing again so he could have her to himself. Well, that was OK with her, but it still didn't solve the problem of where they could go.

Just then, as they drew level with the entrance to a dark alleyway between two shops, Pary stopped. He pulled her round so that she was facing him and put his lips over hers again. His tongue quickly resumed its urgent exploration of her mouth and she melted against him.

She felt her skirt being lifted from behind and then Bri's hand moved in to fondle her buttocks. Moving like one giant and ungainly six-legged monster, the two men guided her backwards into the concealing darkness. Her foot stepped on an empty beer can and it loudly rolled away into the hidden shadows.

Pary moved his hand round and pulled her top up over her breasts. His fingers started to squeeze her left nipple while his other hand pulled up the front of her skirt. Behind her, Bri gradually lowered her knickers, and she felt him thrust his fingers between her thighs.

'This is what you wanted, isn't it, Gemma?' Pary had moved his mouth away from hers and placed it over her right ear. His words sent a ripple of lust right through her. 'You've wanted us ever since you got the job as physio for the team, haven't you? Wanted to feel our cocks pushed up in you?'

'Yes. Oh yes.' She squirmed at his words. Dirty talk always did it for her. Her nipples formed into hard pebbles between his fingers.

Whimpering in her excitement, Gemma raised her own trembling hands and unzipped Pary's fly. She wanted to touch his cock. Her groping fingers slid inside the opening and quickly released his penis from the tiny pouch he was wearing. It was hard and thick, thicker than she would have believed possible. She traced one fingertip over his glans, marvelling at its well-formed ridge, and then on down the solid stem with its raised cords of engorged veins. His pubic hair was thick and fluffy, so unlike her own wiry curls. She ran her fingers gently through it and reached down further to caress the swell of his heavy balls.

Pary was nibbling her earlobe, sending sweet shivers right through her body. As she caressed him he shifted restlessly from one foot to the other and she felt his hot breath sighing inside her ear. Behind her, Bri opened his zip and she could feel him begin to pump his cock back and forth between her legs while his inquisitive fingers explored all her secret places.

Back in the main shopping precinct, footsteps approached and stopped. A beam of light shone blindingly down the alleyway and a deep, male voice called out: 'Anyone there?'

The six-legged beast froze, cowering motionless in the scant safety of a narrow doorway. Gemma could feel Bri's cock jerking impatiently between her thighs and Pary's stubby manhood seemed to twitch between her fingers.

The torch explored the far wall and then hovered curiously over a bulging black bin bag in the centre of the alleyway. A lump formed in Gemma's throat and her heart was pumping so rapidly that she was certain the policeman would hear it thudding. Bri's cock twitched again, so fiercely that she almost cried out. She felt him start to move back and forth again, his lust clearly overcoming his fear of discovery. Terrified that the policeman would hear his movements, Gemma clamped her thighs, trapping him. She almost squealed as Pary pushed his warm tongue into her ear.

The torch beam went out, leaving them blind in the

darkness. The heavy footsteps faded and Pary began to chuckle.

'Jesus!' Gemma could feel her whole body shaking with the after-effects of her fright. She could clearly imagine the headlines in the newspaper:

YOUNG PHYSIO CAUGHT IN PUBLIC PLACE WITH RAMPANT HOCKEY PLAYERS
ICE HOCKEY HEROES SCORE HOME GOAL IN ALLEYWAY!

If Roland could see them now she'd be out of a job like a shot.

Pary started to tweak her nipples again and the tremors of pleasure soon overcame her panic. Both men seemed to be as hard as ever. Didn't anything put them off their stroke? Obviously not. She gasped aloud as Bri increased his urgent thrusting and Pary took his own cock and started to rub it round her sensitive clit.

She felt another urgent thrust from behind, so hard and deep that Bri's long, snakelike penis was rammed right through between her legs. Immediately, she lowered her hands and touched the tip protruding in front of her. An erotic thrill enveloped her. It was as if she had suddenly grown a penis of her own, poking out, swollen and ready. She squeezed it between her fingers, smoothing his dribbles of lubrication all over the soft round tip. Pary continued to caress her clit with his own cock and she felt the tingles of her arousal deep inside her. Her pussy spasmed as an unexpected orgasm overcame her and she felt her juices dribble down her legs.

Bri groaned desperately as her fingers slid frantically up and down his tip and Gemma felt the first spurt of his come shoot out between her fingers. She pumped harder as burst after burst poured from him and the stem of his cock writhed and jerked between her hot, wet thighs.

'Hey, watch where you're pointing that thing, will

you?' Pary stepped back to avoid the sudden shower of semen spurting up into the air in front of her. He laughed softly as he smoothed a condom down his rigid shaft. 'Now that you've shot your bolt, why don't you get out the way and watch a real artist in action?' he muttered.

Before Gemma knew what was happening, Pary stepped forward and swung her up into his arms. As she locked her fingers around his neck, he moved his hands down under her and lifted her legs. Following his lead, she wound them tightly round his waist and groaned as she felt his left hand pushed between them, guiding his huge cock into her. She was so wet that it slipped in easily, despite its unaccustomed circumference.

'Oh Christ,' she moaned with delight as he sank up into her, filling her completely. Despite having so recently climaxed, she could already feel another orgasm building as his cock pummelled her and his fingers continued to tease and caress her clit.

'Oh yeah, baby,' Pary grunted urgently, as she began raising and lowering her buttocks, sliding herself up and down his hard pole. 'Feel good?' he mumbled in her right ear. The words enflamed her further.

'Feels great,' she whispered. 'Just great.' Another pang of lust engulfed her. 'Harder,' she begged. 'Harder.' She felt him respond to her voice, thrusting his cock in and out like a piston.

Gemma turned her head and glanced down at Bri. He was standing so close to them that, even in the almost non-existent light of the alleyway, she could see the gleaming white flesh of his naked lower body. His eyes were fixed on her buttocks and she saw that his long, thin cock was rapidly swelling once more.

Bri looked up at her and grinned. Deliberately, he reached down and grasped his cock between his fingers. Without taking his eyes off hers, he began to knead and caress his tip and stem. His cock grew even longer and Gemma was reminded of how she had felt with it poking out between her own thighs. She licked her lips, then gasped again as Pary increased the pace and depth of his own thrusting.

'Almost there baby,' Pary breathed. 'Almost there. You ready for it?'

'Ready for it!' What with the way he was ramming himself into her and the sight of Bri wanking away, Gemma was almost fit to bust. She bit her bottom lip to stifle the deep moan that was welling up inside her as her vagina went into spasm again. She sensed the first burst of his own release, hot and hard inside her, at the same time as she felt another shower of Bri's spunk splashing across her buttocks and thigh. Pary gave a final long thrust and she felt his cock twitch violently as he let go.

Finally, it was over and Pary lifted her gently off him and lowered her carefully to the ground. No one said a word as they wiped themselves off as best they could and tried to readjust their dishevelled clothing.

'All we have to do now,' Pary muttered as the three of them re-emerged from the alleyway into the deserted town centre, 'is to figure out how to get back into the hotel without getting sprung.'

Roland paced up and down furiously, his face contorted in anger. Stephen Jackson sat passively, as if mentally steeling himself for the outburst to come. Roland finally turned and glowered at the coach, his face black as thunder.

'What the hell went wrong, Stephen? 5–2, for Christ's sake! This match should have been a doddle. My fucking grandmother could have run rings around them. Another one like this and our chances for the Championship will be over.'

Stephen shook his head. 'I realise that. I don't understand it. The lads were in such good form during training last week. I don't know if it was nerves, or . . .'

'Or what?' Roland snapped.

Stephen shrugged. 'Oh, I don't know. Just a feeling that one or two of the lads were a bit sluggish out there today. Maybe they were too keyed-up to sleep properly last night or something? I mean, there's a lot riding on them at the moment. We've never been this close to getting into the finals. I think they're just a bit stressed-out. Don't worry. I'll sort it.'

'You'd damn well better. That's what you're paid for, after all. There's no point in having the best players going if they can't take the pressure of being at the top. You should have seen this coming and sorted it before the match.'

Stephen's eyes narrowed dangerously. 'If you want my opinion, you ought to keep a tighter rein on them. Maybe they'd play a damn sight better if there was a lot less fucking around going on. I know for a fact that several of the lads were out boozing and whoring last night when they should have been resting.'

'You're their coach,' Roland snapped.

'And you're their manager. Why don't you get off my back and start acting like one?' Stephen stood up and stamped furiously out of the room.

Roland stood, fuming. How dare Stephen talk to him like that? If he didn't need him so much right now he'd kick his arse right out of the squad. As for the players! He'd read them the riot act. They were under contract and they'd bloody well better remember it or else.

Maggie! She had turned him down the previous evening so that she could have dinner with some of the team. She and Troy were obviously far too interested in each other. His jealousy burned at the idea. The little slut. Troy might as well have been playing with his eyes closed out there today. He'd probably screwed the bitch silly all last night.

Maybe he would have a little chat with Justin about Maggie. He remembered that Justin and she had something going between them too. Shit! The bloody woman was nothing but trouble. Using him to get free tickets to the matches, manipulating the rink manager for her own benefit and now interfering with the players' training and costing them vital points. She would have to go. Somehow, he'd have to find a way of making Justin see what a liability she was. An idea began to take shape in his mind and, as it grew, he started to feel much better.

'Yeah. You'll rue the day you turned me down, you little whore,' he muttered softly.

Chapter Eight

'I've never known you to be so evasive. It's like getting blood out of stone.' Maggie glared impatiently at Jan. 'Don't forget it was because of me that he came to you in the first place.' It was the first time Maggie had seen Jan since they had got back from Bristol and she was still burning with curiosity to find out about Tor's house hunting.

Jan smiled. 'I know. I know. How many times do you want me to say thanks?' She sipped her drink. 'How's your coffee? I made it hot and black, just the way you like it.'

'Don't keep changing the subject,' Maggie complained, doing her best to ignore Jan's pointed comment. Did Jan fancy Troy as well, or was she just being deliberately provocative? Maggie wasn't in the mood for playing games. She was too worried about what Justin had said to her earlier.

Jan shrugged. 'I don't know what else you expect me to say. You're the one with all the hot news. You haven't said anything about Nottingham yet.'

Maggie shrugged. She wasn't sure that she was ready to talk about herself and Troy. Besides, she was determined to find out what had happened between Jan and Tor, and she was more than a little anxious to know if Tor had said anything about her to Jan. If anything serious was going on between them, she certainly didn't want her friend to find out how wantonly she had behaved with him in Bristol that night. It might have been a fantasy come true but fantasies were private!

'Was it just Tor you showed round, or did any of the others come with him?' Maggie questioned. In her mind, she could almost picture Jan pleasuring all of them, including Troy. Her jealousy burned.

'It was only Tor,' Jan replied with a dreamy look in her eyes.

So, she hadn't been with Troy. Maggie felt much better. Mind you, she was still consumed with curiosity as to exactly what had gone on between the two of them. Tor hadn't really mentioned Jan at all at the weekend, although he had said that his new house was just what he'd been looking for. Was Jan planning to see him again? If so, would she admit to it?

'Sod it.' Maggie swore as a drop of coffee splashed down the front of her dress. She brushed at the stain angrily. 'I've only just had this dress cleaned.'

Jan peered at her curiously. 'What's got you so ratty today, anyway? You've had a face like a thundercloud ever since you arrived. Have I done something?'

Maggie shook her head. 'Sorry. It's not you. It's work. Some money's gone missing from the ticket office till and Justin is in a real rage about it.'

'So? What's it got to do with you? It's his problem.' Jan took another sip of her coffee. 'Do you fancy a biscuit? I think I've got some somewhere, if Marcus hasn't scoffed them all.'

Maggie shook her head again. 'No thanks.' She frowned. 'The thing is, he was acting really weird when he told me about it. It was almost as if he suspected that I might have taken it.'

'Surely not? Justin knows you better than that. You must have imagined it.'

'Yes, I suppose so. It's just that I can't see who could or would have. I mean, a thief,' Maggie reiterated. 'It just doesn't bear thinking about, does it?' She pictured each of her colleagues in turn. There were only two or three who officially had access to his office but then nobody ever bothered to lock up, so it could have been anyone. 'It's horrible to think that one of your workmates can't be trusted.' Maggie tried to force a smile. 'Maybe I will have that biscuit, after all.'

Jan stood up and opened a cupboard to reach for the biscuit tin. 'How about another coffee?' she suggested. 'Then I want to hear all the lurid details about your weekend in Nottingham.'

Justin shrugged. 'I just don't know what else to say, Maggie. I'm sorry.'

It was two days after her conversation with Jan when a message had been delivered by one of the office juniors to tell Maggie that Justin wanted to see her in his office immediately. Annoyed at being summoned in such an offhand manner, Maggie had hurried to obey, wondering what was so urgent that it couldn't wait until her shift was over. He had not kept her wondering for long. As she had listened to what he had to say, she had felt herself growing cold all over. It was like some ghastly nightmare.

'You can't seriously believe that I would do something like that, Justin. You know I wouldn't.' Maggie protested feebly when he finally fell silent.

'If it was the first time but, well, there was the money from the till as well.' Justin replied awkwardly.

'I've already told you that I didn't have anything to do with that,' Maggie retorted angrily. 'It could have been anyone. Shit. This is ridiculous. Why on earth would I want to steal some petty cash for Christ's sake?'

'Hardly anyone else knew that the money was in my office,' Justin reminded her. 'Apart from myself, only you and Stephen. And he's not been around for several days.'

'If Stephen knew, then Roland probably knew as well, didn't he?' Maggie persisted.

'Of course. But it was his money! You're not suggesting that Roland would sneak into my office and steal his own money, are you?' Justin demanded incredulously.

'Why not? It's no more ridiculous than suggesting that I sneaked in and took it.' Maggie glared at him. 'So, what are you going to do now? Have me arrested?'

Justin looked pained. 'No, of course not. Look, the thing is, Roland agrees with me that we don't want any bad publicity. If we call the police in, it will be all over the local papers and might reflect badly on the squad. With the Championship going so well, we don't want that.'

'No, of course not,' Maggie interrupted him sarcastically. 'What the hell has all this got to do with Roland anyway?'

Justin frowned. 'Please don't make this any more difficult than it already is, Maggie.' He drummed his fingers nervously on the desk. 'Look. The staff have to see that I'm not prepared to tolerate this sort of thing. I'm sorry, but I'm going to have to let you go.'

Maggie gasped. 'You can't. If you sack me for alleged thieving, without any proof, I'll have you up for unfair dismissal,' she threatened. 'See what that does for Roland's precious publicity image!'

'I'm not letting you go for thieving,' Justin told her coldly. 'Your contract is up in a couple of months and I've decided not to renew it. Call it downsizing or staff rationalisation, if you like. Our recent internal review has revealed that we just don't need so many part-time staff.'

'You bastard!' Maggie spluttered, finally realising just how well she had been stitched up. Had Roland known that her contract was due for renewal too, or was that just a lucky coincidence? She felt a blaze of hatred. Just because she had turned him down! The slimy, stinking bastard had had her sacked because she wouldn't go to bed with him. Justin obviously didn't realise. Maggie tried to explain what had happened.

Justin listened in silence then looked wary. 'Did anyone see or hear any of this?' he asked her.

'No.'

'I'm sorry Maggie. You'd never prove a thing,' he told her.

'You know I didn't steal anything, Justin. You know I didn't!' Maggie could feel the tears welling up at the corners of her eyes.

'You can have your two months' pay, of course.' Justin ignored her appeal. 'I'll even throw in an extra month's bonus. No need for you to work out your contract.'

'I have no intention of working it out,' Maggie yelled. 'I wouldn't stay here another minute – whether you paid me or not.' She stood up and started to turn towards the door.

He gave her a feeble smile. 'I hope we can still be friends, Maggie?'

She tossed her head and stamped haughtily out of the room before he caught a glimpse of the tears that began openly trickling down her cheeks. She was damned if she would give him the satisfaction.

As soon as Sara had served Roland his breakfast and cleared up in the kitchen, she headed into town to meet her friends for coffee. She had a lot to tell them. They didn't know about her new job yet. Maggie was probably wondering why she hadn't been at the rink lately.

Her mind was in a whirl. Roland had invited some of the team around again that night to discuss their next match, and Sara was wracking her brain trying to think of something really special to cook for them. She was also wondering if Ean was to be one of the guests and, if so, whether he would slip away to see her again. She knew she ought to feel a bit guilty about her behaviour with Ean. After all, it wasn't exactly the way Ms Jamison would expect her to conduct herself. She smiled. Ms J. had said Roland wanted someone discreet. No one had said anything about her not having any fun.

Roland had brushed himself up against her in the kitchen again that morning. It had happened too often now to be put down to coincidence. She would have to draw the line there, she decided. After all, he was her employer, wasn't he? Besides, without being unkind, Roland wasn't exactly irresistible.

Not like Ean. Had they really thrown dice for her company? It was an incredibly exciting thought. She wondered if they would do it again. Sara pictured herself naked and helpless in front of them all while they competed for the pleasures of her body. Perhaps she should visit the beautician later and have a complete facial. She could afford the odd luxury now.

She was so caught up in her daydreams that she almost walked straight past the table where Maggie and Jan were seated. An impatient shout brought her back to her senses.

'Sara! Over here.'

'Whoops, sorry.' Sara hurried back to their table and plonked herself down beside Maggie. 'Sorry, I'm a bit late. Have you already ordered?'

'You looked as if you were in another world,' Jan teased her. 'I sense a man. Just what have you been up to?'

Sara felt the sudden rush of colour to her cheeks. What would Maggie and Jan say if she told them about Ean? No, she couldn't. Well, not in so many words, anyway. She could tell them about her job though and maybe drop a few hints. They could draw their own conclusions.

'You'll never believe this,' she began, 'but I've been reassigned by the agency. That's why I wasn't at the ice rink this week.' She drew a deep breath and tried to make her voice sound matter-of-fact. 'I've got a new job as Roland Donaldson's housekeeper. In fact, I'm cooking dinner for him and several of the Trojans tonight.'

'You poor bitch. I'd watch my back if I were you.' Maggie's voice was dripping with sarcasm and Sara stared at her in surprise, wondering what she was so mad about. It wasn't like her at all.

'Don't mind Maggie,' Jan told her. 'She's not feeling very happy at the moment. So, tell all. Are you staying with Roland? I mean, actually living in?'

Sara nodded. 'He insisted,' she told them. 'He said it was silly for me to travel back and forth every day when he had plenty of room. He's been very nice.'

Maggie raised an eyebrow. 'Nice?' she questioned icily. 'Nice is not the word I'd use to describe that stinking rat. Has he tried it on yet?'

Sara frowned again at the venom in Maggie's voice. Something was obviously very wrong. She thought about Roland's advances and felt a tingle of apprehension.

'I just meant that he's been very considerate and that he's paying me a more than generous salary,' Sara replied cautiously.

Maggie snorted rudely and took a sip of her coffee. Jan shrugged her shoulders apologetically. 'As you might have gathered, Maggie doesn't like Roland very much,' she said.

'Like! I could tell you what I'd like to do to him,' Maggie interjected. Her face was twisted with hatred.

'What's going on?' Sara demanded as she stared in confusion from one to the other.

'Maggie's been given the push. Some money went missing from the rink and, well, Justin suspects she might have been responsible,' Jan explained bluntly.

'What? But that's ridiculous! Justin would never . . . I mean, why Maggie?' Sara was lost for words.

'Because your precious new boss wanted Justin to

think it was me, that's why,' Maggie retorted loudly. 'He probably took the money himself to make me look guilty. Just because I wouldn't fuck him,' she yelled.

The café suddenly fell silent and several heads turned to stare in curiousity.

'Shush! You don't know that, Maggie,' Jan replied softly. 'You've no proof.'

'Nor has Justin. That didn't stop him, did it? I know it was Roland. It had to be him. It's his way of getting back at me.' She snatched her bag and fled sobbing towards the loo.

Sara stared at Jan. 'Could you please tell me exactly what's been going on?' she demanded. She really didn't want to believe what Maggie had seemed to be implying.

Later that day, Maggie stood outside Tor's rented house and asked herself what on earth she was doing there. It was Troy she really wanted to see, but somehow they had never got around to swapping addresses. Was he in there with Tor now? They were often together. He had even told her that he was thinking of moving in with Tor and sharing the rent. What was she going to say to them? She hadn't seen them since Nottingham and she had no idea what they had heard or thought about what had happened at the rink. Surely they wouldn't believe that she was a petty thief, would they? But then again, why shouldn't they? Justin obviously did, and he knew her better than any of the Trojans.

Bugger it. Maggie put her hands on the gate and shook her arms angrily. It was all so humiliating and so bloody unfair. The gate began to swing open and Maggie hesitated. Her thoughts were so confused. She was angry and hurt and she wanted revenge but, most of all, she just wanted to be comforted. She desperately wanted, needed, to be believed.

Maggie slipped inside and pushed the gate shut behind her. As she walked down the driveway, she examined the house enviously. If only she could get a few of the right breaks maybe she could live in a place like this, instead of shacking up in a poxy flat barely big enough to swing a cat. Fat chance of that now. The way things were going, she would be lucky if she could even afford her flat for much longer. She had to find another job.

Funny, she had never before thought that her job at the rink was very important to her. She had often told Jan that one job was the same as another. Now, she was beginning to realise how much it had meant to her. She was good at it too. If she didn't organise everything for Justin the place would fall apart; now she hoped it would. Serve him right.

As she approached the house, Maggie could hear voices coming from the front room. She was certain that one of them was Troy. Deliberately avoiding the front door, Maggie followed the narrow pathway round to the back door and tried the handle. The door swung open on to a dark, narrow passageway. She called out but received no response. What were they up to? She waited to allow her eyes to adjust to the gloom, then took a few steps past the open kitchen door. An ear-splitting wail just behind her almost scared her witless. She froze as rapid footsteps approached the door in front of her.

'I bet it's Roland trying to sneak up on us.'

'Maybe it really is a burglar? Do you want me to go first?'

The male voices were coming closer by the second. It was too late to do anything except brazen it out. If only the goddamned alarm would shut up so that she could think. Maggie stood up straight, pulled her stomach in and thrust her breasts out.

'I don't suppose you know how to shut that bloody thing up?' she yelled as the door swung open and Tor and Troy appeared.

'Maggie? What are you doing here?' Tor pushed past her and reached up to punch a few numbers into the alarm console. In the almost overpowering silence following the racket of the alarm Maggie could hear her heart thumping.

'I'd better give the local cops a bell too,' Tor muttered. 'We don't want them bursting in on us as well.'

'Are you sure? I mean, you don't think she's dangerous or anything, do you?' Troy was staring at her in open amusement and Maggie could feel the blood flooding to her cheeks.

'Oh, I think we can handle her, between us,' Tor responded softly. Maggie turned her head to gaze up into his sparkling grey eyes.

'Nice to see you,' Tor told her. 'Next time though, do me a favour and just knock on the front door like everyone else.'

'Sorry. I wanted to surprise you.' Maggie suddenly felt stupid. What in the world had possessed her to sneak in like that? Just like a thief. Her bottom lip started to tremble. Troy immediately stepped forward and took her hand in his. She could feel that she was trembling but was powerless to stop herself.

'What's wrong Maggie?' he questioned. 'Shouldn't you be at work this morning?'

Maggie flushed even deeper red. So, they hadn't heard. 'I don't work at the rink anymore,' she responded softly.

Troy stared at her a moment then turned to Tor and nodded his head towards the door. Tor nodded in reply. 'I'll just go call the police,' he muttered, as he moved through the door and closed it behind him.

Troy gave Maggie's hand a gentle squeeze. 'How come you've deserted us? The rink will never run properly without you there.'

'Maybe you should ask your boss,' Maggie snapped.

'Roland? What's he got to do with it?' A look of sudden understanding came over his face. 'What's he been up to? Look, how about a coffee or something? Then we'll sit down and talk this over. I'm sure we can sort things out.'

Troy took her arm and steered her into the front room where Tor was waiting for them. Troy signalled for him to pour them some drinks. Maggie was surprised and deeply touched by the look of concern on both their faces. She perched herself on the arm of the couch and waited in silence while Tor poured them each a Scotch. As soon as he handed her a glass, Maggie took a quick sip, grimacing as the fiery liquid scalded her tongue. She had never been fond of neat spirits. At least she wasn't trembling quite so much any more.

'So, what exactly has Roland got to do with you leaving the rink?' Troy asked her. 'If he's been making a nuisance of himself you just shouldn't take any notice. He tries it on with everyone.'

Maggie was tempted to lie. It was horrible having to admit that she had been sacked and that Justin thought she was a thief. What if she lied and then they heard what had really happened? Wouldn't that just make her look even more guilty?

'Someone helped themselves to some money that I was responsible for and Justin fired me,' she hastily admitted.

'Shit. That's a bit off, isn't it?' Troy commented. 'Doesn't sound like Justin at all.' Maggie shrugged.

'I don't see what it's got to do with Roland, though,' Tor persisted.

'He set me up,' Maggie said, flaring up angrily. 'I know he did. He and I had a bit of a disagreement and this is his way of getting rid of me.'

'What kind of a disagreement?' Troy demanded.

'He wanted me to screw him, if you must know,' Maggie blurted out. She took another gulp of her Scotch. 'Look, can we just leave it? It's bad enough that everyone thinks I'm a thief without keeping talking about it.'

Troy moved over and put his arm around her. He gave her a hug. 'I don't think you're a thief,' he assured her.

Tor shook his head. 'I had begun to suspect that Roland could be a bit sharp, but I never thought he'd do something like this.'

'I don't have any trouble with the idea of him trying it on,' Troy replied, 'but I really don't think he's clever enough to come up with anything devious. There has to be some other explanation for the money.'

'Even so,' Tor continued, 'he shouldn't get away with it. Do you want us to have a chat with him?' He cracked his knuckles.

Maggie shook her head. 'No. Just forget it.'

Tor shrugged philosophically. 'OK. It's too bad, though. We'll really miss you. Where are you working now?'

'I'm not. There don't seem to be too many options for an ex-receptionist who doesn't have a reference.'

Troy gave her another squeeze. 'I'll give you a reference. You were the best hostess we ever had!'

Maggie giggled, already feeling much better. These two men were just the tonic she needed right now. She was suddenly very glad she had come. 'Thanks, but I don't see how that's going to be much help, unless I decide to look for a job at the local escort agency!'

'Now, there's a thought,' Tor smiled. 'You'd make a fortune.' He stared at her body thoughtfully. 'Hey! I don't suppose you can dance, can you?'

'Dance? What do you mean, dance?' Maggie glanced around the room and was grateful that she could see no sign of a CD-player. For one crazy moment she had thought that he was about to ask her to waltz with him or something!

'Dance. You know. I've got a friend who runs a night-club not too far from here. A fellow Canadian. I bet he'd be only too happy to take you on as a dancer if you were interested.'

She was just about to retort angrily that she was not planning on becoming a stripper, when she noticed the expressions on their faces. Although she had no intention of taking work as a dancer, she found that she just couldn't resist the opportunity to take advantage of them just a little.

'I've never really thought about it,' she lied. 'I mean, I suppose anyone can dance, can't they?' She thought about what she had done to Justin at the Cellar and a tingle of lust ran down her spine.

'Not the sort of dancing I had in mind,' Tor murmured softly.

'Why don't we all go out somewhere this evening and you can judge for yourselves whether or not I can dance?' she suggested brightly. A night out with these two was just what she needed to boost her spirits.

'What's wrong with dancing for us here?' Tor objected.

'What, now?' Maggie looked around the room again. 'For a start, you don't seem to have any music, unless you were planning to hum?'

Tor moved across the room and opened a heavy wooden cabinet to reveal an expensive-looking MiniDisc system. He flicked a couple of switches and the room was immediately filled with booming disco music. He sat himself down on the arm of a thick leather chair and an expectant grin spread over his face.

Maggie stood up and stared at each of them in turn. The men were watching her the way a cat watches a mouse, as though at any moment they might pounce on her. The loud music was insistent and compelling and she found herself beginning to sway her slender hips from side to side, thrusting her crotch forward suggestively as she moved. She heard Troy draw a sharp breath and was immediately overwhelmed by a desire to exert her power over them.

Gyrating faster, Maggie shuffled in front of Tor so that her crotch was almost touching him. She raised her arm and pushed firmly on his shoulder. Overbalanced, Tor slipped down into the leather chair and Maggie positioned herself in front of him, with her legs spread wide apart.

Bending forward from the waist, she thrust her breasts in front of his face and started to caress them through the thin material of her top. Her flattened palms made wide, circular movements across her chest and she felt her nipples harden in response. When she saw his eyes widen she knew that he had noticed, too.

Still rubbing her breasts with one hand, Maggie slid her other palm down over her mound. She could feel her clit swelling and sense the hot dampness of her own arousal. A quick glance downwards told her that she was not the only one. Tor's flies were already straining as his cock pushed hard and urgent against them. She leaned closer to him, so that her mound was hovering just inches above his groin, and smiled as she saw him involuntarily lift his buttocks off the chair, thrusting his crotch up towards hers. There was definitely more to lap dancing than she had thought!

Still smiling suggestively, Maggie wiggled back from him and swayed seductively across the room to stand in front of Troy. She put her hands behind her and ran them over her buttocks, then round her hips and up her stomach to her breasts. Troy watched her avidly, his white teeth gleaming and his black eyes burning.

'Don't you think you're a bit overdressed,' he muttered, reaching out to take hold of her waistband. His fingers began to tug clumsily at her button and Maggie shuffled out of his reach and moved back in front of Tor. As she repeated the suggestive caresses of her breasts and groin for his benefit, she experienced a rush of power that made her feel invincible. They were both already practically wetting themselves. She could see it in their eyes, their faces, and the way they were shifting their bodies awkwardly from side to side. She had them totally under her spell – yet again – and she intended to take full advantage.

Moving back into the middle of the room, Maggie started to undo the buttons on the front of her blouse. As soon as it was open, she slipped her arms out of the sleeves and let the garment drop slowly to the floor, leaving her in just her bra and skintight trousers.

Troy walked over to stand in front of her. He started to sway his hips in time with hers, his body not quite touching hers. His cock was a solid bulge behind the taut zip. Maggie put her hand on his waist and began to undo the buckle of his belt. As soon as it came loose, she tugged the leather strip out of his trousers and started to caress herself with it. As she pulled it tantalisingly back and forth between her legs, she heard his small sigh.

'Take your trousers off,' Troy whispered. 'Or let me take them off for you.' He stepped towards her again.

Maggie dropped the belt and opened her own trouser button. She kicked her feet free of her shoes and then began to peel the tight material over her buttocks and thighs. She took her time, posing carefully. Her skimpy silk panties were so damp with a mixture of sweat and lubrication that they clung to her body like a second skin, hiding nothing. She could smell the musky warmth of her own arousal wafting around her to mingle with another scent – the heady scent of fresh masculine sweat and sexual stimulation.

She stepped out of her trousers and kicked them up into the air with her left foot. They landed on Tor's knee but he didn't seem to notice. She slipped her feet back into her shoes and resumed dancing. Her fingers repeated their suggestive journey around her body, over her breasts and between her legs. The music seemed to grow louder and more insistent, throbbing and pulsing through her.

Maggie moaned softly and pushed her hand under the wet silk at the front of her crotch. Her fingertips encircled her engorged clit and she felt another rush of moisture on her already damp thighs. She pushed her hand down deeper, collecting the lubrication on her fingers, then pulled it out and raised it to her mouth. Slowly and deliberately, she inserted one finger between her pink lips, sucking on her own juices.

'Jesus Christ!' Troy had put his hand down the front of his trousers and wrapped his fingers around his rigid cock. As he moved it away from the zip, Maggie could see that he was gently squeezing himself. His face was flushed and his breathing ragged. She smiled provocatively and put her hand back down inside the front of her panties.

Her own need was like a searing burn deep inside her. She only just stopped herself from crying out as her fingertip remade contact with her hard little bud. Rubbing it rhythmically, she clamped her mouth closed to keep herself from panting and used her other hand to caress her aching nipples. She could feel the little ripples of excitement running up and down her body and raising goose bumps all over her tingling flesh. Troy stepped closer and wrapped his arms around her waist.

'Look, but don't touch,' she commanded as she twisted out of his gasp and pirouetted across the floor, closer to where Tor was still sitting in the big leather chair. Giving him a cheeky grin, she perched herself across his knees with her own legs spread wide. Fixing her eyes on his face, she reached behind her and undid the catch of her bra. She placed her other hand over the front and gradually slipped each strap in turn off her shoulders and down her arms.

Tor had had his eyes fixed on the dark, wet patch of silk between her open legs. Now, he raised his head and stared expectantly at the arm holding her bra in place. Maggie arched her back, thrust her chest forward and raised her arms above her head. The bra fluttered down on to his lap and her firm breasts bounced free, the nipples already dark and swollen.

Tor grinned appreciatively and stretched his neck out

towards her. She could see the tip of his pink tongue protruding between his lips: soft and wet. She could almost feel its satin caress on her hot, tingling skin. She longed to feel him suck her aching nipples into his mouth. Not yet, though. She wasn't finished teasing them yet.

Pushing her hands against his chest, Maggie leaped nimbly to her feet and twirled across the room with her naked breasts wobbling up and down in front of her. She came to a stop with her back against the door to the hallway and, her lips parted, looked around her. Slowly, she raised one leg and ran her hand teasingly down her bare thigh.

Tor was still sitting forward on the edge of his chair, while Troy was now standing in front of the settee. He still had his hand down the front of his trousers and was shifting restlessly from one foot to the other with his mouth partly open. She glanced down at his crotch and her own eyes widened at the size of the bulge. It looked as if he had stuffed a pair of socks down his front!

Troy's eyes followed her gaze and he gave her a knowing grin that was so suggestive she almost lost her balance.

'What have you stopped for, baby?' he challenged her. 'I was just getting into the beat.'

Maggie grinned. 'Not dressed like that, you weren't. Now it's you with too many clothes on.'

'We can soon fix that.' Troy pulled his hand out of his flies and started to tug his zip open.

'Not so fast. I want to enjoy this,' Maggie said.

Tor chuckled. 'You don't expect us to do the Full Monty for you, do you?'

'You got a problem with that?' Maggie retorted.

The two men exchanged glances and then Tor stood up. 'No problem at all,' he assured her.

Without taking her eyes off them, Maggie glided sensuously across the room and perched herself on the arm of a chair with her legs slightly apart and one hand absent-mindedly playing with her nipples. She put her hand over her mouth to stifle her little gasp as they stood side by side in front of her and then simultaneously spun around, lowered their trousers and raised their gyrating buttocks towards her.

Without breaking their stride, the two men whipped their shirts off and tossed them in the air. Turning in unison, they presented her with two pairs of over-tight briefs, each pair filled to bursting with a flatteringly enthusiastic hard-on. As the current track reached its final crescendo, Tor and Troy grinned and slowly lowered them. Two new dancers, one white, the other almost purple-black, took up the beat, swaying up and down in time with the men's gyrating hips.

It should have been funny. Maggie could feel a giggle building up inside her but, for some reason, her mouth was too dry to make a sound. She felt another tingle of lust between her legs and immediately crossed them, squeezing her tormented sex bud tightly between her thighs.

Without breaking his rhythm, Troy sidled closer and pushed his erection up towards her breasts. Without even thinking about it, Maggie leaned forward and sucked him up into her mouth. She slipped her left hand between his legs and cupped his massive balls in her palm. Slowly, teasingly, she slid him deeper and deeper into her mouth, using her tongue to caress the pronounced ridge of his shiny-smooth glans.

For the first time since they had begun to dance, she sensed Troy falter and lose his synchronisation with the rhythm of the music. With a soft sigh of pleasure, he tightened his buttocks and thrust himself into her, rocking gently back and forth on his heels and savouring the smooth wetness of her mouth and lips.

Out the corner of her eye, Maggie saw Tor edging in closer to her with his eyes riveted on what she was doing to Troy. She reached out and took hold of his cock. As she continued to run her tongue up and down Troy, she started to pump Tor with her eager fingers.

Troy crouched lower on his heels and stretched his arm out towards her until his fingers made contact with the crotch of her sopping wet panties. Unerringly, he homed in on her clit and started masturbating her.

'So, how did you like our dancing?' Tor murmured as he pushed his gigantic penis even harder into her willing fingers.

Even if she had not had her mouth full, Maggie would have been hard-pressed to think of a suitable reply. Her brain seemed to have abandoned her head and settled between her legs. She could think of nothing but the sensation of Troy's knowing fingers tormenting her clit. Her climax was already inevitable. She could feel the little tremors of pleasure running down her legs like electric shocks. The muscles inside her were contracting violently, creating further spasms of delight that seemed to travel all the way up to her nipples.

'Oh yes,' she breathed softly, as a surge of pure ecstasy swiftly engulfed her. She felt another rush of moisture pouring from her to coat Troy's fingers, but was too exhilarated by her climax to feel more than the tiniest twinge of embarrassment for her loss of control.

'Don't stop now,' Troy whispered.

With a start, Maggie realised that her fingers and tongue had both stopped moving. She had been so engrossed in her own gratification she had all but forgotten about them!

Troy pulled himself out of her slack lips and patted her on the top of the head. 'Maybe we should amuse ourselves for a bit and give Maggie time to recover.' His words made it quite clear that he was in no doubt about what they had done to her. Well, it was too late now to feel bashful!

She watched without comment as he took his still rigid

penis in his hand and started to fondle himself. If men only knew how exciting it was for a woman to watch them jerking off. She smiled to herself. Perhaps it was a good job they didn't?

Tor pulled himself back out of her half-hearted grip and begun to wank himself slowly and deliberately. Maggie stared silently from one to the other; she was mesmerised by the sight of them and not surprised to feel the first stirrings of renewed lust between her still-trembling thighs.

'Do you like to watch us wank, baby?' Troy questioned as he moved closer to her and began to fondle her nipples. 'You do, don't you? I can see it in your face.' He moved his hand up and down his shaft even faster. 'Maybe you'd like to watch us wanking each other?'

Her eyes widened as he reached out and grabbed Tor's cock, pushing Tor's own fingers away and then jerking him up and down at the same time as he continued to pump himself.

'That turn you on, eh, babe?'

Maggie nodded silently. She had never seen two men touching each other like that before. She was amazed at how stimulating it was. Her eyes grew even bigger as Tor slipped his hand underneath Troy's buttocks and started to fondle his huge black balls. He pushed his finger round until it was between Troy's solid buttocks and began rhythmically pushing his fingertip into Troy's arse crack. Maggie's eyes bulged.

'You like that, too?' Tor grinned. 'Want to watch me stick it in him? Or, maybe you want me to stick it in you again?' He pulled away from Troy and reached to grab her.

Maggie rose, unresisting, to her feet and allowed him to twist her round and push her stomach down over the arm of the chair. By twisting her head slightly, she could still see Troy pumping himself. Both men's balls seemed to have swollen to twice their previous sizes and the tips of their cocks were already wet and shiny.

She groaned again as she felt Tor forcing his cock between the backs of her thighs, using her own juices to slide back and forth against her skin. In the background, she could still hear the music thumping and pulsating urgently, feeding her passion. She felt a pricking, tingling sensation between her legs and knew that she was close to another climax.

Without warning, Tor pulled back from her and grabbed her firmly round the waist. Lifting her effortlessly, he swung her up high into the air and spun round on his heels, holding her out in front of him. As if this manoeuvre had already been rehearsed, Troy was standing up right in front of her, with his hips spread wide.

Grinning, he reached out and grasped her panties, tugging them down her thighs and over her knees and ankles in one, fluid motion. He tossed the skimpy damp silk over his shoulder and thrust his groin forward invitingly as he spread her thighs apart with his hands.

Tor lifted her even higher, took a couple of steps forward and lowered her gently on to Troy's awaiting cock.

'Oh my God,' she muttered softly, as Troy's manhood delved deeper and deeper inside her warm, welcoming embrace.

As Troy began to thrust firmly in and out, Tor continued to support her from behind. Every time he brought her down on to Troy's shaft, she felt his own hard cock prodding urgently against her buttocks. Maggie shut her eyes and gave herself up completely to the beat of the music and the multiple stimulation of her body.

Troy groaned urgently and pushed himself even deeper into her pliant cunt, and Maggie opened her eyes again just in time to see his face contort, then relax, as his pleasure consumed him. She felt her body slip effortlessly from his still twitching organ as Tor tumbled backwards and collapsed on to the chair. He pulled her sweat-drenched body tight against him and forced his rigid cock up between her slippery wet thighs. Maggie pushed her hand down between her legs, caressing his blood-engorged tip with her fingers while her thumb pushed hard on to her own tingling bud.

His grunt of release was masked by her own urgent cry as they climaxed together. She felt his come splatter powerfully on to her legs to mingle with her own flow of moisture. She whimpered again, a gentle sigh of complete and utter fulfilment, and relaxed her tense body against his hot damp chest. Almost as if on cue, the music came to an end and the sudden silence was only broken by the sound of heavy and irregular breathing, gradually dying away as they recovered.

'Well, I guess we've proved that she can dance,' Tor whispered hoarsely.

They were still laughing when they heard the sound of a car pulling up on the driveway.

'It's Roland,' Tor groaned. 'I recognise the sound of the engine.'

Troy jumped to his feet. 'Oh Lordy.' He rolled his eyes dramatically and flapped his hands around in mock terror. 'Massa Boss gonna whip my black ass if'n he catch me wid mah dick out. Oh Lordy!'

Tor and Maggie both howled with laughter, clutching on to each other helplessly as the tears of mirth trickled down their cheeks. Outside a car door slammed and Maggie began to pull herself together.

'Look, I'd better go. I'll leave the way I came,' she told them. 'I don't think Roland and I have anything to say to each other just now.' As she struggled into her sweaty and crumpled clothing, she couldn't help noticing that the two men were every bit as skilful at dressing quickly as they were at everything else she had seen them do.

* * *

To Sara's great disappointment, it was not Ean but Roland who came into the kitchen while she was stacking the dishwasher that evening. She kept her distance as he congratulated her on the meal and asked her if she was happy or whether there was anything else she needed. Her ears were strained for the slightest sound that would tell her what the others were up to, but the house seemed strangely still and quiet.

'Where is everyone?' she questioned finally.

'I believe they've all gone home,' he informed her. His voice sounded slightly huffy and she knew he was beginning to get the message that she was not interested in him. She started to imagine Ean tucked up alone in his bed, naked under the sheets. If only she were his housekeeper. She imagined herself popping up to his bedroom to see if he needed anything.

'Well, if you're sure you don't want anything, I guess I'll go and do some paperwork. It's a full-time job, just keeping up with the lads' expenses. I'll be in the library if you need me.'

After he had gone, Sara quickly finished her chores and then decided that she would have an early night. As she tiptoed softly past the open library door, she saw Roland huddled over his accounts, sipping a large Scotch. She remembered Maggie's bitchy comments about him and wondered if her friend's accusations could possibly be true. It didn't make sense. Why would Roland bother to have Maggie fired? Perhaps she would give the library a thorough clean tomorrow and tidy up Roland's messy desktop for him. Who knew what she might find?

Chapter Nine

Roland rubbed his weary eyes and ran his finger down the long column of figures. He nodded to himself in satisfaction. As always, he had done a neat job of hiding his tracks. Even someone who was good with figures would have trouble spotting any discrepancies. A bunch of brainless dickheads like the Trojans wouldn't stand a chance. Apart from Troy of course. Roland's eyes narrowed. That one was too clever for his own good. Roland still resented the fact that Maggie preferred Troy to him. Just look where that had got her though! If Troy ever gave him any trouble, he'd get rid of him just as quick. There were plenty of other good hockey players on the market and another transfer deal would help boost his own retirement fund.

Roland opened his personal account book and feasted his greedy eyes on the balance. Even with his heavy gambling losses, he was doing pretty well. If it kept up like this, he was going to be a very rich man before long. Those stupid prats had no idea how much they were raking in from sponsorship this season. He rubbed his hands together, polished off his Scotch and reached for his jacket. He had a little business to take care of at the bank. As he made his way down the hall, he could hear Sara singing to herself in the kitchen while she prepared his lunch.

Roland smiled. He had a little business to take care of there as well. With Maggie out of the way, he needed to turn his attentions elsewhere. It was ages since he'd had a woman. Stupid cow, Maggie. He could have shown her a much better time than Troy or any of the others. Still, one cunt was as good as another and Sara would probably do him just as well.

By the time her doorbell rang that evening, Jan was almost beside herself with nervous anticipation. Thank heavens Marcus was away on business again for a few days. Not that she should allow it to worry her. She was quite certain that he would not be sleeping alone while he was away. One day she would have to confront Marcus about his double standards where her sex life was concerned!

She checked her appearance one more time in the hall mirror, then opened the door.

'Hello Jan.' Tor was holding a huge bunch of flowers out in front of him. They must have cost a fortune. Jan could hardly believe her eyes. No one ever brought flowers on a date any more. It seemed almost ridiculously old-fashioned and totally unexpected.

'They're beautiful. Thank you.'

'Just my way of saying thanks for helping me out.'

Jan took the flowers from him and headed for the kitchen. 'I'll just put them in water.' She was very aware of Tor following along behind her. As she filled a large vase and fussed with the flowers, she could feel his eyes watching her, like a hungry lion ready to pounce.

She couldn't believe how awkward she was feeling. Like a teenager on a first serious date. It was quite ridiculous for someone of her age and experience.

Especially so, considering what had happened the last time they'd been together.

'So, what do you have in mind for us this evening then? I mean, where are we going?' she rephrased her words quickly.

'Well, I don't know this area very well yet but there's this nice little pub I came across, not too far out in the country. I think it's called the Blue Wren. I thought we might go there first, if that's all right with you?' Even his voice sent little shivers of desire coursing through her.

'Yes, I know it. I'll just get my coat.' Jan finally gave up fiddling with the flower arrangement and turned to walk past him into the hallway. Tor watched her silently and she had a feeling that he was tempted to touch her. She contemplated falling into his arms and making it easier for him. However, she knew that once they started neither of them would be able to stop. Well, so what? There was a big double bed in the other room, just waiting for them, and plenty of food and drink in the fridge if they were hungry later.

As she passed him, she looked up into his face and saw the lust smouldering in his eyes. She remembered his urgent desperation for her the last time and how he had lost it almost as soon as she had touched him. The memory caused a surge of fire in her loins. She wanted to do that to him again, wanted to see him squirming with his need for her. There was plenty of time. Why rush? They had the whole evening in front of them.

Jan picked up her coat. 'Ready?' she called.

Tor took the coat from her and held it open. As she shrugged her arms into the sleeves, he ran his hands teasingly over her shoulders. His touch made her feel quite weak at the knees and she was sorry when he let her go to open the front door. Once outside, she was pleased to see that he had borrowed Roland's flashy red sports car. She hadn't fancied the grubby old van she had sometimes seen Tor and a few of the others driving round in.

'Nice of your manager to let you use his car,' she commented as he helped her in.

'Yes. I'm sure he will be only too happy, once he knows how generous he's been,' Tor responded with a cheeky, almost boyish grin.

Tor drove fast but carefully and Jan sank back into the deep leather upholstery and allowed herself to enjoy the speed and comfort. She was both surprised and disappointed that he kept his hands to himself but consoled herself with the fact that his eyes kept darting down on to her thighs in a very flattering way.

The pub was only half full and they soon found a small table for two in a secluded corner. Tor fetched them both a drink and picked up a menu. After a few awkward moments, they both began to relax and chat comfortably about nothing in particular. They sat side by side and the table was small enough for her to be able to feel the slight pressure of his thigh against her own. It was just enough to remind her of what was bound to happen sooner or later. The warm glow she was feeling right through her body had little to do with the alcohol.

They decided to order a cheese and pâté platter for two, washed down with a carafe of red wine. While they were waiting for the food to arrive, they continued to chat aimlessly. She found herself telling him all about her plans to open an estate agents of her own in the near future while in return, he described his life in Canada after his parents had inherited some money and decided to emigrate. Jan learnt that he had always been good at athletics and had originally planned to be a runner, until, that is, Canada introduced him to its favourite sport and he discovered he had a talent for skating.

'Of course, I did think about becoming a Mountie for a while too,' he told her with a twinkle in his eyes, 'but there was a slight problem with that.'

'Why, because you're British?' she questioned.

'No, because I can't ride,' he chuckled. As they both laughed, he casually slipped his arm around her shoulder and she snuggled up against him, enjoying his masculine scent.

'How do you fancy seeing a film after?' he suggested.

After what, Jan thought to herself as her excitement intensified. It had been a long time since any man had made her feel so damned horny as Tor did by simply being there. Her knickers already felt slightly damp and he hadn't so much as kissed her, yet.

'Yes, if you like. I've no idea what's on, though.'

'I do,' Tor assured her. 'Ah, great. Here's the food. I'm famished.'

During the meal, Tor moved his hand under the table and lightly on to her thigh. The action was so casual it almost seemed as if he was unaware that he was even touching her. Jan couldn't have felt more aroused if he had pushed his fingers down inside her knickers. The yearning was so intense, it was almost more than she could bear. She had never felt anything quite like this before.

When he finally removed his fingers in order to pay the bill, her sense of loss was like a physical blow. As she stood up to put her coat on, she found her limbs were trembling. It was as much as she could do just to walk across the room. She took his arm for support.

'Whoa! That wine must have been stronger than I thought,' she muttered as she swayed slightly, and Tor quickly steadied her with an arm around her waist.

The cold night air helped a bit but, as he helped her into the car, the touch of his hands on her skin sent another wave of desire washing over her, leaving her flushed and breathless – almost nauseous with the strength of her longing.

She didn't speak as he started the car and headed back into town. She didn't trust her voice not to betray her emotions. She could feel her heart thumping painfully in her chest and was intensely aware of the ache in the pit of her stomach. She closed her eyes and tried to make herself relax.

'Here we are then.' Tor had stopped the car and she heard the click of his door opening. She opened her eyes and looked out of the windscreen. They were parked in front of the gates of his rented house. Tor was already opening them.

When he climbed back in, she stared at him curiously. 'I thought you said a film?' Was he feeling as wound up as she was? Perhaps he had decided just to skip the film and take her back to his bed. Her desperate longing swept over her again, almost making her gasp.

'The TV and video are already set up and waiting,' he responded as he selected first gear and edged the car through the open gates. 'I thought it would be more fun, just the two of us. If that's OK with you?'

Jan nodded mutely, her mouth suddenly too dry for her to answer.

As soon as he had let them into the house and reset the alarm, Tor took her arm and guided her up the stairs and along the landing. His hand felt as if it were burning her skin through her clothes. Tor pushed a door open with his foot.

'The second largest bedroom with a lovely view of the back garden,' he mimicked her own words. 'Of course, it's a little too dark to appreciate the view now.' He grinned again.

Oh, I don't know about that, Jan thought, as she eyed him up and down. Would he think her too forward if she just started ripping his clothes off him now? Did she care what he thought, just so long as she got her hands on him?

'Make yourself comfortable,' he suggested. 'I'll just put the film on.'

She slipped out of her coat and looked around. The TV

and video were set up on a table at the end of the bed. There was nowhere else to sit. She sat down and swung her legs up on to the springy mattress. Tor was bent over the video and she admired the tightness of his trousers across his buttocks and thighs, longing to tug his trousers off him and sink her teeth into his solid flesh.

'Do you fancy a drink? I've got some champagne on ice in the bathroom.'

'Please,' she responded softly.

Now, that's what I call style, she thought, as he returned from the bathroom with two tall glasses of ice-cold bubbly. He sat down beside her and handed her a glass.

'I hope this is good,' he commented, pushing the video button. 'Troy had it sent to him from somewhere in Europe. He reckons it's terrific.'

Who cares about the film, Jan thought as she sipped her drink and placed the glass on the bedside table. There's only one thing I want to watch right now. She rolled closer to him and put her hand on his chest. As she began to fiddle with his top button, she glanced up at the TV and her fingers stopped moving.

The film had already started. Two muscle-bound men were knelt on the floor, wearing nothing but jock straps. Stretched out between them was a pretty young girl dressed in a skimpy, button-through white dress. Her hands and feet were bound with ropes and she had a blindfold over her eyes. The blond man on her left picked up a piece of velvet ribbon and trailed it softly up her bare legs. The girl writhed her hips and moaned softly.

Tor slipped his arm under her and pulled her closer. Jan rested her head on his chest and tried not to over-react as his fingers stretched round and found the swell of her right breast. She glanced down his body to the bulge of his groin and shivered at her memories of last time.

The girl in the film was moaning louder, her breath

sobbing from her. Jan looked back at the screen and saw that the man with the ribbon had unbuttoned her dress to reveal her tiny breasts. He was trailing the end of the ribbon round one of her nipples, which was already swelling and hardening. The girl arched her back, thrusting her breasts upwards. The man moved the ribbon on to her other nipple and teased it erect too.

Jan sighed gently. She could feel her own nipples rubbing against her bra and she rolled slightly so that Tor's fingers slipped further on to her breast. She felt his fingertip touch her own super-hard nipple and sighed again. A little tremor ran down her chest and stomach, like a small jolt of electricity. Her clit began to tingle expectantly.

The blond man pushed the hem of the girl's dress up, exposing a tiny triangle of white material, hardly big enough to cover her. The camera moved in closer so that they could see a few fluffy wisps of blonde pubic hair poking out each side. The second man had picked up a vibrator. He switched it on and placed it over the white triangle.

The girl's body jerked as if she had been stung by a scorpion. The camera panned back to show her face. She was rolling her head from side to side and groaning urgently. Her lips were slightly parted and the tip of her pink tongue repeatedly licked her ruby lips.

Jan turned her head and glanced up at Tor. He was staring avidly at the TV screen, totally engrossed. She lowered her eyes and examined his groin again. The bulge under his zip was much larger than before, and the sight of it caused another surge of desire to rush through her body. She forced her eyes back to the film.

The second man had slipped the vibrator under the girl's panties and was making small circular motions around her clit. The blond man was still tormenting her breasts with the velvet ribbon.

'Please. Stop. Oh please. I can't. I . . .' The girl was

rolling her whole body from side to side and drumming her heels against the floor. A close-up revealed a few droplets of perspiration trickling down between her breasts. She appeared to be about to climax.

Suddenly, both men stopped and sat up. The darker one switched the vibrator off and put it down. With the camera full on him, he pulled his briefs down and wrapped his hand round his already huge erection. Kneeling up over the girl, he began to pump himself up and down.

'Jesus!' Jan's gasp was out of her mouth before she could stop herself. She had watched plenty of porno films before, but never one with a fully erect cock.

Tor turned his head. 'What's wrong?' he asked.

'Eh. Nothing.' Jan could feel herself perspiring. 'Where did you say this film came from?'

The dark-haired man was still pumping himself enthusiastically while the blond man watched him and fondled his own groin. His other hand was gently caressing the bound and blindfolded girl, who was still trembling. Jan thought it was a good job the girl was blindfolded. If she'd been close to coming before, seeing what was happening now would certainly have set her off.

'Troy sent for it from somewhere. Holland, I think. Are you enjoying it?' His fingers moved gently over her breast again and Jan felt an expanding dampness inside the crotch of her panties. The camera had moved up even closer to the dark man. She could actually see the tip of his cock glistening with his lubrication. His penis looked purple and swollen and his balls were hard and tight with his need. It was difficult to see how he could be faking it. Without breaking his rhythm, he pushed his other hand down inside the girl's panties and started rubbing her.

The girl jumped again and pushed her hips up off the ground, grinding herself on to his palm. Without taking her eyes from the screen, Jan reached down and put her hand over Tor's bulging flies. She heard his breath catch and felt his fingers pushing harder on to her breast. Her own fingers fumbled to open his zip and his trousers parted easily. She slipped her hand into the opening and closed her fingers around his cock.

Tor turned his head and pushed his tongue into her ear. Jan shuddered from head to foot as hot shivers of passion raced through her. On the TV, the dark-haired man ripped the girl's panties down her thighs and leaned forward to run his tongue over her sex lips. The girl cried out and her face and chest flushed red. The man smiled and resumed pumping himself. The other man whipped his own cock out and crouched over the girl's chest, using his hands to push her breasts up around his erection. Tor's cock was hard and urgent in Jan's trembling fingers. His tongue continued to probe her ear and his fingers had somehow found their way under her blouse and bra to torment her nipples.

Jan rolled round against him and pushed herself hard on to his thigh. Just the pressure of his body against her clit was enough to push her over the top. With a long, desperate moan, she climaxed violently, her whole body convulsing from the intensity of it. It was one of the most powerful orgasms she had ever had and it left her weak and trembling as she sucked in ragged breaths, waiting for her head to stop spinning.

'A bit sensitive, aren't we?' Tor whispered mockingly. 'I take it you are enjoying the film?'

Jan could think of no suitable reply. Her hand was still wrapped around his erection, although, lost in her own gratification, she had long ago stopped moving her fingers. Now, as she felt him twitching, she sensed her own strength returning.

She wriggled down his body slightly, undid his trouser button and eased him out. His cock was every bit as rigid and purple as the man's in the film, and twice as big. Jan ran her tongue down his length and smiled at the enthusiastic response. On the TV, the blond man was now sucking and licking the girl's clit, while the dark man had pushed his cock between her lips and was pumping rapidly in and out of her mouth.

Jan licked her fingers and encircled Tor's glans. She started to pump him up and down, gradually building up speed until she felt his body stiffen. Immediately, she stopped pumping and squeezed him firmly. Tor groaned and pushed his hips up against her hand, trying to force her to continue. She moved her hand from top to base, centimetre at a time, then back up just as slowly.

The girl in the film cried out urgently, but neither Jan nor Tor looked up. Jan could feel Tor's whole body shuddering with his need for release. She increased her speed again, relentlessly bringing him back up to the brink.

'Oh Jesus!' Tor's words were faint, desperate. She slowed her hand again, waiting. Suddenly, he twisted out from under her. With all the agility of his profession, he rolled her on to her back and yanked her sodden undies down her thighs. Before she knew what was happening, he was on top of her and she felt the hot tip of his cock begin to enter her.

'Yes!' His cry was a mixture of desperation and triumph as he slid himself in effortlessly. The girl on the TV cried out again and Jan sank back on to the pillow and arched her back to meet Tor's relentless thrusting.

When he finally started to come, she felt herself responding yet again, so that their combined moans drowned the film out completely. Oblivious to the loss of their audience, the two men and the young girl continued to pleasure each other enthusiastically.

Sara's heart was thumping so hard in her chest that she could barely draw breath. She knew that it would be more sensible to wait until Roland was out of the house, but Maggie had been pushing her for days now to help her, and she didn't want her friend to think she didn't have any gumption. Though, just what good Maggie thought it would do, she had no idea. If Roland had been responsible for getting her fired, something Sara was not entirely convinced about, he was hardly likely to leave any evidence lying about the house. What did Maggie expect her to find anyway? A labelled envelope full of the missing ice rink money or a signed confession, perhaps?

Sara turned her head and strained her ears. Roland and a few of the squad were in the main living room with the coach, discussing tactics for their next game. Tor and Pary were both there and they were obviously annoyed about something because they were both shouting angrily. She could hear Roland's honeyed tones trying to soothe them, clearly unsuccessfully. It sounded as though they would be a while yet.

Sara looked around the library thoughtfully, wondering where to start. She eyed the safe door and smiled ruefully. If Roland had hidden the stolen money anywhere, which was extremely unlikely, then that was the most obvious place. Fingers shaking, she pulled the desk draw open and rummaged around for the keys. Her hand found the big black book she had seen him working on most days. On impulse, she pulled it out and opened it.

As Roland had suggested, it was an account book and Sara was flabbergasted by how much money was involved. No wonder Roland lived like a lord, with lavish roast dinners every night and a huge cooked breakfast most mornings. She felt slightly aggrieved when she saw just how much Butterflies were charging for her services. Why, she didn't even see a half of that in her wage packet! At least it helped to explain why Ms Jamison had been looking so pleased with herself lately.

With frequent nervous glances over her shoulder, Sara

continued to work her way down the neat columns of figures. She didn't really have the first idea what she was looking for, of course. Maggie had also hinted that she thought Roland was probably on the fiddle but, if he was, evidence of the fact would hardly be obvious to her inexperienced gaze.

Sara's eyes came to rest on a recent sponsorship entry and her brow crinkled thoughtfully. Although the figure entered was an awful lot of money, it was not anywhere near as much as she had overheard Roland discussing with a smart-looking businessman a couple of evenings previously. She stared at the figures again in bewilderment. She was certain that the man had been the one whose company was responsible for the donation. Why would he and Roland discuss one figure and then Roland enter a much smaller amount in the accounts? It didn't make sense. Perhaps she had misheard, or perhaps the company had had second thoughts about how generous a donation they were prepared to contribute?

The living room door slammed and Sara heard footsteps in the hallway. She shut the book quickly and shoved it back into the drawer. She had hardly closed it, when the library door was flung open and Roland stomped into view.

'Sara? What are you doing in here?' he demanded.

She shook her feather duster in the air in front of her. 'Just a spot of dusting.' She flicked the duster over the top of the telephone on the desk as if to prove her point. 'Actually, I'm just about finished, so if you've got some work you need to be getting on with, I'll leave you to it.' She took a few steps towards the hallway.

Roland put his hand out and caught hold of her arm as she passed him. 'No need to rush off. How about a little drink?'

'Oh, eh, no thank you. It's much too early for me. I really should be getting on with lunch.'

'Do you like working here, Sara? I mean, would you consider making it a more permanent relationship?'

'I, um. Why, yes.' Sara was flustered. As far as she knew, Roland had only hired her services until the end of the current season. It was a much better job than working in the café at the rink. 'If it's all right with the agency, of course.'

'Never mind the agency. It's me you have to please.' Roland's voice was as sweet as syrup, but his eyes looked dark and dangerous. His meaning was quite clear and Sara felt her heart sink. Obviously, she wouldn't be able to stay on if he was going to start adding extra, unwritten, clauses to her contract.

'Well then, I'd better make sure I get your food on the table on time, hadn't I?' she responded brightly, as she shook his hand from her arm and backed away. Head down, she scurried from the room.

'Hey! You look as if you just stepped on something nasty. What's up?' It was Tor's voice. Sara had only just stopped herself from walking headlong into him.

'Oh, excuse me. I was miles away.' She said and gazed up into his rugged face. She wondered how it was possible to find one man so repugnant and another so attractive that it made her weak at the knees.

'Roland's in a bad mood, is he? Sorry about that. It's probably my fault. We were just arguing about our next match. Don't worry. His bark's worse than his bite.'

Sara smiled at the image, thinking how apt it was. Roland reminded her exactly of a great slobbering Rottweiler.

'Lunch won't be long,' she told Tor breathlessly. 'I hope you and the others will be staying?' She felt a rush of excitement when she saw the ravenous look on his face. Of course, he was thinking about her cooking not her body – but a girl was allowed to dream, wasn't she?

* * *

As soon as she had cleared the lunch things away, Sara phoned Maggie and arranged to meet her at their usual coffee house. She slipped out without anyone noticing.

Maggie was already waiting impatiently outside when Sara arrived. As soon as they had found a table and fetched some drinks, Sara told her friend what she had discovered.

Maggie's eyes glittered triumphantly. 'Your see! I told you the bastard wasn't to be trusted, didn't I?' she exclaimed excitedly.

Sara looked dubious. 'I still don't see that it proves anything. It's more likely that I just misheard the sum involved or he made a mistake.' Sara took a quick sip of her coffee and glanced around the almost-deserted coffee house.

Maggie shook her head impatiently. 'More likely he pretends to receive one amount, the amount he puts in the accounts, and then just keeps the rest for himself,' she suggested.

'It's taking one hell of a risk. It would be so easy for someone to catch him out. If I heard the sum involved, you can be sure others would, too,' Sara argued.

Maggie grunted angrily. 'Well, hell, I don't know. Maybe he's got two sets of books. The one he shows the squad and the taxman and the one he lines his own pocket from.'

Sara continued to look unconvinced. The conversation was giving her a bit of a headache. She decided that she wouldn't make a good private eye. All this creeping around and speculating was far too confusing.

'What else did you notice?' Maggie demanded.

'Well, nothing really. I didn't have much time and, anyway, I don't really know what I'm looking for.' Sara tried to imagine just what Maggie hoped to get out of all this. Roland was a low-life, certainly. She was finding that out all too well for herself. But, even if he was dishonest in his dealings with the Trojans, why would he have had Maggie fired from the rink? It was all too much for her. She didn't really want anything to do with it, yet she could clearly see how much her friend was hurting and she desperately wanted to help.

'I'll have to get back,' she excused herself. 'I've still got a lot of work to do.'

After Sara had left, Maggie continued to sit on her own, lost in thought. If Sara could just find a second account book she might have the proof that she needed to nail Roland. Without it, she was certain that the Trojans would not believe her. Troy had already more or less laughed at her suggestion that Roland was responsible for the missing money, assuring her that their manager was too stupid to try and get one over on anyone.

She thumped the table angrily. It just wasn't fair. She knew that Roland had been responsible for having her sacked. He had more or less told her he would. So far, she had had no luck in finding herself another suitable job, and money was already becoming tight. Besides, if she didn't clear her name, everyone would always half-believe that she was a thief. She had to prove her innocence to Justin. Not that she would ever have anything to do with him again after he had treated her so badly, but she had to prove him wrong.

'Well, well. Hello Maggie. How are you? No, don't get up.' Roland's voice broke into her thoughts and caused her to jump visibly.

'What are you doing here?' Maggie could feel her temper rising. After what he had done to her, where did he get the gall to come over to her now, all crocodile smiles? She was sorely tempted to punch him on his smug nose. Had he seen her talking with Sara? Maybe his guilty conscience was getting the better of him. Not about her, of course, but perhaps he was worried about what Sara might know – or find out.

'I was just passing when I saw you sitting here, all

alone,' he replied cheerfully. 'I wondered how you were getting on. I was sorry to hear you had lost your job. Complete nonsense, of course. I'm sure you would never do anything dishonest. I told Justin as much.'

Maggie swallowed. His concern was so blatantly insincere as to be sickening. She knew he had to be responsible for getting her fired, no matter what he said now. She was about to get up and walk off, when it occurred to her that this might be the opportunity she was looking for. If she lulled him into a sense of false security, maybe she could trap him into inadvertently saying something incriminating.

'Would you like some coffee?' she asked him politely.

'No thanks.' Roland shook his head and perched his ample backside on the chair opposite her. 'I've just had some.' He bared his large teeth at her and Maggie immediately understood how Little Red Riding Hood must have felt. She tried to suppress a shudder of revulsion.

'I really wish that there was something I could do to help you,' he told her. 'If I had any jobs going, but well, money is a bit tight at the moment.'

Maggie snorted. 'With all the sponsorship money you've been raking in? I find that hard to believe.'

Roland suddenly looked wary. 'I don't know where you got that idea from. Sponsorship money is extremely difficult to acquire and, with so many expenses, it really doesn't go very far,' he told her.

'No. I would imagine your XK8 put quite a dent in the coffers,' Maggie retorted sharply, before she could stop herself.

Roland frowned. 'I don't know what you're implying. My personal expenditure has got nothing to do with the squad's sponsorship money.' He pulled a grubby handkerchief out of his top pocket and mopped his brow.

'If you say so.' Maggie's tone made it quite clear that she did not believe him.

Roland's eyes narrowed and his mouth became a hard line. He stood up abruptly. 'Considering your own situation, young woman, I wouldn't have thought that you were in any position to start making insinuations about other people. You're lucky Justin didn't hand you over to the police.'

'Yes. I'm surprised you didn't arrange that, too,' Maggie replied. 'Or, perhaps you were reluctant to have them poking around the rink, in case they uncovered more than was to your own best interests.' As soon as the words were out of her mouth, Maggie wanted to bite her tongue off. The last thing she wanted to do was to warn Roland what she suspected. Why the hell had she allowed him to provoke her so easily?

'I think this conversation's gone quite far enough,' he snapped. His eyes flashed dangerously. 'I would advise you not to interfere with things that have nothing to do with you, my dear, or . . .' He stopped.

'Or what?' She hoped that he couldn't hear the tremble in her voice.

'I don't let anything come between me and business, Ms Lomax. Or anyone. You would do well to remember that if you know what's good for you.'

'Is that a threat?'

'I never make threats my dear. At least, not idle ones.'

Maggie stood up shakily.

'Nice to have talked with you.' He held out his hand. She ignored it and he grinned. 'I'm sure we understand each other better now.' He turned on his heel and strode away without looking back.

At least she knew that she was right now, anyway. Her rash comments had certainly found their mark. Had he really been threatening her? Surely not? What more could he possibly do? He'd already had her fired. He'd just been hoping to scare her off. Well, it took more than a fat pig like him to stop her, once she had made her mind up about something. She would have to get in touch with Sara again and push her a bit harder. One way or another, she was going to fix Roland Rat for good.

Chapter Ten

Maggie uttered profanities under her breath as she tried to ease her car out from in between two others that had thoughtlessly been parked much too close to hers. She and Jan had spent all evening talking over her job situation without getting anywhere, and Maggie was tired and grumpy. All she wanted to do was to get home to bed. As she pulled away, she was dazzled by a set of high beams from behind, reflected in her mirror.

'Sodding idiot!' Maggie flicked the rear-view mirror up to protect her eyes. The road was empty and she pulled out quickly, turning left towards home. Glancing in her wing mirror, Maggie saw the other car pull out behind her, driving much too close. Its headlights were still blazing, making it impossible to tell what make or colour it was. She increased the pressure on the accelerator, attempting to pull away. Reaching the end of the road, she slowed down and indicated right.

The other car was so close behind her that she could almost sense its presence, like when someone stands too close behind you, breathing down your neck and encroaching on your personal space. Thankfully, there was nothing coming and she pulled out too quickly, feeling the rear wheels slide as she fought to keep the turn under control. Her unwelcome shadow followed, riding her boot.

'That's it!' Maggie's temper snapped. She could feel herself shaking with a mixture of anger and fear and her heart was thumping erratically inside her ribcage. Flicking the left indicator on, she slammed her feet down on the brake and clutch and spun the steeringwheel towards the kerb. As she came to a stop, she heard a squeal of brakes and then the roar of an engine as the driver behind her shifted down.

The car shot past her so close that she half-expected her wing mirror to be ripped off. Staring wide-eyed through the side window, she caught a brief glimpse of the silhouettes of two large, well-built figures in the front of the big black car. With its boot level with her bonnet, the car slowed and stopped. She could see the two figures in the front twisted around to stare back at her. They seemed to be arguing and gesturing towards her.

Really frightened now, Maggie shoved her foot on the clutch and rammed the gearstick into reverse. Before she could move, the other car's engine revved loudly and it shot off into the night with its tyres screaming. Taking the next left, it disappeared from sight.

Trembling so much that she could barely control her limbs, Maggie put the car into first and moved off warily. As she passed the left-hand turn, her heart was in her mouth and her foot was poised over the accelerator, ready to make a sudden dash if the other car should be lying in wait. The road was completely deserted. She laughed shakily.

By the time she reached her flat, Maggie had almost got herself under control. After all, it had probably only been a couple of joyriders messing about. She parked her car and hurried inside. After throwing her jacket over the back of the settee, she kicked her shoes off and curled up wearily in her favourite chair with a book. Although she had been so tired earlier, suddenly, she didn't feel like sleeping at all.

Two days later, Maggie was on her way round to Jan's again. It was late afternoon and she had had a very bad day. All three interviews she'd attended that day had been a complete waste of time and she was beginning to think that she was never going to get another job.

If only she could bring herself to ask Justin for a reference. She was fairly certain that he would give her one, no matter what he suspected her of, but she just couldn't swallow her pride. She had been surprised at just how much his lack of trust in her had hurt, no matter how much Roland had twisted his arm. She hadn't realised that she cared that much.

As she pulled out, she glanced in her mirror and saw what looked like the strange black car behind her again. She felt her stomach churn. If it was the same car, then it couldn't possibly be just be joyriders, could it? Roland's threatening words popped unbidden into her mind: 'Don't interfere with things that have nothing to do with you or . . .'

Maggie tried to grin. It certainly wasn't Roland following her. She would recognise his portly build and flashy red car anywhere. But who was it who had been trying to call her yesterday evening? Twice, when she had answered the phone, no one had been on the other end. Honestly! Talk about an overactive imagination. There must be dozens of big black cars like this one, and wrong numbers were not that uncommon.

Maggie turned left towards Jan's house. She tried not to notice that the car was still behind her. If it was someone pissing about, she refused to play any more of their silly games. As she took another left turn, the car suddenly sped up and overtook her. She saw that it was a Ford Cosworth. As before, two shadowy figures lurked inside but they could have been anyone.

Her foot lifted slightly from the accelerator and she realised that she was still half-expecting the car to skid in front of her and block the road, like on TV police chases. The Cosworth continued to accelerate away from her at high speed and she smiled with a mixture of relief and disappointment as it disappeared from view. In a strange kind of way there had been something exciting, almost stimulating, about imagining she was being chased.

Maggie slowed and turned right into Peacock Lane. A man was crouching at the side of the road and she instinctively pulled out to avoid him. As she drew closer to him, she could see that he was fiddling with what looked like a reel of wire fence. Seemingly oblivious to her approach, the man stood up and threw something across the road. Maggie had no chance of stopping.

'Stupid bloody idiot,' she exclaimed angrily as she heard a peculiar rattle under the wheels. She slowed to turn left and glanced back at the man. He was already picking up whatever he had thrown. What kind of nut was he?

As she began to turn the steering wheel, Maggie felt the back of the car drift from under her. She fought the wheel, struggling to correct the skid. The vehicle was behaving like a bucking bronco. She had practically no control of it at all. Damn it to hell, she must have picked up a puncture. Cursing loudly, she managed to guide the car into the grass verge and come to a stop. Fortunately, it was less than a mile to Jan's place if she were forced to walk.

'Of all the stupid, idiotic morons!' She was trembling with both rage and fright as she got out and stared at the now very flat tyres. She might have been killed. She moved round to the near side. All four tyres were ruined.

As she turned her head, she saw the man hurrying towards her with whatever he had thrown tucked under his arm. So he should come over to apologise. Bloody fool. For the first time, it dawned on her that it might not have been an accident. The man had deliberately thrown that wire fence thing out in front of her. Didn't the police use some sort of spiked tyre-mat to stop joyriders? Her heart did a complete somersault. Were the police after her? Christ Almighty, perhaps the rink were going to bring charges against her after all!

'Get a grip on yourself, girl,' she muttered under her breath. Her alleged crime wouldn't warrant this kind of response, would it? The man was rapidly drawing closer and suddenly she was quite certain that he was not a policeman. She grabbed her bag and started to run down the road towards Jan's house. A quick glance over her shoulder confirmed her fears. The man was running in pursuit. She ran faster. If she could just get round the next corner there was a footpath that cut straight through some waste ground to Jan's road.

Running flat out, she reached the corner and glanced back. He was being left behind. If that was the best he could manage, she could easily outrun him. She rounded the corner and raced for the safety of the footpath. Soon, she would be out of sight altogether.

As she scrambled over the style, her skirt caught on a rusty nail and she heard the sound of it tearing. Yanking herself free, she lost her balance and tumbled awkwardly, winding herself. Before she could move, two hands grasped her round the waist and helped her to her feet. Maggie screamed.

'Are you all right?'

She peered up anxiously at the man. He was dressed in jogging pants, jacket and trainers. His hood was pulled up so that she could not see his face properly. 'Sorry,' she blurted. 'You made me jump.'

Out the corner of her eye, she saw her pursuer round the corner and start down the pathway. She grabbed the jogger by the arm. 'Please help me.' She pointed back down the path. 'That man is following me.' She gripped his arm tightly and tried to move round behind him.

As her pursuer reached the style and started to climb over it, Maggie felt the jogger flex his biceps. He was very well built. Very attractive in a rugged kind of way. She felt a wave of relief wash over her at the realisation that she was going to be all right.

The jogger smiled. 'It's OK,' he assured her. 'I'll take care of you. We wouldn't want anything to happen to you would we, Maggie?' He shook off her hand and took hold of her arm.

The blood in her veins turned to ice. She stared back at the original pursuer and saw that he had pulled a balaclava on over his head. He continued to advance slowly but surely. His eyes were two dark holes filled with menace.

Stupid bitch! She had run straight into their trap. A small whimper of fear and despair burst from her lips as she swivelled her head round, desperately seeking a way out. Back on the road, someone might have driven past; here, there was no one to help her.

Maggie shrank away from the jogger, tugging her arm to free herself. He gripped her harder and twisted her round so that her arm was pinned behind her back. Another sob welled up inside her.

'You've been sticking your nose in where it isn't wanted, Maggie.' She heard the man wearing the balaclava speak for the first time. His voice was as cold and menacing as his eyes.

'I don't know what you mean. Let me go.' Maggie had deliberately relaxed her body, hoping to catch the jogger off-guard. Now she used all her strength to try to break free. She almost succeeded. Blindly, she kicked out at his knee but he sidestepped her easily and increased the pressure on her arm. Her eyes began to water with the pain.

'Ow! Stop it. You're hurting me.' She was forced to lean over to find some relief. Drawing her stomach in, she pushed back as hard as she could. Her buttocks smashed into the jogger's crotch but he barely seemed to notice.

'Now, behave yourself Maggie. We're just here to give you a message. A warning.' He stressed the word. 'It's nothing personal. Just a job.' He relaxed his grip enough for her to stand up straight once more.

'Normally, we'd just break a leg or an arm. Nothing too serious.' He looked around at the woods and fields thoughtfully. 'If anything like that happened to you here, it might be some time before anyone found you. That would be a pity.'

'A great pity,' the man in the balaclava agreed softly. His words seemed more gentle and Maggie felt a glimmer of hope. She was determined not to let them see how scared she was.

'OK. So you're not going to break my legs,' she responded stiffly. 'You've done your job. You've ruined my tyres and I've got your message. From now on, I'll mind my own business.'

They had to have been sent by Roland. Although she could hardly believe he would dare pull a stunt like this, at least it proved she was right about him.

'There. I knew you would be sensible about this. I could tell as soon as I saw you.' The jogger squeezed her wrist.

'Oh yes. Very sensible,' she agreed. 'Feet always firmly on the ground.' Her attempt at bravado sounded rather lame, even to her.

'Well that's good,' he replied. 'But, the thing is, we have to make sure that you understand. I mean, it's all very well saying it now, but what about later? What about once you've had a chance to think it over and get all sure of yourself again?' The jogger tugged on her arm and she stumbled. Immediately she lashed out at him again with her left foot. Again, she missed.

'See what I mean, Maggie? No, you are going to have

to be taught a lesson.' He twisted her arm savagely and Maggie cried out in pain as again she doubled over.

'If that kick had found its mark, I would do more than hurt you. I'd break your fucking legs.'

She knew that he meant it. As he eased the pressure and let her straighten, she could feel her eyes brimming with tears.

'It would be a pity to break such lovely legs.' The man in the balaclava stepped closer and reached down to run his hand up under her skirt and on to the tops of her stockings. Why the hell hadn't she worn her old jeans? Maggie gritted her teeth as his other hand began to explore the curve of her buttocks.

'We have ourselves one very sexy lady here,' the man informed his colleague. Maggie flinched as his fingers ran across the tops of her thighs. She tried to wriggle out of his reach but that just seemed to encourage him. She stood perfectly still and feigned disinterest.

They wouldn't dare do anything bad to her. Not really bad. Roland might be a creep but it wasn't as if he were a real hardened criminal. No, they were just going to scare her a bit, then let her go. Of course, there would be no way to tie any of this to him.

'Why don't you let us have a look at your tits? Have you got nice tits, Maggie?'

Maggie hated the way they both kept using her name. Like they owned her or something. She felt the jogger release her arm and wrap himself around her. His hands cupped her breasts.

'They feel good to me.' He flipped open one of her buttons and pushed his fingers inside her bra. His hand felt icy cold against her skin. She heard a rip as his other hand tore the next two buttons free. His fingers pinched her left nipple and she squealed.

'Bastard!' She felt him pinch harder in response and she bit her lip to stop herself saying anything else. Goose bumps sprang up all over her body and she could feel her legs trembling with conflicting emotions.

'Very nice.' His words galvanised her into action. She was tired of being treated like a piece of meat and angry with herself for responding to their caresses. She twisted out of his grasp, raised her hand and slapped his face with all the force she could muster. Her hand started to throb.

Caught off-balance, the jogger stumbled backwards. Not waiting to see what the other man was doing, Maggie started to run. Before she had gone three paces, she felt a sharp tug on her skirt and she stumbled on to her knees. There was another tug at her skirt and it ripped up one side to the belt. She felt herself being lifted up and pushed and pulled back and forth between the two of them as they toyed with her, like a couple of cats playing with a captive mouse. Her head began to spin.

'Stop it. Please stop it,' she begged. Her blouse was gaping open and her skirt was hanging in tatters. They were laughing at her and she hated it. She had to get away before it was too late.

The jogger grabbed her by the neck, pressing her head down, then dragged her across the grassy path. She twisted and turned, scratching and kicking. Her feet flailed out in all directions, seeking a target. The man with the balaclava crouched down in front of her, just out of reach, and spoke in a calm but threatening voice.

'The more you fight us, the more fun we're having,' he said. Maggie saw him reach into his pocket and pull something out. The click the blade made as it opened sent a cold chill right through her. She held her breath and stood completely still as he put his hand on her stomach and pushed her down to the ground.

'Lie still or I'll cut you.'

His words terrified her. All her remaining courage evaporated. She stared helplessly up at the shiny blade, too scared even to blink.

'Please. Just let me go,' Maggie whimpered.

He ignored her and continued waving the knife around, making jabbing gestures at her but stopping short of actually touching her.

Maggie couldn't take her eyes off the blade as its owner smiled at her fear.

'Now keep very still. I don't want to slip and have an accident.' He rubbed the blunt edge of the knife across her throat.

Maggie shook her head wordlessly. She was shivering with fear and her mouth was too dry to speak. She tried to plead with her eyes.

The pressure of the knife disappeared and Maggie heard the blade snap shut. The relief was so great she almost wet herself. The breath whooshed out of her tortured lungs and she began to gasp. Tears pooled in the corners of her eyes and dribbled down her cheeks as she lay there, horrified at what might happen next.

The jogger reached down and patted her shoulder. 'Do you think she's got the message now?' he questioned his companion.

'I'm not sure.' The other man took her hands and tugged her to her feet. 'Look me in the eyes, Maggie.'

Maggie didn't move. She stood in front of him with her head lowered.

'Now!'

Her head jerked up as if it were on strings. She watched his eyes devouring her naked body.

'You've got a very nice body, Maggie. Haven't you?'

She said nothing.

'Haven't you!'

She flinched. 'Yes,' she mumbled.

'You wouldn't want it to be scarred now, would you? You wouldn't want us to leave you so no man would ever want you again?'

She shook her head.

'Good. Then get up. Now.'

'I'll get the car,' the man in the balaclava muttered. He headed back towards the road.

'Come on, Maggie.' The jogger took her arm and Maggie found herself being dragged along beside him. 'Please let me go.' Whatever happened, she knew she mustn't dare get in the car with them. As they reached the style, she saw the car pull up and the other man begin to reverse it towards them.

'Look. You've got what you wanted. I'm scared. I'll forget everything that happened. I won't tell anyone. Just let me go,' she wailed.

'Shut up.' The jogger reached the car and opened the boot. He picked up a strand of rope and quickly tied her hands together. He reached back into the boot and picked up a black hood. Before she could react, he shoved it down over her head. She screamed.

'I told you to shut up.'

She felt herself being lifted into the air then dumped down on her back. There was a loud thud as the boot closed, trapping her inside.

Maggie tugged frantically at the ropes on her hands. She was sobbing uncontrollably. Jesus Christ. What were they going to do with her? 'Please God, don't let them kill me,' she whispered. She screamed again as she felt the car moving off. Where were they taking her?

A few minutes later, the car stopped again. She heard the doors slamming and then felt the cold evening breeze on her naked flesh as the boot opened. Hands lifted her up and she started kicking with her feet. She opened her mouth to scream but her throat was so dry with terror that she couldn't utter a sound.

'Remember, Maggie. Keep your nose out of things that don't concern you in future. We won't be so nice next time.' The disembodied words petrified her. She felt herself falling and something sharp grazed across her leg. The car doors slammed and the engine revved up. They pulled away with a squeal of tyres and a handful of gravel flew up and stung her bare skin. Everything grew silent.

Mustering all her remaining strength, Maggie struggled with the rope. The knot was not very tight and, after a few minutes, she managed to work her wrists free. She pulled the hood off her face and blinked as she stared around. She was lying in a ditch at the side of another lane and it didn't take her long to recognise where she was. She was only a couple of miles from where she had been attacked. If she remembered correctly, there was a telephone box at the far end of the lane. No more than half a mile.

Maggie glanced down at herself. She was dressed only in the remaining tatters of her skirt and her stockings. The stockings had not even laddered. A bubble of hysterical laughter escaped from her lips at this thought. She had to do something. She couldn't just lie semi-naked in a ditch forever.

It was a quiet lane with few houses and very little traffic. Maggie scrambled up the grassy bank and hurried along the lane as fast as her stockinged feet could carry her. After twenty yards or so, she broke into a kind of desperate jog. She felt terribly vulnerable and very scared. When she heard the sound of a car coming, she leaped into the ditch and huddled behind a small bush. What if it was the two men coming back for her? She held her breath, willing the car not to stop. She couldn't face anyone. Another small sob welled up inside her. Her whole body was shaking with the reaction to her ordeal, and the cold evening breeze chilled her right through.

The car passed without slowing and Maggie slipped out of the ditch and resumed her desperate dash for safety. The phone box was already in sight when she heard another car approaching. Maggie dived back into the ditch and ducked her head. She was panting hard and tears of fear and humiliation trickled down her pale cheeks. She just couldn't bear the idea of anyone seeing her like this.

Oh God! If only she had never got involved with the Trojans, or their sleazy manager. She didn't want anything more to do with any of them. From now on, she would forget all about ice hockey and just get on with her own life. Roland could do what he liked.

As soon as the car engine faded away, Maggie stood up and stared nervously at the phone box. It was so exposed, especially now that the daylight was fading and a light had come on inside. Still, what other choice did she have? Glancing all around her, she dashed for the phone box, picked up the receiver and dialled the operator.

While she waited for the operator to call Jan's number, Maggie huddled herself up as small as possible, tugging the tatters of her skirt around her and putting her arm protectively over her breasts. She continually scanned as far as she could see, and her ears strained for the slightest sound. She would just die if anyone found her in this state. As soon as she heard the operator ask if Jan would accept the charges, she started sobbing down the phone, begging Jan to take it.

'Yes. I'll take the call.' Jan's calm, sensible voice was like a lifeline. 'Maggie? Is that you? What's wrong? Are you all right?'

'Jan, please help me.' Her voice was no more than a feeble squeak.

'Where are you? Are you OK?'

'I'm in the phone box by the fields on Market Road. I need you to come and get me. Please hurry.' Maggie's nerve broke. She slammed the receiver down and scurried out to the comparative safety of the ditch. She crouched down behind a bush and rubbed her arms with her hands to try and keep warm. She would be all right soon.

Jan arrived about ten minutes later. She parked her car by the phone box and opened the door to climb out. 'Maggie? It's me. Jan. Where are you?'

Maggie started to sob with relief when she saw her friend. She stood up and scrambled up out of the ditch.

'Oh my God, Maggie. What's happened?' Jan took her coat off and wrapped it around Maggie's quivering shoulders. She helped Maggie over and into the car, then ran round to the driver's side. She started the engine and turned the heater up full.

'It won't take long to warm up,' she promised reassuringly, as she put the car into gear and headed for home.

Maggie huddled down in the seat. Now that she was safe, her last resolve disappeared and she could only sob helplessly as she tugged the coat around her nakedness. Thankfully, Jan didn't push her to tell her what had happened. She couldn't find the words to explain anything just yet.

By the time they arrived at Jan's house, Maggie had almost managed to stop crying. Jan helped her inside and steered her in front of the gas fire in the living room. Tiny sobs still wracked her body as she crouched in front of the welcoming warmth. Jan's coat slipped from her shoulders and fell to the floor.

'Here. Drink this.' Jan thrust a large glass of brandy in to her hands. Shakily, Maggie raised it to her lips and gulped the fiery liquid down. She gasped and started to cough, then drained the remaining drops. For the first time, she noticed that Jan was dressed only in a skimpy slip.

Jan followed her gaze. 'I was about to take a bath when you called,' she explained. 'I just grabbed my coat and keys and came running.' Her eyes anxiously scanned Maggie's semi-naked body.

'Are you hurt, Maggie? You have to tell me what's happened. Have you been raped? Do you want me to call the police or send for a doctor?'

Maggie shook her head, feeling stronger as the heat of the fire and the warmth of the brandy took effect. She was safe now. She sank down on to a nearby chair.

Jan knelt beside her and slipped her arm around Maggie's shoulders. 'Do you feel like telling me what happened?'

Maggie shuddered as she remembered lying in the boot of the car, wondering if they were going to kill her. Another small sob fell from her lips.

'OK. Never mind. Let's at least get you cleaned up.' Jan took Maggie's hand and led her unresisting upstairs to the bathroom. Passively, Maggie allowed Jan to peel her stockings and the remaining threads of her skirt from her trembling body. Jan topped up the now cooling bath water and motioned for Maggie to climb in. Gently, she soaped and rinsed her friend all over, before helping her out and drying her with a large fluffy towel. The remaining chill gradually left Maggie's body, and she was able to raise a feeble smile as Jan helped her into a warm dressing gown. The two women went back downstairs in front of the fire and Jan poured them both another brandy. She gave Maggie another small hug.

'Now can you tell me what happened?'

Maggie stared at her in silence for a few seconds, then looked round the room. 'Where's Marcus?' she whispered.

'Don't worry. He's not here. He won't be back until tomorrow at the earliest. It's just us two girls.' Jan pulled Maggie's head down on to her breasts and gently stroked her tousled hair. 'It's OK. You're safe now.'

At last, Maggie started to speak. As the words gradually tumbled out of her, the tears began to trickle down her cheeks.

Jan listened in silence until Maggie had finished speaking.

'You're certain it was Roland who arranged it?'

Maggie shrugged. 'Yes. I'm quite sure. But I can't prove it.'

Jan frowned. 'You're not going to let him get away with it are you?'

Maggie stared at her in surprise. 'Well, what do you expect me to do?'

Jan shook her head. 'I don't know yet, but if that bastard thinks he can do this to my best friend and get away with it, he's in for a nasty shock.'

Maggie had never heard Jan sound so angry or so determined. It made her feel strong and safe. 'I guess you're right. I don't see what I can do, though.' Another little tremor shook her body.

Jan stared at her. 'This can wait for now. You look completely done in. You'd better stay here tonight. I know it's a bit early, but you've had a bad scare and you could do with some sleep.'

'I don't want to be alone, Jan.'

'You'll be fine. I'll set the alarm and double check all the locks. Besides, I could do with an early night myself.'

Upstairs, Maggie quickly donned one of Jan's nighties and then snuggled down gratefully in Jan's big double bed. Jan stripped off and climbed in beside her. She pulled her close and Maggie snuggled up against the warmth and comfort of her friend's body. She could feel Jan's arm around her waist and her hand resting just under her breasts.

Maggie closed her eyes and tried not to think about what had happened, but it was impossible. At least she had not been the complete victim. Nevertheless, the whole ordeal was unforgivable. How dare Roland arrange to have her treated like that! Christ Almighty! She had been abducted, manhandled, threatened at knifepoint and dumped in a ditch. She might have been seriously hurt, even killed. How could she even think about letting him get away with it? Jan was right. Roland had to be taught a lesson. What was it that he was so scared of her finding out, anyway?

Of course, it was easy to think like this now that she was lying safe and warm in Jan's arms. Maggie relaxed her body, pulling Jan's arm tighter around her. As she drifted towards sleep, she realised that Jan's hand was now covering her breast. She remembered the feel of Jan's hands soaping her body. She could feel her fingers gently teasing her nipple. Her touch felt very good. Warm and comforting.

Chapter Eleven

Maggie opened her eyes and gazed around in confusion, trying to remember where she was. As the events of the previous evening flooded back, she felt another rush of fear for what might have happened. A small whimper fell from her lips.

'Maggie? What is it? Are you all right?'

She turned her head and found herself staring into Jan's concerned eyes. She forced a feeble smile. 'Hello. Yes, I'm all right.'

Jan sat up and wiped the sleep from the corners of her eyes. She yawned widely and glanced around her. 'What time is it? Did you sleep OK?'

Maggie nodded. 'Yes, thanks. I must have gone out like a light. Brandy always has that effect on me.' She hesitated, uncertain what else to say. Her thoughts were so jumbled and confused. Her last memory was of her own hand on Jan's breast and of feeling safe and protected. She remembered thinking that touching Jan that way seemed right and natural, something she had wanted to do for a long time. Had Jan noticed or realised what she was thinking? She felt a faint flush of colour to her cheeks.

'It's only seven-thirty.' Jan had finally found her glasses and was peering through them at the bedside clock. 'There's no need for us to get up just yet. Do you fancy a cuppa?'

Maggie nodded. 'Yes please. I'd love one.' She watched without further comment as Jan climbed out of the bed and walked across the room to pick up her dressing gown. Her short nightie had ridden up over her thighs, exposing the swell of her buttocks, and Maggie found herself wondering what it would be like to run her fingers over all that soft, smooth flesh. She felt a tingle of excitement in her loins that both embarrassed and excited her.

Jan slipped her gown round her shoulders and padded silently out of the room to make the tea. Maggie pulled the duvet back and scurried across the room towards the bathroom. She rinsed her face and used her finger to brush round her teeth before gargling with mouthwash to freshen her breath. Her hair was still tangled and she ran a comb through it, surprised and pleased at how well she looked and felt, considering what she had been through. She must have slept like a top. She took a quick pee and was surprised to find that relieving the pressure on her bladder did little to ease the insistent tingling between her thighs. Hearing Jan's footsteps returning up the stairs, she dashed back into the bedroom and propped herself up in bed with a pillow.

Jan came back into the room, carrying a tray. 'Tea and toast in bed,' she announced with a smile. Maggie grinned.

'I feel like royalty,' she laughed. 'I can't remember the last time I had breakfast in bed. Probably not since I left home.'

Jan placed the tray over Maggie's knees, then pulled her dressing gown off and moved round to slip under the duvet beside her.

'No more than you deserve after what you've been though,' she commented.

Maggie grimaced, then forced another smile. 'Oh, it wasn't all that bad,' she protested, trying not to remember how terrified she had felt when she had been trussed up in the boot of the car. 'You should see the other guys,' she laughed flippantly.

Jan gave her a hard stare, then reached for the tray. She lifted it up on to the bedside table, then turned back and slipped her arm round her friend's shoulders. 'Poor love. You've had a pretty bad time of it lately, one way and the other, haven't you,' she murmured softly, as she pulled Maggie into her comforting embrace.

Maggie gulped back the ready tears and snuggled gratefully against her friend, so that her head was resting on Jan's soft breasts. She closed her eyes and tried to relax. Jan's hair brushed against her face; it felt soft and gentle and smelt fresh and clean, like a summer's day. Maggie felt a little tremor of excitement run down her spine. Tentatively, she lifted her hand and brushed her fingertips lightly over Jan's breast.

Jan flinched but didn't pull away. Maggie peered anxiously up into her friend's face. 'You, you don't mind, do you?' she whispered huskily.

Jan shook her head. 'No, I don't mind at all,' she responded softly.

Maggie smiled. 'You've got lovely breasts,' she murmured as her hand resumed its slow exploration of Jan's body. 'I want to . . .'

'Yes? Want to what?' Jan asked.

'I want to run my tongue over them,' Maggie admitted.

Jan wriggled out from under her and drew back the duvet. Slowly, she raised her arms and tugged her nightie off over her head. Her naked breasts fell free in front of her, bouncing delightfully. Maggie sighed with pleasure and bent her head forward. Slowly, she ran the tip of her tongue down Jan's shoulder and on to her left breast. As her lips gently caressed the nipple, she felt it harden in response and heard Jan's quiet sigh. Her stomach flipped and her own nipples began to stiffen.

'Oh yes,' Jan breathed. 'That feels so good.' She arched her back, pushing her breast up harder on to Maggie's lips. Maggie sucked the rigid nipple into her mouth and circled it with her tongue. Jan sighed again and Maggie felt another powerful surge of lust between her thighs. Impatiently, she sat up and pulled her own nightie over her head. Her own breasts were already aching with her passion and her nipples were hard, dark buds. She gasped with delight as she felt Jan's silky smooth tongue exploring them. Her thighs dampened and her clit started to tingle.

'Pinch me, somebody. I must be dreaming. Unless I've died and gone to heaven?' Marcus was standing beside the door, watching them. Maggie gasped with shock and horror. Quickly, she pulled back from Jan's caress and tugged the duvet up over her nakedness.

'Marcus?' Jan looked distinctly surprised and uncomfortable. 'I wasn't expecting you back until later.'

'So I see.' Marcus took a step into the room and Maggie could see the lust blazing in his eyes. She tried to imagine what it must be like for him to creep up into his bedroom, expecting to find Jan asleep, and catching her and her girlfriend. Despite her embarrassment, Maggie couldn't help but see the funny side of it. She could also imagine the affect it would be having on him. She was now well aware of how men fantasised about this sort of thing. This thought made her feel even more horny. Marcus or no Marcus, she wanted Jan more than ever.

Marcus took a few more steps, so that he was standing at the foot of the bed and Maggie no longer had to imagine his reaction. She could see the outline of his cock, already hard and rigid beneath his trousers. Another ripple of longing raced through her.

'Maggie's had a bit of a shock,' Jan explained. 'I was just comforting her . . .'

'I could see what you were doing,' Marcus interrupted her. His voice sounded strange. Hard and tight. A bit like his trousers, Maggie giggled to herself.

'Don't stop on my account,' he continued. 'Just pretend that I'm not here.' As he spoke, he pushed his hand down the waistband of his trousers to adjust himself and Maggie shivered again, both at the sight of his obvious arousal and at the implication of his words.

She was already nervous enough about what she and Jan had been doing. How could she possibly carry on now, with him watching? On the other hand, how could she possibly stop? She was feeling more and more aroused by the second. Her body was burning to feel Jan caress her again and, if she was perfectly honest, the sight of him so obviously turned on by watching them was only adding to her passion. It was just what she had been secretly fantasising about for some time. Maybe not with Marcus, but the result was the same.

Jan sat up and pulled the duvet around her. 'Do you want some breakfast?' she questioned him brightly, just as if there was nothing unusual about the situation.

Marcus shook his head. 'I'm not hungry.' He licked his lips. 'At least, not for food.' He moved round beside Jan and pulled the cover back down, exposing her. As she went to get up, he pushed her back on to the bed and pulled the cover off Maggie as well. Both girls watched his face silently.

Marcus placed his hand over Jan's left breast and pinched her rigid nipple between his fingers. Jan groaned and her body writhed with pleasure. Marcus pushed her towards Maggie. 'Suck her nipples,' he ordered hoarsely.

Jan shook her head but did as she was told, and Maggie felt another rush of dampness between her tightly clenched thighs. She stared up at Marcus, watching him watching them. He leaned over her, his face flushed with desire.

'Now you, Maggie. Suck her tits,' he commanded.

Quite unable to stop herself, Maggie lifted her head and sucked Jan's right nipple into her mouth. Jan moaned, arching her back so that the duvet slipped right down off her, revealing the damp, blonde curls of her pubes. She reached out and gently caressed one of Maggie's tingling nipples.

'Oh yes!' Maggie shuddered from head to toe and sucked harder on Jan's breast, using her tongue to make small, circular movements around the puckered nipple. She heard Marcus groan and, out the corner of her eye, saw him struggling with the zip of his straining trousers. Was he going to climb in bed with them? Maggie had never really thought about sex with him. He was certainly attractive enough, but she had secretly always thought him a bit of a wimp. Besides, he was Jan's lover and nothing but trouble ever came of playing around with your best friend's man.

Jan pushed them both away and sat back up. Her face was flushed and her eyes were sparkling with desire. 'One thing at a time, I think,' she whispered. She turned towards Maggie and winked mischievously. 'Since Marcus wasn't actually invited, I think he should sit back and wait his turn, don't you?'

Maggie stared at her friend in surprise. She had always thought that she was the more adventurous of the two where sex was concerned. Look at what she had got up to with the Trojans! Mind you, she didn't know for sure what Jan had done with them, did she? She was bloody certain something had happened between her and Tor, at least.

'What do you mean?' she muttered, doing her best to ignore the way Marcus was devouring her body with his eyes. Didn't Jan mind? Did she mind?

'I'll show you.' Jan climbed off the bed and took hold

of Marcus' arm. She led him unresisting across the room to a wooden chair and pushed him down on to it. 'I think you should be able to see everything from here,' she told him as she tugged the cord out of her dressing gown and calmly tied his hands to the back supports.

Maggie stared at them both in silence, realising for the first time the hidden advantages of Marcus' passive nature. Had Jan done this sort of thing with him before? She felt a slight twinge of jealousy at the idea of her not being the first.

Jan stood naked in front of the bound-up Marcus, with her hands on her hips. 'Hmm. Not quite right. You must be uncomfortable with so many clothes on.' She bent down and finished undoing his trousers. 'Lift up.' As she whipped both trousers and pants down his legs, his swollen cock sprang out in front of him, hard and desperate. Jan took no notice of it at all, while Maggie stared at it in astonishment.

After tugging his clothing free from his ankles, Jan moved across the room and removed the cord from his dressing gown, which was hanging behind the door. Without another word, she secured his ankles and then climbed back on to the bed beside Maggie.

Maggie stared at her shyly, her mouth gaping. Jan grinned. 'I often tie Marcus up like that while I pleasure myself for him,' she confessed softly. 'I like the idea of knowing that he can look but not touch. Not just me, but himself too. Don't worry. He likes it too.'

Another ripple of lust crawled down Maggie's spine at the implication of Jan's words. No matter how excited Marcus became, there was nothing he could do about it, until Jan allowed it. The concept appealed to Maggie enormously. She would have to try it with Justin. Her good mood evaporated as she remembered that it was all over between her and Justin.

'Now, where were we?' Jan edged closer to her and put her hand back on Maggie's breast.

Maggie shook her head. 'I don't know, Jan. I'm not sure . . .' Despite her change of mood, Maggie could still feel the little shivers of desire rushing through her body. Jan's fingers were so soft and so knowing. She moaned softly as she felt Jan's other hand creeping down her stomach towards her mound.

'You don't really want me to stop now, do you?' Jan whispered. Her hand reached between Maggie's legs and her fingertip unerringly sought for and found her hardened clit. She caressed it softly and Maggie moaned again, closing her eyes as she gave herself up to the exquisite little tremors of arousal coursing through her. Dumbly, she shook her head again.

Jan increased the pressure of her caress, rubbing Maggie's bud in a way no one had ever rubbed it before, except Maggie herself. However, she couldn't believe how much better it felt than when she pleasured herself. It was incredible. Already, she could feel the tingle of her mounting orgasm building deep inside her. She writhed her hips from side to side, moaning with delight.

Marcus groaned. 'Jesus!' he spluttered. His voice was a high-pitched squeak. 'Jan. Please untie me. I can't take this.'

Maggie opened her eyes and turned her head towards him. Marcus was leaning as far forward on the chair as his bindings would allow. His face was bright red and contorted with his lust. She lowered her gaze and feasted her eyes on the sight of his rampant cock, engorged with his need and twitching hungrily as he gazed pleadingly at the two women.

Jan peered round at him and smiled teasingly. 'Of course you can,' she contradicted him, clearly revelling in her position of power over both of them. 'If it gets too much, just close your eyes and think about something else.'

'I can't. Shit. I mean it, Jan.' Marcus strained harder against his bindings, causing the chair to rock forward on to its front legs, so that Maggie was afraid that he was about to tumble on his face. He had clamped his thighs together as tightly as possible and was wriggling his hips erratically in a desperate effort to rub his tortured cock. 'I have to . . . I want to . . . Oh God!'

Jan smiled and turned back to Maggie. Slowly and deliberately, she ran her tongue down Maggie's stomach and over her shaved mound. Maggie sank back on to the mattress and gritted her teeth. Jesus Christ! It felt so good. Jan's tongue was as soft and light as a feather and she seemed to know exactly where and how to touch for maximum effect. Maggie's clit was on fire and her orgasm inevitable. She could feel it welling up inside her dripping cunt, building like a thunderstorm. Any second now, it was going to burst and engulf her whole body; she could already feel the scream of ecstasy in the back of her throat as her chest heaved with her pent-up emotion and longing.

Jan lifted her head away from Maggie's cunt and put her hand between her own legs. Maggie groaned with frustration as her climax was halted right on the brink of engulfing her. It didn't seem possible to be so close to release and yet not to come. Every nerve in her body seemed to be on edge. One more caress was all it would take; just one more touch and she would be there. Her longing overwhelmed her and she rolled her hips from side to side again, savouring the exquisite torture of her desperate need.

'Please, Jan,' she sobbed. 'Please don't stop.' Already, she could feel the immediate urgency receding, although the need burned stronger than ever, so that her passion was consuming her.

Jan reached out and took Maggie's hand. Firmly, she placed it over her own mound, lifting her buttocks so that she could rub herself against Maggie's pliant fingers. Maggie could feel the warm dampness of Jan's juices trickling out on to her skin, and another surge of lust shook her body. Slowly, she moved her hand down between Jan's silky lips and pushed her middle finger up deep inside her friend's welcoming dampness.

Jan clenched her buttocks and thrust herself down hard on Maggie's hand; rolling her whole body from side to side as she savoured her pleasure.

'Oh God, Jan. You have to untie me,' Marcus begged again.

Maggie looked at him once more and almost gasped aloud at the look of sheer desperation on his face. His cock was jerking up and down as if on strings and his balls were so hard and swollen that they looked like they were going to burst. She could see the dampness of his lubrication glistening on the hot, purple tip of his shiny cock and, still burning with her own desperation, could imagine only too well how he was suffering.

'Don't stop,' Jan begged her, pushing herself even harder on to Maggie's fingers.

Maggie looked back down at her friend and smiled. Just one look at Jan's face was enough to tell her that she was almost there. Teasingly, Maggie withdrew her finger, trembling all over with her own passion as she watched Jan writhe and shudder with the intensity of her need.

Jan sat up and grinned shakily. She climbed off the bed, moved over to Marcus and knelt down in front of him. Raising her arms, she cupped one hand round the base of his trembling penis and began to slide it up and over the swollen head. As she began to glide it back down the other side, she used her other hand to follow her first, so that she was effectively stimulating him with one long continuous stroke; over and over, without ceasing.

Marcus moaned, his whole body shaking. Maggie stared at them both in fascination, shivering with her own desire. Marcus seemed to be deliberately clenching himself, as if he could physically stem his approaching eruption with his pelvic muscles. Jan grinned at him and started to slap his engorged cock lightly back and forth with the palm of one hand. Maggie could have sworn that it was growing even harder and darker with every tap. Marcus groaned again.

'Naughty boy,' Jan chided. 'I should give you a really good spanking for watching us like this.'

'Please, Jan. Untie me.' Marcus pleaded again.

Jan gave his cock another light tap and sat back on her heels. She shook her head. 'Not yet, my lover,' she murmured. 'Not yet.' She stood up, walked back across the room and climbed onto the bed, positioning herself so that she could place her tongue back between Maggie's still trembling thighs, while Maggie could now do the same for her. As the two women lowered their heads eagerly over each other's sex lips, Maggie heard Marcus groan again, and the sound of the chair bouncing along the floor as he edged himself ever closer to the bed.

Maggie flinched as she felt Jan's tongue run over her aching bud and then slip up inside her welcoming cunt. Tingles of ecstasy ran up and down the backs of her legs, and her overdue climax rapidly began to build again. Whimpering with delight, she pushed her own tongue deep inside Jan's hot dampness and began to thrust it firmly in and out. There was a hard thump as Marcus' chair collided with the edge of the bed.

When she finally came, Maggie's orgasm was so intense that she could not even cry out. The spasms of pleasure enveloping her were so strong and so powerful that the top of her head felt as if it was coming off. Her whole body shook, and she was so overwhelmed with her own gratification that she only just registered the fact that Jan was crying out as she also came.

As the last little tremors of her climax died away, she lifted her head to look at Marcus. His face was swollen with his passion and she could see the sweat literally pouring off him. His cock was stuck up in the air in front of him like a mast.

'I think he enjoyed himself too, don't you?' Jan chuckled.

Maggie couldn't resist. She licked her finger and, leaning over, ran it down his erection towards his balls. Marcus groaned urgently and she pulled back with a surprised yelp as his seed began spurting helplessly from him to shower his chest and thighs.

Maggie could feel the satisfied grin on her face as she snuggled back down on the bed and savoured the warmth of Jan's body and the unmistakable scent of their combined enjoyment. It was a pity about the tea and toast though, she thought sleepily, they must be stone-cold by now!

In the end, Maggie stayed with Jan and Marcus until the end of the week. She used the time to work through her confused and conflicting emotions about what had happened to her. By the time she was ready to go home, the fear, anger and humiliation had been almost completely consumed by her appetite for revenge. Before, she had only been partly serious about catching Roland out, now she was deadly earnest.

It was an interesting time in many ways. By the end of it Maggie no longer had any lingering questions about what it would be like to make love with another woman. No questions, only lots of happy memories and a much closer relationship with Jan than ever before.

Her opinions about Marcus had changed too. He really was a very sweet and delightful man. Jan was lucky to have him. Maggie felt slightly guilty at how she had treated him during her stay. Not that he appeared to mind. On the contrary, he seemed to enjoy her abuse almost as much as she had enjoyed abusing him. Still, she had never used anyone for her own gratification like that before. She had teased him unmercifully and it was almost as if every act of humiliation she had made him suffer had served to make her stronger and more determined to seek her revenge on Roland.

As she had hoped, Jan was not lacking in ideas for exposing Roland. Three days after Maggie had been attacked, the two of them had just about completed their overall strategy. All that remained now was to take care of a few details. It was time for them to have a little chat with Sara and Claire. If the plan were going to have any real chance of success then Sara's co-operation would be vital.

Chapter Twelve

'Maggie?' Sara's whisper was barely audible. 'Are you there?'

'Finally!' Maggie stepped out from behind some bushes and brushed a couple of twigs from her dress. The mild spring weather had taken a recent turn for the worse and her teeth were almost chattering. 'About time too. I thought you had forgotten all about me. It's freezing out here.'

'Shush!' Sara put her fingers to her lips. 'Sorry. I had to wait until everyone had arrived and been served with drinks.'

The thought of all her friends supping drinks in the warm with the Trojans, while she shivered outside in the undergrowth like an outcast, did little to improve Maggie's temper. 'I'm surprised you didn't wait until you'd all had something to eat and watched a movie as well,' she snapped sarcastically. She stepped up to the French windows and peered in at Sara, who was wringing her hands together and shooting nervous glances over her shoulder. Don't say she was going to lose her nerve now.

'Where's the Rat?'

Sara's lips twitched. 'Jan's just about to take him off somewhere for a little chat.'

Maggie grinned. Good old Jan! Knowing her friend, Roland should be well out of the way for the time being. 'OK, then.' She stepped into the room. 'Lead the way. Let's have a good look at those accounts of his, and find out what dirty little secrets he keeps in his safe.'

Jan moved across the room and touched Roland's shoulder. She stood on tiptoe so that she could whisper in his ear. 'Have you got a few minutes? I've got something I'd like to discuss with you.'

Roland grinned lecherously at her and gave her bum a familiar pat that made her clench her teeth to hide the anger. 'Of course, my dear,' he answered. 'I can always find time for a pretty lady. Why don't we adjoin to the library? We can be quite alone there.'

'Um, no. Not the library,' Jan replied. She thought quickly. 'I hear you've got a tank of tropical fish somewhere. Do you think I could see them? I love fish.'

'Why not?' He tucked her arm in his and led her down the passageway towards the far end of his luxurious house and into his immaculate drawing room. He turned the wall lights down low and guided her over to the wide, comfy couch, which rested in front of a blazing fire.

'Would you like a drink?' He indicated a well-appointed bar in one corner of the room.

'Please. A gin and tonic if you have one. Ice and lemon.' Jan ignored the couch and moved over to stand in front of the large fish tank set into the far wall. She peered curiously into its murky depths. 'They're lovely. Somehow, I didn't really picture you as an animal-lover.'

'I'd hardly call fish animals,' Roland laughed. 'Actually, I find them very soothing. The fish, I mean.' He walked across and stood beside her. 'Here's your drink.'

He nodded at the tank as he handed her a glass. 'It's a wonderful way to unwind, just watching them.'

Jan took the glass from his outstretched hand. 'Thank you.' She deliberately allowed her fingers to brush lightly over his knuckles and pretended not to notice the way his eyes lit up. 'You really do have a beautiful home, Roland.' She let her eyes wander around the room. 'I had no idea ice hockey managers were paid so well.'

He took her hand and led her back over to the couch. He sat down beside her so that his thigh was touching hers. Jan smiled coyly over the top of her glass, then licked her lips seductively. 'Cheers.' She sank back on to the soft cushions and smiled contentedly.

'You said that you had something you wanted to discuss with me?' he remarked, and took a long gulp of his own drink before leaning back on the couch with his arm behind her. Jan grinned to herself as she felt the pressure of his thigh against hers increasing. She knew he wanted her, but suspected there might be something he wanted even more.

'Yes.' She smiled encouragingly. 'I've recently come into some money,' she told him. 'An inheritance from a maiden aunt. I'm looking for the best way to invest it.' It sounded a little corny but he didn't seem to notice. Besides, there was nothing like a bit of flattery to get to his ego. 'The lads all said you were the one to talk you.'

Roland dropped his arm so that it was resting lightly across her shoulders. His fingers started toying with her hair. 'I see. Just how much money are we talking about here?'

'A lot.' She forced herself to let her body relax against his.

He took another swig of his Scotch and stared down at his almost-empty glass. His face was slightly flushed and Jan could smell his perspiration. She glanced at the carriage clock on the mantelpiece and estimated that she needed to keep him occupied for at least another fifteen minutes.

He dropped his hand over her shoulder so that his fingers were resting on the top of her breast. Jan glanced down at his groin and saw that his flies were already straining. Two over-excited pricks together, she thought to herself. How delicious. She rested her hand casually on his thigh and suppressed a grin at the way his muscles immediately twitched.

'What type of investment did you have in mind?' he questioned. 'Long-term secure or short-term high risk, high return?'

'No risk. Just a sure, steady return.' She paused, then played her ace. 'Actually, I think I could be interested in investing in the Trojans,' she told him coyly. 'If the incentives were right.'

Roland's eyes sparkled greedily. 'Incentives?' he questioned carefully.

She nodded. 'I'd have to have a vested interest, wouldn't I? Something too irresistible to ignore.'

Roland grinned hungrily and leaned forward to place his lips over hers. Jan returned his kiss with as much pretence of passion as she could muster. She wondered how Maggie and Sara were doing. Maybe just another ten minutes would be enough.

'I think I can provide that,' Roland muttered as he increased the pressure of his fingers on her breast.

'Why don't you unzip yourself and show me just what you have to offer?' Jan whispered huskily. She had a feeling that it would not take much to satisfy him. Most probably just a few words and suggestions would do it. She set herself the challenge. Could she make him come without so much as touching him, before Maggie and Sara got through? It was an interesting concept. She could feel her thighs and buttocks tingling with anticipation.

* * *

When Maggie and Sara finally walked into the living room, Maggie couldn't hide the smug satisfaction on her face. The evidence against Roland was overwhelming and spoke for itself. Once the Trojans saw it and heard what she had to say, they could be in no possible doubt that their manager was fleecing them. She had even found two entries for payments she was certain he had made to have her taken care of. One was shortly before her ordeal, the other the day afterwards. She would never be able to prove that part of it, of course.

Claire rushed over to them excitedly. 'What took you so long?' she hissed. 'I was getting frantic.'

'Where's Roland?' Maggie questioned breathlessly.

'Over there. He and Jan reappeared a couple of minutes ago. He doesn't look very happy,' Claire giggled. 'I don't think Jan's proposition agreed with him.' She glanced anxiously at Maggie. 'Well? Did you find anything?'

'You could say that,' Maggie nodded. She turned her head as she saw Justin moving towards her with a questioning look on his face. Her temper flared at the memory of how he had treated her. After what she had been through, she was definitely going to enjoy the rest of this evening.

'Maggie! What on earth are you doing here?'

Ignoring Justin completely, Maggie stepped into the middle of the room and cleared her throat. She turned to face Roland and held up his personal account book that she had been concealing behind her back. Roland was staring at her in astonishment. When he saw what she was holding, his eyes bulged and his face drained of colour.

'Where the hell did you get that?' Roland made a lunge for the book, but Maggie side-stepped him easily. 'Give it here. I should have thought that you would have learned your lesson . . .'

'What? From your thugs?' Maggie smiled sweetly.

'Didn't they tell you? They had a bit of a change of heart when they realised that they were on the wrong side. In fact, you could say that we became quite friendly . . .'

'Would somebody mind telling us what the hell is going on here?' Tor was staring in bewilderment from Maggie to the enraged Roland.

'I'm sure Roland will be only too happy to explain,' Maggie replied. 'You do have an explanation for why you keep a second set of accounts, don't you, Roland? And, I'm sure there's a perfectly good reason why a large percentage of the squad's sponsorship money never gets any further than your own pocket. On the other hand, I know that you were prepared to go to great lengths to keep it quiet. Your pet gorillas proved that.'

'I don't have the faintest idea what you're talking about,' Roland mouthed through gritted teeth. 'You're not making any sense, whatsoever.' He glared angrily at Sara. 'What's this silly bitch doing in my house?' he demanded.

Maggie threw the account book to Tor. 'Go on. See for yourself.'

Tor flicked the book open and stared at the figures in silence. His face hardened as he quickly checked a few entries against dates and the implications of what Maggie was saying began to sink in. He swung round and stared questioningly at their manager. 'Well?'

Roland shrugged.

'There do seem to be rather a lot of deposits,' Tor continued softly.

'I don't think this is the time, or the place,' Roland muttered. 'I don't know what she's talking about, but I promise you that there's a perfectly logical explanation for everything. There are no irregularities. You know I do a lot of investment.'

'Yeah, but all I can see are deposits,' Tor persisted. 'All one way. Your way.'

'Never mind that. What's all this talk about thugs?' Troy demanded as he stared curiously at Maggie.

'When Roland realised that Maggie was growing suspicious, he sent a couple of bruisers round to teach her a lesson,' Jan responded angrily. 'They stripped her, knocked her about, threatened to rape her and damn-near half-killed her.'

Troy swung round on Roland. 'Is that true?' His voice was as cold as an icicle and the side of his mouth twitched dangerously. His hands closed into tight fists as he struggled to control his fury. He took a few menacing steps towards the now frightened-looking manager.

Roland shook his head frantically. 'No. The woman is clearly deranged,' he stuttered. 'I have no idea what she's on about.'

Tor moved himself deliberately between Roland and Troy. 'I think you're right, Roland. This isn't the place to discuss it. I suggest we arrange a meeting with the chairman as soon as possible. The sooner the better. You can explain everything to him.' He turned to Maggie.

'If even part of what you've suggested is true, I expect we all owe you an apology. I suppose Roland was responsible for having you sacked from the rink, too. I never did believe you were a thief.'

'I never believed that Maggie was guilty either,' Justin interrupted quickly. 'I told you that, didn't I, Maggie? I just didn't have any choice in the matter.'

'Just a minute. You can't be seriously intending to take this crazy woman's word over mine,' Roland blustered. 'Not after everything I've done for you. I made you. You owe me.' He made another grab for the account book.

Tor held it easily out of his reach. 'From the look of it, you've been collecting for months. You could say that you owe us. Do you want us to collect?' He raised an eyebrow. One or two of the other Trojans took a couple of steps towards him.

'You'll be sorry. You won't get away with this. You'll never play again. Any of you. I've, I've got friends.'

'Not here you haven't,' Tor assured him.

Roland glared furiously at Maggie. 'It's a pity they didn't really take care of you, you interfering little bitch,' he hissed under his breath.

'Why, you sodding bastard!' Troy side-stepped Tor before anyone could react. With an angry snarl, he hit Roland full in the gut. Roland squealed pitifully and doubled over, gasping for breath.

Tor quickly grabbed Troy, pulling him away. 'Let it go, Troy. Half killing him won't help.'

Troy struggled furiously. 'I'll tear his fucking head off,' he yelled.

Maggie reached for his arm. 'Troy. It's OK. I've got my revenge. I just wanted to clear my name. There's no need for any more violence.'

An uncomfortable silence fell over them all. Jan looked at Maggie and winked, and Maggie smiled weakly. Her whole body was trembling so much that she could practically feel her knees knocking together, and her stomach was churning queasily. She looked up at Troy's angry face. 'Come on, let's go out and get some fresh air,' she suggested gently.

Maggie led Troy along the hallway, through the kitchen, and out of the back door on to a wide patio. It was a cloudy night with a distinct chill in the air and Troy pulled her closer as he felt her shivering.

'Looks like some kind of seat over there.' He guided her down some wide steps on to a velvet-smooth lawn. As they sat down side by side on a comfy garden hammock, Troy took her icy hands in his.

'I can't believe that bastard,' he muttered. 'Look. I'm really sorry I didn't believe you before. I just thought you were upset. I should have listened to you. I'm sorry.'

Maggie was surprised at the genuine anguish in his

voice. She shuddered as she remembered the terror she had endured in the boot of the car. 'It's OK,' she told him, 'there was no real harm done and it's all over now. I've got my name back.'

'You should have let me shove his teeth down his throat,' Troy ranted.

Maggie smiled. She leaned across and kissed his cheek. 'What, and risk hurting yourself before the big game? Besides, it doesn't matter now. The important thing is that he's been caught out.'

'What made you suspect he was conning us, anyway? And, how did he realise that you were on to him?' Troy shook his head. 'I can't believe all this was going on and we never noticed a thing. If only I had listened to you before. How did you know?'

Maggie laughed. 'I don't know. I just knew. Let's just call it women's intuition, shall we?'

Troy pulled her into his arms and put his lips on hers. A surge of lust raced down her spine as she felt his soft tongue slipping into her mouth. She put her hands behind his head and buried them in his short wiry hair.

Without breaking the kiss, Troy reached up and started to lower the zip on the front of her dress. He pushed his hands inside and cupped her left breast. Maggie moaned with pleasure as her nipples started to pucker. Her thighs began to prickle with anticipation.

Troy groaned and started to tug his own zip open. He took one of her hands and pushed her willing fingers inside his fly. He wasn't wearing any underpants and his cock was already hot and hard. Maggie wrapped her fingers round it and squeezed gently. Her clit burned as she felt him trembling to her touch.

'Jesus. I have to have you. Now,' he mumbled desperately.

'Aren't you supposed to be in training, or something?' Maggie teased.

'I don't need any training for what I'm going to do to

you,' Troy assured her softly, and Maggie shivered as she felt him lift her up and swing her round so that she was standing in front of him. Urgently, he tugged her dress down her arms. Before it had even dropped to the ground, he was already stripping her panties down over her thighs. Maggie whimpered as she felt his tongue probing her damp pussy. Automatically, she spread her legs, falling forward over him so that her breasts were pressed flat against the top of his head.

Troy moaned again and raised his buttocks off the seat so that she could peel his trousers down his hips. His dark skin glistened and his already damp-tipped cock seemed to be steaming in the cold night air. He grasped her hips and lifted her up into his arms. In one smooth, fluid motion, he lowered her down over him so that she was perched astride his lap and Maggie felt his rigid shaft beginning to penetrate her. She put her hands on his shoulders and ground her pelvis on to him, pushing his cock up even harder and deeper into her.

Still holding her around the waist, Troy started to thrust his buttocks up and down, raising and lowering her body as his cock pumped in and out of her. His tongue caressed her nipples and his fingers dug into her skin.

Maggie threw her head back and thrust her breasts harder on to his lips as she used her inner muscles to tease and caress his hard wet cock. She could already feel her climax building and sending little ripples of fire right through her.

'I'm going to fuck you until you can't stand up,' Troy threatened her hoarsely. Maggie shuddered at the note of longing in his voice, and increased the pressure of her muscles around him. Troy laughed and his hot breath steamed in the icy chill. 'You'll have to do a lot better than that, baby,' he told her breathlessly. 'Not that it will do you any good. You can't possibly win. I'm going to make you come at least three times before you get the better of me.'

Just the threat was enough. With a sharp cry, Maggie felt her clit spasm as her first orgasm enveloped her. She cried out again, shuddering all over as the little tremors of her pleasure shook her whole body. Troy laughed again.

'One,' he taunted her, as his cock thrust even harder and deeper into her pliant dampness. 'Two more to go. I hope you're feeling strong.' He sucked her right nipple back into his mouth and nibbled it softly.

Maggie drew a deep breath and tightened her grip around his muscular thighs. She rolled her hips, grinding herself on to his shaft and willing him to lose control. Troy chuckled knowingly and pumped himself even harder into her.

'Oh Christ. That feels so good,' she simpered. 'I love to feel your hard hot cock shoved right up inside my cunt like that.'

'Nice try, Maggie. Talk as dirty as you like. It won't work.' Troy lifted her up into the air so that his cock sprang free. He twisted her round and pushed her down face forward over the seat. 'Let's see how it feels from this side,' he suggested as he stood up behind her and started to guide his cock between her thighs.

Maggie grunted and sprawled forward over the seat with her buttocks thrust up in the air. She whimpered as she felt his hardness gliding back up into her. Gradually, she felt him building up speed again until he was pumping rhythmically in and out. She reached round behind her and grabbed his buttocks, pulling him harder on to her so that she could feel his groin slapping against her thighs. She pushed one hand down underneath them and cradled his massive balls in her palm.

Troy groaned with delight and took her breasts between his fingers. As he started to tweak her aching nipples in time with his thrusting, his other hand homed in on her clit and she instantly knew that he was about to win again.

'Oh Christ!' she cried out as she felt another powerful climax engulf her. She tensed all her muscles and her whole body spasmed in response to her pleasure. She felt the sudden rush of moisture trickle down her thighs and she slumped forward on to the seat and took a long, shuddering breath. Troy's cock slipped out from her dripping cunt and rubbed itself teasingly all over her tingling buttocks.

'Two,' he counted triumphantly. 'Do you concede yet?'

Maggie shook her head wearily and pushed herself upright. She tugged him down on to the seat and pushed his legs apart. Crouching between his thighs, she took his cock in her fingers and ran her tongue softly down his length.

Troy groaned softly and closed his eyes. She saw him lift his buttocks up off the seat to push himself up towards her lips, and she smiled with satisfaction. Even he would not be able to withstand this. Maggie closed her lips around him and sucked him deeper into her mouth. With her eyes fixed on his face, she started to pump him in and out.

Troy's mouth tightened and she saw the beads of sweat breaking out on his brow as he struggled to keep control. His cock twitched urgently between her lips and she tasted the saltiness of his lubrication. Immediately, she pushed her hand under him, cupping his balls in her palm again. They were tight and swollen. It wouldn't be long now.

'Put your hand between your legs and play with yourself. I want to see you wanking.' His voice was nearly as tight as his balls. The words enflamed her. Without breaking the rhythm of her mouth, Maggie slipped her hand down her stomach and over her mound. Her clit was still swollen like a grape and so sensitive that she whimpered as her fingers caressed it.

Her sex lips were still engorged and damp from her previous orgasms. Slowly, she pushed her middle finger up inside her smooth, wet cunt and started to pump it back and forth.

Troy leaned forward so that he could watch what she was doing. His cock jerked inside her mouth and she felt his body stiffen, fighting her. She pumped harder, revelling in the double sensation of his cock twitching in her mouth and her own finger tormenting her cunt and bud. He was about to come. She knew that he just couldn't hold out any longer. She moaned urgently, then moaned again as yet another orgasm of her own took her by surprise.

'Three,' Troy muttered hoarsely. 'I warned you. Oh shit!' He thrust himself so deeply into her mouth that she could feel the tip of his cock in the back of her throat. 'Oh yeah.'

Maggie tasted the first powerful spurt of his climax. She swallowed hard and sucked him again as she felt another jet of spunk burst from him, then another. She kept sucking, pumping him in and out of her lips until he had nothing left to give.

'I win,' Troy told her softly as soon as he had recovered his breath. Maggie laughed.

'It's the final tomorrow night,' she reminded him. 'Will you win that, too?'

Troy gave her a fierce hug. 'Of course. With you back as our mascot, how could we possibly lose?'

'I don't think I shall go back to work at the rink, though,' Maggie told him, surprised to discover that her mind was made up. She thought about the little girl with the sprained ankle and remembered her words of encouragement to the youngster. 'I've got a chance to start over and I'm not going to waste it. It's too late for me to become a doctor now, but I think I might train as a nurse, or perhaps a physiotherapist.'

Troy kissed her on the nose. 'Any time you want to

play at doctors and nurses is fine with me, baby,' he teased.

Maggie noticed that it had started to snow. She smiled contentedly as she snuggled up against his smooth, broad chest and watched the soft flakes melting on his hot skin – ebony and ivory, fire and ice. Definitely a winning combination.

BLACK LACE NEW BOOKS

Published in June

ANIMAL PASSIONS

Martine Marquand

£5.99

Nineteen-year-old Jo runs away from the strict household where she's been brought up, and is initiated into a New Age pagan cult located in a rural farming community in England. Michael, the charismatic shaman leader, invites Jo to join him in a celebration of unbridled passion. As the summer heat intensifies, preparations are made for the midsummer festival, and Jo is keen to play a central role in the cult's bizarre rites. Will she ever want to return to normal society?

ISBN 0 352 33499 1

IN THE FLESH

Emma Holly

£5.99

Topless dancer Chloe is better at being bad than anyone David Imakita knows. To keep her, this Japanese-American businessman risks everything he has: his career, his friends, his integrity. But will this unrepentant temptress overturn her wild ways and accept an opportunity to change her life, or will the secrets of her past resurface and destroy them both?

ISBN 0 352 33498 3

NO LADY

Saskia Hope

£5.99

Thirty-year-old Kate walks out of her job, dumps her boyfriend and goes in search of adventure. And she finds it. Held captive in the Pyrenees by a bunch of outlaws involved in smuggling art treasures, she finds the lovemaking is as rough as the landscape. Only a sense of danger can satisfy her ravenous passions, but she also has some plans of her own. A Black Lace special reprint.

ISBN 0 352 32857 6

Published in July

PRIMAL SKIN

Leona Benkt Rhys

£5.99

Set in the mysterious northern and central Europe of the last Ice Age, *Primal Skin* is the story of a female Neanderthal shaman who is on a quest to find magical talismans for her primal rituals. Her nomadic journey, accompanied by her friends, is fraught with danger, adventure and sexual experimentation. The mood is eerie and full of symbolism, and the book is evocative of the best-selling novel *Clan of the Cave Bear*.

ISBN 0 352 33500 9

A SPORTING CHANCE

Susie Raymond

£5.99

Maggie is an avid supporter of her local ice hockey team, The Trojans, and when her manager mentions he has some spare tickets to their next away game, it doesn't take long to twist him around her little finger. Once at the match she wastes no time in getting intimately associated with the Trojans – especially Troy, their powerfully built star player. But their manager is not impressed with Maggie's antics; he's worried she's distracting them from their game. At first she finds his threats amusing, but then she realises she's being stalked.

ISBN 0 352 33501 7

To be published in August

WICKED WORDS
A Black Lace Short Story Collections

£5.99

This is the third book in the *Wicked Words* series – hugely popular collections of writings by women at the cutting edge of erotica. With contributions from the UK and USA, these fresh, cheeky, dazzling and upbeat stories are a showcase of talent. Only the most arousing fiction makes it into a *Wicked Words* compilation.

ISBN 0 352 33522 X

A SCANDALOUS AFFAIR
Holly Graham
£5.99

Olivia Standish is the epitome of a trophy wife to her MP husband. She's well-groomed and spoilt, and is looking forward to a life of luxury and prestige. But her husband is mixed up in sleazy goings-on. When Olivia finds a video of him indulging in bizarre sex with prostitutes, her future looks uncertain. Realising her marriage is one of convenience and not love, she's eager for revenge!

ISBN 0 352 33523 8

BLACK LACE BOOKLIST

All books are priced £5.99 unless another price is given.

Black Lace books with a contemporary setting

THE NAME OF AN ANGEL £6.99	Laura Thornton ISBN 0 352 33205 0	☐
BONDED £4.99	Fleur Reynolds ISBN 0 352 33192 5	☐
CONTEST OF WILLS	Louisa Francis ISBN 0 352 33223 9	☐
FEMININE WILES £7.99	Karina Moore ISBN 0 352 33235 2	☐
DARK OBSESSION £7.99	Fredrica Alleyn ISBN 0 352 33281 6	☐
COOKING UP A STORM £7.99	Emma Holly ISBN 0 352 33258 1	☐
THE TOP OF HER GAME	Emma Holly ISBN 0 352 33337 5	☐
LIKE MOTHER, LIKE DAUGHTER	Georgina Brown ISBN 0 352 33422 3	☐
ASKING FOR TROUBLE	Kristina Lloyd ISBN 0 352 33362 6	☐
A DANGEROUS GAME	Lucinda Carrington ISBN 0 352 33432 0	☐
THE TIES THAT BIND	Tesni Morgan ISBN 0 352 33438 X	☐
IN THE DARK	Zoe le Verdier ISBN 0 352 33439 8	☐
BOUND BY CONTRACT	Helena Ravenscroft ISBN 0 352 33447 9	☐
VELVET GLOVE	Emma Holly ISBN 0 352 33448 7	☐
STRIPPED TO THE BONE	Jasmine Stone ISBN 0 352 33463 0	☐
DOCTOR'S ORDERS	Deanna Ashford ISBN 0 352 33453 3	☐
SHAMELESS	Stella Black ISBN 0 352 33485 1	☐

TONGUE IN CHEEK	Tabitha Flyte ISBN 0 352 33484 3	☐
FIRE AND ICE	Laura Hamilton ISBN 0 352 33486 X	☐
SAUCE FOR THE GOOSE	Mary Rose Maxwell ISBN 0 352 33492 4	☐
HARD CORPS	Claire Thompson ISBN 0 352 33491 6	☐
INTENSE BLUE	Lyn Wood ISBN 0 352 33496 7	☐
THE NAKED TRUTH	Natasha Rostova ISBN 0 352 33497 5	☐

Black Lace books with an historical setting

FORBIDDEN CRUSADE £4.99	Juliet Hastings ISBN 0 352 33079 1	☐
A VOLCANIC AFFAIR £4.99	Xanthia Rhodes ISBN 0 352 33184 4	☐
SAVAGE SURRENDER	Deanna Ashford ISBN 0 352 33253 0	☐
INVITATION TO SIN £6.99	Charlotte Royal ISBN 0 352 33217 4	☐
A FEAST FOR THE SENSES	Martine Marquand ISBN 0 352 33310 3	☐

Black Lace anthologies

PANDORA'S BOX 3	ISBN 0 352 33274 3	☐
WICKED WORDS	Various ISBN 0 352 33363 4	☐
SUGAR AND SPICE £7.99	Various ISBN 0 352 33227 1	☐
THE BEST OF BLACK LACE	Various ISBN 0 352 33452 5	☐
CRUEL ENCHANTMENT Erotic Fairy Stories	Janine Ashbless ISBN 0 352 33483 5	☐
WICKED WORDS 2	Various ISBN 0 352 33487 8	☐

Black Lace non-fiction

THE BLACK LACE BOOK OF WOMEN'S SEXUAL FANTASIES	Ed. Kerri Sharp ISBN 0 352 33346 4	☐

------✂-------------------

Please send me the books I have ticked above.

Name ....

Address ....

....

....

.... Post Code ....

Send to: **Cash Sales, Black Lace Books, Thames Wharf Studios, Rainville Road, London W6 9HA.**

US customers: for prices and details of how to order books for delivery by mail, call 1-800-805-1083.

Please enclose a cheque or postal order, made payable to **Virgin Publishing Ltd**, to the value of the books you have ordered plus postage and packing costs as follows:

UK and BFPO – £1.00 for the first book, 50p for each subsequent book.

Overseas (including Republic of Ireland) – £2.00 for the first book, £1.00 for each subsequent book.

If you would prefer to pay by VISA, ACCESS/MASTERCARD, DINERS CLUB, AMEX or SWITCH, please write your card number and expiry date here:

....

Please allow up to 28 days for delivery.

Signature ....

------✂-------------------